ANOMALY

SOME SECRETS SHOULD STAY BURIED

HUGO NAVIKOV

SEVERED PRESS
HOBART TASMANIA

ANOMALY

PROLOGUE

The room at the Pentagon had been swept twice for sound-recording devices as well as for fiber-optic cameras, chemical detectors, heat sensors, or anything else that might allow anyone outside the room to know anything about what was inside the room. Every Pentagon office, meeting room, and kitchen and dining area was regularly swept for bugs, but of any single location within the world's largest office building, Meeting Room 1138 was the most secure.

It had been designed as an n-cube floating within the rectangular cuboid of the actual room, this "floating" created by a magnetic field array that blocked any electromagnetic signals attempting to enter or escape. A near-vacuum created between the two Matryoshka-like rooms prevented any vibration from the inner cube from being detectable. A two-foot-long retractable gangway extended from the floor where Elden stood to the floating cube as he approached; it stretched over what could be described only as a "silence moat."

Those whose presence was requested in the room not only had to turn in any weapons before entering 1138, of course; but they also had to leave behind their cellular phones, which were switched to airplane mode, then shut off completely, batteries removed, and deposited with security, who kept them within a signal-blocking lead-lined box. Also, any ferrous-metal items had to be given up as well, since the vigorous magnetic field all around the inner cube would literally rip any such material (ferrous metal was different from metal medically implanted in a person) from one's pockets—if the owner was lucky. If the object was tucked away so as not to be torn out, the owner would become stuck inside the imaging cylinder, shoved and held fast against the wall by that magnetic object, until the power could be interrupted.

Major Elden, USAF, wondered with amusement about the lead-lined box: *Was the top brass concerned about Superman coming for their phones?* The amusement turned into speculation—if there was anyone in the world who would really know whether superheroes actually existed, it would be those with free access to Room 1138. It was where the biggest of the big secrets were shared—and with only those who absolutely needed to know.

Elden himself wasn't allowed inside this room-within-a-room unless continuously in the presence of an individual who *was* authorized to enter. For this meeting, Elden was to be briefed by the mysterious Colonel John Ash on something "of vital national interest," which could mean whatever Ash wanted it to mean.

Rumors circulated that anyone disclosing even the tiniest sliver of classified information obtained in Room 1138—plus whomever it was disclosed to—would meet with mortal misfortune made to look like an accident. In any group as big as the Pentagon's 26,000 workers, some necessarily die in accidents every so often, just due to the laws of probability. However, some of these "accidents" (the persistent rumors held) were actually the murders of those with loose lips. No one knew exactly who was getting whacked; and with no logbooks of any kind detailing who used the ultra-secure room, no one of a security clearance lower than those with Above Top Secret "Compartmented" clearance knew who went in or out.

Major Elden had seen his entire life taken apart over the past two weeks, piece by piece, every fact examined and adjudged secure before moving on to the next. If Elden had to describe the experience—which he was forbidden from doing, anyway—he would have called it "an IRS audit on steroids, but with everyone you've ever known interrogated by agents of military intelligence like they're at Guantanamo Bay."

It had been exhausting and a nightmare of scrutiny he thought would never end, but finally he was granted access to Specialized Compartmented Information, information that even the president was not privy to.

Now, in front of the door, Elden looked to either side, wondering what he should do. He had no ID card, no key, nothing. Should he knock, or would that be ridiculous?

He wanted you in on this for a reason, Elden told himself. *You are a resourceful, insightful man. Think. There is one chance to ace this final test.* He just had to *think.*

The gangway had extended for him even though he had no transceivers or such on his person to signal his presence. Now that he had stepped to the door, the gangway retracted.

He thought about the extreme military security outside the door to the hallway leading to 1138. They didn't ask for ID—he doubted they even possessed any information about whom they were allowing or refusing entry—Elden imagined that was so they never learned the names of those who sought access to the mysterious room. Name known or not, he had been scanned and x-rayed so many times just now that he thought they were going to give him cancer.

Elden noticed there were no windows in any hallways this far deep inside one of the rings of pentagons that made up *The* Pentagon. He didn't actually know where he was in the giant complex, since the elevators to this level had one button only, an illuminated plunger as large as Elden's palm, and they could move parallel as well as perpendicularly to the ground. There were also no security cameras. There was nothing at all to show he was here. He didn't even know where "here" was.

That meant the point of entry to this hallway was the last checkpoint. And *that* meant that if someone made it as far as Elden had, there were no other security measures necessary—or perhaps even possible without giving away the existence of this room ... or its location.

That meant anyone approaching the door would trigger the extension of the gangway.

That meant the door was open. It had to be—it didn't even have a knob, let alone a lock.

Elden pushed on the door, and it gently opened. A second door faced him on the other end of what Elden could think of only as a tunnel of plasma. Was it a force field? Did those really exist? He put his trust in

Uncle Sam and extended his right foot out and then down onto the "surface" of the tube.

It held. He took two steps forward and pushed on a second door, which opened to reveal an almost-smiling Colonel John Ash, wearing earbuds leading to a rugged case–protected smartphone, probably of CIA design. Seated in one of the chairs opposite Ash was Captain Davidson, an intelligence expert Elden had worked with several times. They nodded congenially to each other. Davidson was also wearing earbuds plugged into the device on the table. Elden entered the room and was immediately disoriented. It was eerie ... what was it?

Silence. All there was in the room with them was utter silence. Elden saw that Room 1138 was not only unconnected physically to anything else and floating within a vacuum to keep any concussive waves from traveling out of the inner cube; it was hellishly, fiendishly quiet.

Room 1138 was an anechoic chamber, the kind that they use to test the sound of everything from surround-sound speakers to the buzz of a single LED. The walls, floor, and ceiling of the room were crisscrossed with low-density gray foam that absorbed every sound, allowing nothing to even touch the walls, much less vibrate them.

He could hear his own heartbeat pounding in his ears. He could hear the saliva glands inside his mouth working to keep his mouth and lips moist. And he could hear something else, something like ... the ocean? Crashing waves?

After a moment, he realized that these sounds came from the colonel's and the captain's earbuds, which were *inside their ears*. But Elden could hear them over his own body's cacophony. Ash motioned for Elden to come to him, saying something that the major couldn't hear over the buzz and ringing coming from his ears themselves. The room ate the sound. Still, he could hear the ocean surf from Ash's and Davidson's earpieces. He wasn't an engineer or a physicist, just a logistics man, so he didn't bother trying to figure out the "why" of it.

Elden went over to Ash and took the set of earbuds with built-in microphone being offered to him. He put them on and plugged into the smartphone. Almost instantly, he felt relief from the maddening, overpowering silence of the protected room. "Sir!" he said, and all three men jumped at the tremendous boom of his voice.

"Whisper," Colonel Ash said in a whisper himself, and this was when Major Elden realized that the device feeding him waves and seagulls was also connected to a unit allowing very quiet communication between the three men. A whisper came through as a shout. He didn't want to imagine what an actual shout would be like. "Major, Captain, I don't need to tell you that the very fact that you're in this room means that any information you receive here is the most secret of Top Secret intel."

Elden nodded, not quite confident about speaking into the transceiver yet.

"That being the case, I can tell you candidly that if any bit, *one iota*, of this information is shared with *anyone* outside this cube, you will be terminated. Not 'fired'—*terminated*, as in 'your widow will receive a check.' That confidential information includes the fact that I have just threatened you with death. Give me a verbal *yes* if you understand and acknowledge this."

"Yes," Elden whispered.

"Yes," Davidson croaked.

"All right, well done." Ash bid Elden to sit in the transparent-plastic chair opposite himself and next to Davidson at the rectangular transparent-plastic table. No bugs or anything of the sort could be planted in, on, or around these clear-plastic furnishings without them being utterly obvious. Ash leaned to reach an impenetrable-looking stainless steel case and pulled it over. Four more just like it remained to Ash's right. He entered a code on the case's keypad, and the lock released with a *click* that might as well have been a bomb going off in the silence of the room.

As Ash opened the case, Major Elden and Captain Davidson instinctively leaned forward. Inside, custom-fitted within shock-absorbing black foam was a brilliantly translucent metallic tablet with indecipherable sigils and squiggles etched onto the surface. The two men examined the slate, then both looked blankly at Ash.

"What you're looking at is an artifact from an extraterrestrial civilization. *Where* the objects inside these cases were found is immaterial, so don't waste your or my time by asking or speculating

5555555555555555

about it. Just know it is central to the mission I invite you to join this day."

"Is—"

"Secure that thought for the moment, Major. Before anyone says anything further, I'm following Compartmentalized Intelligence protocol by telling you that you are required to leave this room immediately if you will not be taking part in the mission. You've both been down this road before, so please take advantage of this opportunity to walk away from this project if you are not fully committed."

Elden had been exposed to and followed this protocol in his intelligence logistics work, only once refusing a mission. However, he had always been given much more information before being asked to make a decision. All he had to go on was the exotic artifact Ash had just shown them. And that was enough: "I'm in, sir."

They both looked to Davidson, who seemed less certain about signing on. No one could know what was going on in his deliberations, but if Elden had to guess, it would be that the captain was unsure about committing to an undertaking in which any intelligence slip would result in death. However, the opportunity to learn and protect must have been too great to pass up, as Davidson nodded and whispered, "I'm in, too, Colonel." He looked to Elden and acknowledged him as well. "Major."

All at the table seemed satisfied with one another, which was a solid way to begin an Above Top Secret operation. Colonel Ash began the briefing anew, but no longer pulling his punches regarding the actual information to be shared: "This … let's call it a *tablet*. We have reason to believe that this tablet contains information coded into its strange alloy's specific and exotic composition."

"Information regarding what, sir?" Elden said, intrigued by the idea.

"The eggheads aren't sure what it says, exactly, but they have been able to work out that these tablets respond to psionic waves."

This was no time for levity, but Ash and Elden cracked a smile as the excited Davidson asked, "Sir, what in the heck is a 'psionic wave'?"

"Psychic energy," Ash said, his crinkly half-smile growing a bit at the sight of his subordinates trying their best not to react to his hoodoo. "But relax, that doesn't mean you can read minds or lift buildings with telekinesis, any of that comic-book garbage. What it *does* mean, as far as our experts can tell without the tablet being 'activated,' is that the information contained within the alloy can be learned experientially. Indeed, it seems that the *only* way that its information can be sussed out is through a sentient lifeform's physical contact. Somehow, this contact brings the psychic information within the tablet into the consciousness of that life-form."

The words hung in the anechoic chamber only because Elden and Davidson were plugged in and blocked against the silence by the continuous feed of crashing waves. After a moment, Davidson said, "If I may, sir: What does that mean, a tablet being 'activated'? Does it require some power source in order to work?"

"An excellent question, Captain. The tablets have no effect this far from their 'power source,' if you will. But in Antarctica, they almost crackle with energy. We believe that the hundred-mile-long gravitational anomaly buried half a mile under the western ice sheet of the continent is an alien spacecraft of tremendous age. Proximity to this spaceship seems to 'activate' the artifact."

"Please pardon my bluntness, sir," Elden said, "but what do you mean 'seems to activate' the tablets? Has no one tried to access the, um, *psychic information*? Have there been no experiments in Antarctica, having some individuals connect with the thing to find out what happens?"

"I don't like questions," Ash said. "However, this is need-to-know intel for you. We have not, in fact, allowed anyone to touch the tablet without wearing latex gloves. We know they forge a connection with the craft under the ice, but we have recruited scientists to do the experiential 'dirty work.' We don't know if the slate's information can be accessed more than once, so we want the eggheads to go in first and glean what they can from the psionic coding within the metal. Then they can tell us, we hope, the nature of the gravitational anomaly before we excavate it and protect it within the United States. I hardly need to tell you that an alien spaceship could contain weapons and defense technology that we want in no other country's hands."

Davidson said, "Isn't there a treaty—"

"We're violating it. This isn't hippie-dippie stuff about measuring climate change or protecting whatever the hell endangered animals live at the ass-end of the world. This may be the most important event in the history of the human race, and we won't let a piece of paper keep us from taking full advantage of it ... before anyone else can."

"So, the scientists touch the tablets in Antarctica, then tell us what they experience?" Elden asked. "It's almost July—that's the *dead of winter* down there—I assume this operation will commence in the South Pole's spring? Maybe in November, or even October, since this is a time-sensitive mission?"

"We leave tomorrow."

Elden and Davidson both started in their seats. "Go down there in *winter*, sir? I thought that was impossible." Elden looked like he was feeling a chill at just the idea.

Ash almost smiled again and said, "We're going to push the boundaries of 'impossible,' Major. Every second of this expedition once we get to the destination will be extremely dangerous, including landing the airplanes on the Wilson Airstrip. Then we'll be exposed to the elements traveling the twenty-five miles to the Wilkes Land anomaly site. And *then* we will be exposed further as our crew builds Criminy Station by snapping together its prefabricated pieces. That sounds simple, but it's a little more challenging when you're facing a wind chill of minus 138 degrees Fahrenheit in complete darkness."

"Of course. But, sir ... *Criminy Station*?" Davidson repeated the name with amusement.

Ash shrugged. "Our building and support crew, the 'icenecks'? They engaged in a bit of gallows humor naming it that—apparently they think this mission might include some ... *frustration*, and they're tough as hell, always up for a challenge. Use the name as a reminder to soberly regard the inherent difficulty of every element of this particular expedition.

"Also, note that these metal tablets have become *extremely* brittle after 200 million years buried in the ice, and so they *must* stay within their cases at all times, even as we have each egghead make contact with it and collect intel to be reported to myself only."

Elden saw that comment as giving himself and Davidson information about where the tablets might have been found, but any explanation regarding *how* they were found was not forthcoming. And ultimately, as Elden knew from previous Top Secret missions, because it wasn't shared, it was probably deemed irrelevant to whatever this mission actually *was*. Scientific? Military? Just an attempt to beat everyone else to the discovery? The reasons really were irrelevant to someone at Elden's pay grade; besides, someone working in military intelligence would only be borrowing trouble to seek out the *how* and *why* of missions that had already been concluded.

"We leave tomorrow, just as soon as the scientists have been collected and brought onboard the aircraft. Any questions?"

Elden had a million questions, but none of them needed to be answered before commencing the mission. That didn't keep his curiosity under control, however, and he sincerely hoped he would know all the answers by the time they returned to the States.

Ash smiled wryly at the lack of queries. "That's it, gentlemen. Congratulations on surviving Room 1138. You will be texted as to what you may or may not bring. You'll also receive notice of the coordinates where we shall meet and board the plane."

Elden and Davidson rose and snapped salutes at the colonel, who returned them.

We might have survived Room 1138, Elden thought as he and Captain Davidson made their way out of the room and onto the extended gangplank, *but surviving this mission won't be so easy.*

00.01: SOUTH

You never know what time it is in Antarctica. Clock time here doesn't mean anything except as a reminder to the winter-overs to sleep and eat.

A single day at the pole—from sunrise, morning, noon, evening, sunset, midnight, to the next rosy-fingered dawn—takes an entire year to unfold. Without astronomical markers to divide a day into twenty-four hours, every expedition to the continent must keep its own time. As long as everyone in a specific camp is referring to the same arbitrary clock time, it doesn't matter what time it "really is" in the rest of the world. The "rest of the world" itself is a vague concept in Antarctica, theoretical, irrelevant.

Some countries use UTC, others GMT, and others don't use any outside reference at all. Those last decide when exactly to begin their twenty-four-hour cycle: watches are synchronized at 00.00 hours and the day is over at the end of 23.59. Like everything else made by men in Antarctica, timekeeping there means nothing to any other living thing on the ice or in the frigid waters around the continent. It means nothing to the ice itself or the slanted sunlight or the cold or the ever-hungry maw of death.

Everything presented here happened over twenty-four hours; but without light and warmth, a human's measure of clock time remains irrelevant. Half a mile under the ice, there's no difference between 100 million years ago and twenty-four hours ago.

At the surface, in winter, you're blind from darkness and ice whipped in your face at eighty knots. You're deaf from the howling winds. You can't feel your hands or your face. And time is as meaningless here as it is a mile down. Come to the dark, and you'll end up disoriented, spinning, lost, never knowing where you are or how little time it takes you to die.

I didn't come to the dark willingly; but here I was, just the same.

＊＊

The first thing I noticed when I regained consciousness was that I was on an airplane. But it wasn't a Cessna, nor a 747; it was something I'd never encountered before. The dimly lit interior was vast, its only seats bolted to the bulkheads on either side. The dips and rumbles told me the plane was in the sky, but to my slowly focusing eyes it looked like I was inside an airplane *hangar*, not an airplane. Reinforcing structures arced across the top. Everything was, at least in the dim light, gray or brown. I definitely was not on a commercial flight. This was a cargo plane. I lay on the floor in a sleeping bag, next to other occupied sleeping bags.

And, my God, my exposed face was cold—*cold* cold, and I hate the frigging cold. That's why I lived and taught in the South, where the mercury rarely dropped to freezing all "winter."

I craned my stiff neck around to see, in a blur, what was going on around me, which was not a whole hell of a lot. Many of the seats, facing inward from either side, were occupied by sober-looking men and women. Their puffy jackets looked designed for some seriously low temperatures. One man wore a puffy black jacket and an LED light on a strap around his head, like an old-fashioned doctor with a mirror or a coal miner with a mounted headlamp trying to push back the blackness far below the surface. He was intently studying a stapled pack of papers on a clipboard. No one spoke to him. Actually, there was precious little talking at all, except for some barrel-chested men with thick beards making amused conversation too far away for me to pick up any words.

My head hurt and my body had stiffened a hundred different ways inside the thick sleeping bag. I could feel that my glasses were in my shirt pocket. They must have been slipped in there while I was out, which made me think that my captors—

Wait, *captors*? That might have been a bit of a logical leap, even for a scientist who made his living researching and extrapolating data to make educated guesses about alien life. I was an exobiologist at [redacted] University, which means that I spent a great deal of time bringing together the disparate fields of biology, geology, astronomy, space science, and any other disciplines I found helpful in making better guesses about who or what is out there.

Who would kidnap an exobiologist? The whole area of study was beloved by the media wanting a fun story, but it was the red-headed stepchild to each of its component disciplines. No one wanting to build a new kind of bomb or end cancer in our time or find a long-theorized particle turned for help to the handful of exobiologists occupying faculty offices. Thus, I had to conclude that this was not a kidnapping and I didn't have "captors." The question then became "Well, then, what the hell am I doing on a brutally cold cargo plane stuffed to the gills with grim-faced operatives and equipment meant for some kind of serious mission?"

The last thing I remembered from before I woke up in this weird plane was locking my office for the night and heading out to my Prius in the faculty parking lot, already sweating in the summer day's leftover heat. Then nothing, then *this*.

What in the hell was going on? Had I been taken by aliens wanting to thwart me because I got too close to "the truth"? That sounded like full-on tinfoil-hat paranoid schizophrenia. I got letters, emails, and calls from the true believers every day, demanding that this self-proclaimed expert tell them "the truth" about our alien overlords. I was not going there. (Spoiler alert: There were no alien overlords. Well, none that I knew of yet.)

Also, the people on the cargo plane were just that: people. Not to mention that it was a cargo plane and not an alien spaceship. I sat up in the sleeping bag and tried to unzip it from the inside. I could feel the fob for the zipper, but it was on the other side of a thick layer of Gore-Tex. I attempted to speak, but nothing came out but a raspy squeak. I collected some saliva and forced it onto my tongue.

It worked. I cleared my throat and said clearly, "A little help?"

A burly man with a white streak right down the middle of his beard turned in surprise. "Hey, welcome aboard, *amigo*!" he shouted over the noise. His accent was somewhere between Scandinavian and British, making the Spanish word sound really weird, and his face was just as inscrutable. "Climb on out of that cocoon and say hi to the rest of the gang!"

I nodded at "the gang," all of whom were taking me in now, and saw six smiles and six expressions of wary blankness. I rustled around the sleeping bag, but to no avail. "Can someone spring me from this thing?"

The burly fellow chuckled, unbuckled himself from his jump seat, and came over. He said, "Pretty warm in there?"

"I'm sweating a little."

"Oh, hell," he said and looked me right in the eye. "This might be … *unpleasant.*"

"Um, okay." What else could I say? "Where the hell am I, anyway? What's going on?"

"First things first, brother. Brace yourself."

"Brace myself for wha—" I said as he grabbed ahold of the outer zipper fob and yanked it down to my waist in one superfast move. *"JESUS CHRIST ON A POGO STICK!"*

Some chuckles, even among the grim-faced passengers. They chuckled because they already knew that the inside of the cargo plane was cold. *Cold.* My slightly damp shirt made it at least twice as bad as it would have been anyway, and I screamed, my mind running the table: heart attack, seizure, frostbite, agonizing horrible death. Once again, I lost the ability to speak; I began shivering like I'd been suddenly submerged in a bathtub filled with ice water.

Except ice water is always exactly zero degrees Celsius. The interior of this behemoth machine was at least ten degrees lower than that. That's ten degrees worse than *a bathtub filled with ice.* Where in the holy hell was I? Where was this plane going, *space*? I almost laughed as my mind screamed *OMG I don't want to say it's aliens … but it's aliens … in a spaceship!*

I *almost* laughed. But I was in too much pain to do anything but shake like a jungle tree during an elephant stampede. "H-help?" I said weakly, tone rising at the end like it was a plea. Which I guess it was.

Faster than I could follow what was happening, my short-sleeve oxford shirt (it was at least 89°F at 8:30 p.m., when I was abducted) was whipped off. Three of my fellow passengers—the burly stripe-bearded man, a weathered but very strong woman who was a head shorter than anyone else, and a man wearing a balaclava with only his glasses and eyes visible—lugged over three heaters with powerful fans and turned them toward me from different directions. The sweat on my exposed skin dried immediately, and before sixty seconds had passed, I wasn't shivering in pain anymore. It was bliss.

"Throw these on," Stripe said (I like anchoring new people in my memory with nicknames) and buried me with a thermal base layer like superpowered long underwear, a layer of fleece, a red cold-weather jacket, and down-filled parka with a waterproof shell. With help, I got these on, and then the process was repeated with my lower half: sleeping bag whipped off to excruciating pain from the cold, the heater fans focused on my legs, giving momentary bliss. I stepped into long johns and my lower body was quickly wrapped in the same layered, thick but lightweight, bright-red items. (The icenecks wore an orange version, the military people black.) A number in white was on each arm of my bright red parka: "51."

As in "Area." As in hidden space aliens and occult government schemes. As in this real exobiologist's pet peeve, not to mention the cause of those daily contacts from the UFOers and conspiracy theorists. And doubly not to mention the amusement of research grant committees.

Great.

The orange parka–wearing crew slipped moisture-wicking thermal gloves and socks onto me, then shoved my hands into a pair of dark green gloves that made my hands look like the Incredible Hulk's. Another pair of socks made of magically thick-yet-light material went onto my feet, followed by insulated boots with Gene Simmons–level thick soles. As they helped me stand at long last, every muscle and tendon in my forty-year-old academic's body screamed, every joint popping and creaking like the wooden beams of an abandoned roller coaster. I managed to straighten myself, and finally I could examine my fellow travelers to wherever the hell we were going. Stripe, Suntan, and Ski Mask checked me for stability and then stepped back.

"Thanks," I said as mildly as I could. "Now can someone tell me what the hell is going on? And where ... are ... we ..." I trailed off as Stripe pointed behind me, toward the rear of the plane.

I followed where he was pointing, and I counted five sleeping bags with their occupants' faces framed by the ultra-insulating material. They were all still asleep—more like *unconscious*, like I had been—and I got a chill even under all my layers.

"Seriously, I'm dreaming, right? I left a fan on, and it's blowing on my bare feet while I sleep, and so I'm dreaming a dream about a freezing plane that makes no sense whatsoever."

"You're not dreaming, Professor Weaver," a deep voice came from behind me. "You have been drafted into service by the authority of the government of the United States of America."

I spun around as quickly as I could in my bulky getup, and I saw a man's face, a hard face, a grim face that looked exhausted and ready for action at the same time. The man was maybe fifty-five? (Not that much older than I, but he probably hadn't spent the last twenty years with his only exercise being standing at the front of a graduate classroom.) Clean-shaven. Angular, pock-marked cheekbones. Gray buzz cut. He couldn't have looked more "military operative" if he were burning down a village. "I've been *drafted?* Into what?"

"That is on a need-to-know basis, Professor."

"Don't you think I need to know why I was *kidnapped* … um, Sergeant …?"

"*Colonel.* You are speaking to Colonel John Ash, United States Air Force."

Ash? I literally bit my lip to keep myself from making an *Evil Dead* joke. But I hardly had to stop the words—the colonel's steely gaze killed any attempts at humor, gallows or otherwise. And I wasn't in a particularly jokey mood anyway.

The colonel didn't put out his hand to shake, which was probably for the best considering we were both wearing layers of gloves thick enough for a stuntman to land on. "You don't need to know jack squat right now. The science draftees will be briefed soon. Information relevant to your role in the operation will be given."

This was illegal on more levels than I could count. I didn't dare say that, of course, but my mind reeled: Did my wife know where I was? The biology department? Did anyone, anywhere at all, even know I was gone? Had I been extraordinarily renditioned? Were we headed to

Guantanamo Bay? At least that would be warm. The only question I could think of actually risking—and believe me, scientists don't shy from asking questions; never go to a movie with them—was "What operation might that be ... um, should I call you 'sir' ... sir?"

"Stop asking questions."

My head vibrated in a double take. "W-what?"

"That's another question," the colonel snapped. "I just told you not to ask those."

"But—"

"Do not follow that 'but' with another question. I promise you that I will shove my $600 Baffin Impact boot right up your ass," he said with no more or less malice than when he told me I wasn't dreaming. "My footwear is rated for minus 100 degrees Centigrade. That's minus 150 in Fahrenheit, Doctor. *Right. Up. Your. Ass.*"

I nodded, lips shut tight. Drafted? More like *enslaved*. Like before-the-Fourteenth-Amendment enslaved. But what else could I do? It wasn't like he was going to share one iota of "intelligence" until he damn well felt like it. I decided to keep my ass boot-free for as long as possible.

He motioned to two of his men—immediately identifiable as military—and barked, "Bishop, Frost—wake those lumps and dress 'em. Then get their asses over here, pronto."

The two airmen did as they were told, quickly and without one unnecessary movement. They lightly shook each of the five "lumps" until the sleeping bag–wrapped people—I'd have bet my sabbatical that they were fellow "draftees"—opened their eyes and tried to speak. Squeaks came out, then raspy coughs, and finally they sat up and felt with shock the extreme cold of the cargo plane. The airmen efficiently shoved each new draftee into the same layered cold-weather kit I was outfitted with.

In less than a minute, the five bleary-eyed people—three men, two women—were mostly awake and all the way in shock as they took in their surroundings. Bishop and Frost led each, one by one, over to where the colonel and I were standing. We all looked like giant tomatoes in our thick red parkas.

"What in the name of God is going on?" The bespectacled fiftysomething had a well-trimmed white beard and a face pink from the cold. As the airmen (Frost, I noticed, seemed made out of protruding muscles even with his gear on) led over the rest of the Sleeping-Bag Brigade, I noticed that *everyone's* face was pink—and mine must have been as well. It was literally as cold as a walk-in freezer in the plane.

"Relax, Doctor Stanton," Colonel Ash rumbled in the least relaxing tone I had ever heard. "My men are leading your colleagues to join us. I will begin your mission briefing at that time."

"*Mission*? Who are you? Who are these other people? Why are we on a plane? Why is it so goddamn *cold*?"

I cringed. That was a lot of questions. I whispered to him, "He doesn't like questions."

"Secure that chatter, Professor Weaver," Ash snapped, then said to Stanton, "I don't like questions."

Bishop, an airman who looked new to the job—a greenhorn on this incredibly dangerous mission made no sense, but that was neither here nor there—brought the last of the five new recruits to the party. The white-bearded Doctor Stanton scoffed at Colonel Ash's dismissal of his inquiries and said, "Surely, you know that those of us in academia are *committed* to the asking of questions? Now, let's try again: Who are—"

"Doctor Stanton," the stone-faced Ash interrupted, "would you please be so kind as to pull back the hood of your parka? We may be getting a bit *overwarm* with all this gear on." Ash must have been warm as well, since he started removing his two layers of gloves as he spoke.

Stanton looked like he was going to make a wisecrack about the irony of *Ash* asking questions but plainly realized it wasn't worth it. He pushed the hood off his head, revealing thick brown hair at the sides, perhaps to compensate for the complete lack of hair on top. He fixed Ash with a querulous expression—

—and the colonel slapped him right across the face.

"*Jesus Christ!*" yelped a woman from under one of the other parkas. "*What in the world is going on here?*" She pulled back her hood to reveal long black hair that was swept into the collar of her gear.

"Doctor Vasquez, I advise you not to ask questions."

She stared at Doctor Stanton, who hadn't made a sound since Ash slapped him. It took Stanton a minute to straighten from the twist of his body forced by the assault; there were tears of pain and humiliation in his eyes.

Doctor Vasquez nodded curtly at the colonel's instructions, not meeting his eyes.

"Does anyone else have a question?" His words were met with a complete lack of anyone making a single peep. "Very good. Captain Davidson—come assist me with the briefing of these indoor kids."

Davidson, a farm boy's wide face appearing from the hood of his parka, attended his superior almost immediately. "Sir," he said with great clarity over the constant loud hum of the cargo plane's engines.

"Ladies and gentlemen," Ash began, without a trace of welcome or warmth. "I will now give you the information about this mission that I deem necessary for you to know at this time. Your questions will be ignored. Do not ask them. I will ask them."

Under his gaze, we all made sure he could see that our mouths were shut very tightly.

"Who am I? I am Colonel John Ash. I have served for thirty years in the United States Air Force. Many of those years were dedicated toward the mission we now undertake."

I took in my compatriots, and indeed, no matter what race or gender, we were each correctly labeled as an "indoor kid." I now saw that the Red-Parka Brigade was comprised of we six academics, professors, or scientists. Well, five—Vasquez was something different; I could tell just by her glasses and what was left of the makeup she must have been wearing when they grabbed her. She looked more hale and hearty than the rest of us, but she had the bearing of an educated professional, serious and calm. (If I were in a situation where joking was appropriate, I would have said I could tell the difference because she seemed to lack the crushed and soiled soul of a university lecturer.) She had to be the mission's medical doctor.

"What is this mission? Human explorers and, later, satellites have, since 1962, been continuously measuring gravitational fluctuations over Antarctica."

All six of us visibly flinched at the last word, each simultaneously connecting the dots between "Antarctica" and the extreme cold on board the cavernous airplane. The eyes under parka hoods goggled with anxiety, even fear. I couldn't tell you what my eyes looked like, but I could say that the rest of me wanted to throw up.

"We have for years detected the existence of and gathered information about a very large gravitational anomaly buried half a mile under the East Antarctic Ice Sheet." He fixed his eyes on the man he had just slapped. "Doctor Stanton may see now why his expertise is needed here."

Stanton didn't acknowledge the mention of his name. In fact, he kept utterly silent as well as perfectly still. It was while I was subtly observing this lack of reaction that it hit me—I'd written a paper with this man! He was one of the world's most influential research geologists. I would have been willing to bet that Stanton had forgotten more about the continent of Antarctica than the colonel (or the rest of us) would ever learn. So, yes, I agreed silently that Stanton's knowledge would be vital to such a mission ... but I had absolutely no idea why Stanton had been dragged here in the flesh. He was hardly frail, but he seemed a bit aged for a covert operation to the harshest place on Earth.

The Amerasian scientist raised his hand politely. At Ash's glare, he said in as neutral a tone as I'd ever heard, "Colonel Ash, I do not have a question."

"Good," Ash said and moved to continue his briefing.

"But I do have a declarative statement: My field is theoretical fluid dynamics—"

"Just say 'meteorology,' Doctor Yutani. This isn't a tenure committee meeting. You don't need to dazzle us with your utter brilliance."

Yutani cleared his throat and continued. "As you say, I am a research meteorologist. But it doesn't take a PhD in theoretical fluid dyn—sorry, *meteorology*—to know that it's July, the dead of winter in the antipodes. It is not possible to conduct any field research or go running around the continent on a so-called 'mission' in July in Antarctica. No *question* about it."

That was clever, I thought. I wondered if Yutani was now next in line for an open-handed slap in the face.

"What you say is true, Doctor." Ash looked first at him, then took the rest of us in, with an inscrutable expression. "There is nowhere on Earth more deadly than Antarctica in winter."

His matter-of-fact tone puzzled everyone—just as he intended, I was sure.

"However, you should all think twice about whining about how 'impossible' it is to do anything but hide inside a plastic-walled research station until the sun rises in a few months. Instead, understand that this 'so-called mission' is of vital, *urgent* national interest. Of *global* interest. Otherwise, we could take our precious time waiting for the balmy 20 degrees below zero Fahrenheit that arrives in January. You are the most accomplished experts in your areas of relevant science, and that is why you were recruited. You must come to the logical conclusion that this expedition is happening *now* because spring will be too late."

We scientists exchanged glances of dread mixed with undeniable curiosity. What role could we possibly play in such an international emergency? Yutani was right when he said *theoretical* fluid dynamics— he was probably more comfortable with a chalkboard and computer simulations than he was walking in the rain to his faculty parking spot. My field, exobiology, was *entirely* theoretical, extrapolating data and speculative ideas from Earth-based biology, geology, meteorology, and more to spin logical webs regarding what extraterrestrial life-forms might be like. Since landing tenure, Stanton had probably spent more time writing theory-based papers with people like me than he had spent out in the field. Whatever the others did, I was willing to bet that they did it in complete collegiate comfort and convenience—the direct opposite of *anything* Antarctic.

Utter darkness, outer-space cold, abduction and enslavement by the government.

I should've listened to my dad back in the day. I should've become a plumber.

THE OTHER-MIND: WEAVER

"Weaver? *Weaver*." Colonel Ash observed the professor's face, watching for any change.

The exobiologist lay on his back on a cot inside Criminy Station's tiny medical ward. His eyes were closed, his entire body in a state of suspension. His heart rate had slowed to a couple of beats per minute, but the EEG showed his brain was *very* active. He was alive—in this state a person could "live" indefinitely, using so little in resources it would have been hard to calculate the amount—but his consciousness was elsewhere, the brain-wave readings spiking and falling as if Weaver were under intense stress.

Seeing no difference, he shook his head and said to Doctor Vasquez, M.D.: "I told him not to touch anything."

"What the heck did he *touch* that did this to him?"

"I don't care for questions, Doctor. He touched *something*. And *something* falls under *anything*, which is what I told him not to touch."

"You want me to treat him? Tell me what he touched. I can't do a thing until I have the whole situation." She must have meant it, too, crossing her arms in a "final answer" position.

"All right, fine, but this is on a purely need-to-know basis." He stomped across the unit's hollow floor and unlocked, then unclamped, a high-tech protective case in which a rectangular metal slate rested in custom-cut foam. "He touched *this*," he said with impatience, holding the case but not, Vasquez noticed, touching the slate itself.

There were unintelligible symbols etched without color into the metal. She looked at it for a moment, but it revealed nothing obvious that would send someone into physical catatonia while his mind went into overdrive. A *human* someone, that was. "This is an alien artifact, isn't it?"

"Do you need to know that to do your job, Doctor?"

"I believe I do, Colonel."

"Then yes, it is. I will not tell you where we acquired it, regardless of any need to know."

"But you brought it with you to Antarctica?"

"Yes."

"Has anyone else—any other *human*—touched it?"

Ash paused, maybe just drawing things out to penalize her for asking, or maybe because he had to sift through his many security clearances to decide whether a mere medical doctor could be trusted with this information. Finally, he said, "Yes. When it was first discovered."

Vasquez didn't want to get shirty with Ash, whom she got the feeling would toss her out into the antipodean night without a second thought, but she sighed in exasperation and said, "Don't you think that would be relevant information for me to know if I'm supposed to bring him back to consciousness?"

"Based on those who have come into direct physical contact with the artifact, he will return from this state with information vital to the success of this mission. He'll wake up by himself with … important intelligence."

"What—he—what kind of information?"

"That is *not* something you need to know."

That cut off the conversation like a meat cleaver striking a butcher block. They both stared at the utterly unmoving exobiologist on the table in front of them. After a minute, Vasquez said in a low voice, "You didn't tell him not to touch it, did you?"

Ash let out a huff of amusement at her deduction. "No. Quite the opposite. We brought the slate for each of our scientists to investigate. By touching it, they … well, we don't know what happens, exactly, but when—*if*, to be honest—they come back, *they know things*."

"Jesus Christ."

"He's a *scientist*. His whole business is extraterrestrial … stuff. No one's going to show him an alien artifact with writing on it and expect him not to go full egghead. This is what he'd been waiting his entire career for, Doctor. He'll no longer wonder. He'll *know*."

Weaver could hear their voices like they were whispers on the wind, *apophenia* his mind tried in vain to make sense of, but he was in the middle of a battle. His hands were splayed and suckered on the ends of his fingers, like a gecko's. In his green hands was a sleek weapon of some sort. When he looked up, he saw saucer-eyed reptilian aliens—

your brothers in arms

—in a semicircle, each of them facing a hissing and spitting monster they had backed into a corner of the valley, under a bleakly overcast orange sky, alongside a river of something that was not water. His field being exobiology, in Weaver's man-brain the area was identifiable almost immediately: Ontario Lacus on Titan—

that isn't what we call it

—but that wasn't possible. Other than the simple impossibility of traveling to Titan, Weaver knew that Titan's surface temperature hovered around minus 290 degrees Fahrenheit. None of the bipedal green men—not *little* green men, as each of them stood at least two and a half meters tall—was wearing anything other than life-support gear, a form-fitting fabric bodysuit, and tall black boots angled out like swim fins. No complex creature should be able to walk on Titan's slushy surface without a damn serious spacesuit ... but ...

Weaver—

who?

—took note of the surface from the view of this alien's eyes. He couldn't control them or any other part of his alien body. The ground wasn't slushy with methane ice. It was rocky, like Mars or Venus. Humans hadn't ever been to Titan or even yet sent a remote-controlled rover. Some part of the surface could have been rocky. But that didn't explain how the atmosphere was warm enough for people (or sentient bipeds, in any case) to walk around and hunt—

capture and contain

—wearing only a breathing apparatus around their necks, breathing through it into a hole in their alien bodies' throats, and no other exoplanet protective gear except that to keep them from being slashed or bitten. Or, rather, it was as if he were experiencing the "breathing" from a third-person perspective: there was "breathing" occurring, but it felt

23

like it hadn't anything to do with Weaver. Like *he* wasn't holding the weapon aimed at the huge but squat, very agitated, dark-pelted thing—

apex predator

—that hissed at them and constantly shifted its feet, looking like it was contemplating a run at them. With its tank-sized body, low to the ground and probably denser than rock, it would knock them over like milk bottles. Why weren't they—

we

shooting? There were at least ten bipeds blocking off any escape route, but as soon as the powerful predator realized it could barrel through them—

us

—anyone in its path would be killed. In fact, now the predator lifted its bison-like head and lowed, a haunting *basso profundo* that echoed through the valley. Was it about to charge?

It lost the chance: a small hoverjet—

antigrav hunt shuttle

—swung into the nook they had corralled the monster into and *boom*—a thick netting shot out and wrapped itself around the reptile-buffalo-predator-thing. It screeched in shock and anger, then stopped for a moment. Analyzing the situation?

"What's it doing?" the soldier—

melee hunter

—next to Weaver's alien body whispered. Wait, no, it wasn't speaking aloud. The words—which were not *What's it doing?* or anything else in any Earth language—bloomed inside the mind that wasn't Weaver's at all.

Weaver's other-mind responded in the same way: *Calling its friends.* This, again, was in no language Weaver had ever heard, but the meaning was clear, both to himself and his compatriot. He had no idea how he was telepathically communicating when it occurred to him that *he* wasn't doing the communicating. He was a witness inside the mind of this sinewy "melee hunter"—an observer. The more he observed, the more he understood what was going on. The more he observed, the less he remembered that he was Weaver.

And the more he knew why they had cornered the Titan Gila. Its name didn't come to him in English, though. It was in the alien's—

our people's

—language, in the alien's mind. Titan Gila was a translation produced by what remained of Weaver's consciousness in this mind, simply the closest English equivalent for the predator's alien name, and the translation was hardly necessary now. Weaver could have spoken in this language if his human mouth could have pronounced the words; if humans possessed telepathy, he could have broadcast in the words of these—

chaos melee hunter pirates

—alien soldiers.

The predator lowed again, making the ground vibrate under their feet. But when it stopped, the trembling of the surface didn't. From far off, Weaver heard the rumble of many, many friends of the Titan Gila. He heard it although he could see from his fellow hunter's head that they possessed no ears.

He was hearing through his feet, or rather through the feet of his host. The swim fin–like "boots" were open in front, he noticed now. They were like sound collectors on Victrolas before electric microphones, concentrating the vibrations into what Weaver's other-mind interpreted as sound.

This race's ears were its—

we hear with our

—feet. Not *in* their feet—the feet themselves were literally the audial sensory apparatus of this race.

He felt the other-mind blast out an excited shout and heard every hunter call back telepathically. The group turned as one to face the approaching thundering herd.

Weaver controlled nothing, he could see that now: if he could, he never would have tried to take on the horde of angry predators. This was suicide. If it were his choice, his body to move, he would have fled and gotten the hell out of there, he was certain.

Except … the alien hunter's thrill at imminent bloodshed took root in Weaver's own mind. He wanted to fight these monsters, kill them! He and his brothers would scour Titan of these enemies and spill their blood, if they had blood. Either way, they would kill every last—

eight

—one of the beasts.

The part of the mind that was still Weaver repeated to itself: eight. *Eight*? Eight *what*?

The hunter's feet were moving now, the group of aliens rushing forward in a thundering herd of its own. They crested a small rise in the terrain—and not 100 meters away were at least sixty Titan Gilas coming at full speed.

Eight, alive
Kill the rest
GO!

At the command, the hunters—

mercenaries

—shifted their weapons from marching to firing position and let fly.

The huge rectangle of his rifle analogue poured out projectiles with barely any recoil at all. But it couldn't be a laser, because there was a definite but small pushback when he fired. The projectile was too fast to see, but the Gila he'd been aiming for flew into pieces.

Becoming more used to being in the other-mind, Weaver realized he could search the alien's knowledge. In seconds, he located a bit of information: the weapon his alien arms held was a railgun. He didn't need to poke into the other-mind to know what that was—a railgun had long been proposed as an Earth military weapon, not to mention being used frequently in science fiction. No explosives, no propellants were needed to shoot the projectile; parallel electromagnets accelerated the bullets almost to the speed of light. To be shot by one would be to die, unless one of your race can live with half its body gone.

Weaver hoped the railgun stored enough projectiles to cut through the Gilas, because there was no time to reload. There was barely time to shoot in the first place. But the fast pulsing and sonic booms created every time a projectile was slung forward by the electromagnets slipped his alien body into a rhythm, and he mowed down six by himself when—*CLACK*—the railgun went dead.

The mind that was still Weaver's shrieked in terror—but the other-mind remained impossibly calm. These aliens didn't have mouths that looked like they could smile, but the ebullient feeling among all of the hunters—

payday

—filled the other-mind and spilled over to Weaver's. His anxiety bottomed out, and if a mind could smile, his would have. But why? His feet could still hear so many Gilas coming, and in front of them was a wall of dead animals! Not relaxing at all … but in a moment the rumbling stopped, replaced by a hundred predators letting out a mournful lowing like the first, netted Gila had made to attract the cavalry.

Then Weaver understood: the wall of dead Titan Gilas really was a *wall*. The monsters couldn't get through to the hunters or to the Gila wailing in distress.

A loud voice sounded in his head: "Air support coming!" (Weaver thought how his new friend Professor Goldsmith would have been wetting himself over hearing an utterly foreign language and not just automatically translating it but also *understanding* the web of connotations and contexts in which the words meant what they meant.)

The alien's legs raced into motion, hurling Weaver forward with every other running hunter—right at the wall of dead predators. The other-mind was too overwhelmed with excitement—

bloodlust

—for Weaver to figure out why they were all rushing *toward* whatever "air support" was on its way. *Didn't soldiers usually run* away *from an air strike?* Even as he thought this, however, he was able to tell that what his mind had translated from the other-mind as "air support" was different from a terrestrial military backup. Its aim wasn't to kill everything in the area. It was to capture—

capture

—it. His mind and the other-mind shared a sympathetic vibration at that moment, and Weaver was awash in the alien's memories of its mission, its training on the tidally locked moons of some great and horrible gas giant, and this, its first assault after the final test on [there was no translation of names of people or places, just the sound in his mind no human could reproduce], where the alien had shown it could handle the Titan Gila for—

chaos

—the outfit's next mission. That mission was the one happening right now. The alien climbed to the top of the barrier of dead Gilas and many parts of other dead Gilas and watched its fellow green-scaled hunters come over the wall of the dead. To Weaver, every one of them looked essentially the same, much like the *Star Wars* bounty hunter Greedo would if he breathed through his neck and spoke through his mind.

Star Wars? Weaver couldn't remember what those sounds meant. His mind and the other-mind were too much in sync now, memories and emotions and sensations bleeding both ways inside the head of the alien.

Alien. He was inside an *alien* consciousness. That meant—

SCREEEEEET!

As one, the hundred or so Titan Gilas let out a shriek and started running haphazardly, caught between the mounds of their dead fellows and … what? It took a few seconds before Weaver could hear the sound of whatever was throwing the monsters into a blind panic, but then the tumult rang out through his alien's feet. Something big was coming at the Gilas, something bigger than any stomp-footed *kaiju*, bigger than everything, if it could rumble the very ground of Titan; but, looking between the hill of the dead and the horizon, Weaver could find no visual sign of what was so greatly terrifying the Gilas.

Then the alien looked up, and Weaver saw through its eyes a massive, insensibly vast blue-steel leviathan dropping from the sky. Its sonic booms were what was rending the air and driving their monstrous catch mad. As it emerged from the hazy orange sky, it slowed to a standstill, blocking out the bleak sunlight and flattening a ring of terrain along every degree of the horizon. (Weaver had written a paper on this usually overlooked consequence of a massive hovering object à la *Independence Day*'s monumental invading spacecraft: nothing can belay the effects of gravity except resistance against the surface. Those giant spaceships would never have had to shoot a single laser to destroy New York and Washington and Sydney; all they had to do was hover, and they would crush flat anything beneath them. *This* megalithic transport, however, pushed back against gravity with virtual legs that crushed the area *around* its hover target.)

The Titan Gilas stood in place now, not making a sound. A massive hatch on the bottom of the blue leviathan slid open in a way that seemed slow to those on the ground but was probably moving at monumental speed from a vantage point aboard the ship itself.

The rumbling of the anxious animals' feet ceased entirely as the mass of apex predators rose into the air toward the yawning opening in the ship.

A tractor beam, the Weaver-mind marveled. If he had ever posited in print that he believed that exo-civilizations would boast *Star Wars* technology, he would have been laughed out of the room.

It would've been the same reaction he'd have gotten from saying space aliens would be little green men. (Or big green men, as he and his fellow 10-footers were.) But there it was, an attractor impulse generator … science lingo for "tractor beam." Weaver was amused.

The other-mind, however, felt only awe as it watched the transfer of the Titan predators. Weaver felt confident that his experience of sharing the alien's mind would get even more interesting from here. The next world they were visiting was Jupiter's icy moon Europa, the closest life-bearing world to Titan, for the next—

chaos

—monster hunt.

After this last deep sharing of the other-mind, the world wavered like something seen at the bottom of a swimming pool. The exobiologist felt a wave of disorientation—or, rather, multiple orientations—as his mind unhooked from the alien's and floated back up to his body on Earth, already mourning the loss of his mind's other half.

***

The EEG and EKG monitors at once regressed to the mean, Weaver's brain waves calming down as his heart rate made a rapid rise toward normal. His eyes opened.

Colonel Ash and Doctor Vasquez immediately took the few steps to Weaver's cot and looked down at the exobiologist, who seemed physically fine now.

"Professor?" Vasquez said in a flat, loud voice. "Are you back with us?"

Weaver nodded and indicated the water bottle on the table at which they had just been seated. He took a sip, then a swig, and finally a couple of gulps. "I'm okay," he croaked. "I'm back."

"Back?"

"Back from where, Weaver?" Ash asked in anticipation, all but holding his breath.

"Saturn's moon Titan. I was an alien on Titan. Hunting."

"The hell, you say," the colonel said through what was quickly becoming a genuine smile. He pulled a chair right up to the edge of the cot and sat, leaning in with eyes that seemed to sparkle. "Tell me everything."

01.25: ICENECKS

The vast cargo plane was not going to land for another two hours at the least, so once we were dismissed by the tyrannical Colonel Ash, I followed Major Elden toward the fore of the cavernous area to meet and possibly commiserate with the drilling crew, who called themselves "icenecks." I wasn't surprised when Elden told me that these four men and two women represented "the very top of the top" when it came to precise, scientific execution of drilling missions in the most extreme conditions. So, we were all billed as "the tops" in our respective areas of expertise: I was the tops, my colleagues were the tops, these ice-drilling experts were the tops, the military types were the tops—all headed to the bottom of the world.

I had already met, informally, the iceneck with the white stripe in his beard, the thirtysomething woman with the sun-browned face, and the huge guy who was still wearing his black balaclava—Stripe, Suntan, and Ski Mask, as they were now stuck in my mind.

The drill crew members introduced themselves, starting with Stripe: "I'm Scott, the oldest dumbass in a dumbass crew doing the dumbest-ass jobs in this dumbass world."

Then Suntan, in a heavy Kiwi accent: "I'm Allison? Smarter than Scott but dumber than somebody who doesn't do this for a living?"

Next was Ski Mask, who spoke with an accent that could be Russian, or maybe Czech. "My name is Ian. I don't like the cold." This got a chuckle out of the whole team, because ice drillers, I would think, don't get a lot of warm-weather work. "I take orders from my Allison. She is scary." They rubbed noses through his balaclava. Retching noises ensued.

Sitting next to him was a tall fellow who looked scrawny next to the hulks that were his crewmates: "I'm Tom, the most qualified member of this crew."

The other five smiled and groaned. I gathered they had heard all this before.

"Check it out—I *gave* for that Vostok expedition, man." Tom pulled off his two layers of gloves and wiggled his fingers at me. At least, the ones that were still there—his smallest digit and a slice of his hand were missing. "Frostbite, my friend. True mark of a dedicated iceneck."

"True mark of a moron who ignored a safety protocol," Allison said, congenially but sincerely.

"Cruel, so cruel," Tom said. "But not *entirely* inaccurate. Learned my lesson there."

In my mind, Tom became "Pinkie." Not terribly original, but I was a scientist, not some fiction writer seeking mnemonics to aid readers' memory of multiple characters.

A small but intense-looking woman sat next to Pinkie. I nodded at her, and she lifted her chin in acknowledgment in a not-unfriendly manner.

"Um … hi, I'm Professor Weaver. I'm an exobiologist and … that means …" I trailed off as she looked away, rather rudely.

"We call this ball of bad attitude 'Michelle Rodriguez,'" Stripe said. "Fast and completely furious."

She hit Stripe with an f-bomb and a couple of hard-to-picture instructions of what to do to himself. Then she looked at me. I wouldn't have said her expression was one of joyful friendliness now, but at least she said, "Name's Ellen. Good to meet you. I don't go for men, all right?"

"Sure, okay, of course," I said in a very cool and collected voice. She was now Michelle Rodriguez (thanks for that, Stripe) in my mind and always would be, I was sure. She *did* look like the actress, which made her seem even more threatening than did her other threatening aspects. I made a mental note to do everything I could not to piss this woman off.

Finally, there was a very large man whose orange parka made him seem inhumanly huge and powerful. He was sitting, but I couldn't imagine he was an inch under six foot six. He put out a giant paw, smiled through his bushy brown beard, and said—in the highest voice I'd ever heard from a man—"I'm John. We'll make sure you science guys get where you need to go. Don't matter how deep."

I glanced at the other icenecks to see if this was a joke, but it was *not*. In fact, they were all checking me to see if I was going to have some smart-ass comment about his voice. (I wasn't. I'd been in academia so long, taught so many people, that I knew never to mock a name or anything else about a person I didn't know well.)

The other icenecks saw I was going to be cool, and we all relaxed. I had to admit, despite his almost-squeaky voice, his physique overpowered that and he projected the air of confidence strong men usually seem to have. In my frozen, possibly concussed brain, I labeled him ... wait for it ... "Big John."

The icenecks weren't credentialed scientists—they weren't scientists at all, actually, although three of them had master's degrees in engineering—but no one needing to get through the thickest ice could do a single thing without people like these. They told me about their central role in the recent, epic drilling operation to reach the waters of Lake Vostok in Siberia. They bored down almost 3,500 meters—just over what this American still thought of as *two miles*—into the ice for scientists to sample the pristine water for evidence of life that branched off from the rest of the world untold millions of years ago. (I was a consultant on that project because of the possibility of the discovery of extraterrestrial life in the lake, a job which allowed me to stay warm and dry in my faculty office.) That made the 825-meter target depth, just half a mile down, of our anomaly seem like a driving-range divot.

But a question nagged at me, so I asked the six of them straight-out, quietly and keeping watch over my shoulder, "Did any of you get ... um ... *kidnapped* for this mission?"

The rugged gang looked at one another like they were passing secrets. Then they looked back at me as one—and started laughing their rugged asses off.

Ski Mask managed to say through his wheezing laugh, "My man, we're being paid so much for this job, we woulda kidnapped *them* if they didn't hire us on."

More laughter at my expense, which was fine. I was part of the family now and all that (I mean, against my will, but it seemed that wasn't the icenecks' doing).

Michelle Rodriguez smirked at me, just like the actress does in movies. "We could set our own price on this one, Weaver. Double time for working outside the U.S., that's normal. Then put another hour's pay—"

"—and this is specialty drilling-rig pay, Doc, which is not low in the first place," Pinkie said.

"Right?" Michelle Rodriguez didn't seem to mind the interruption, and she continued, "Then put another hour's pay on top of that for hazardous duty—"

Pinkie: "Double time on top, Mitch. *Extra*-hazardous duty, working on a science rig in Antarctica. And then—"

"Tom, you mind if I tell this guy the situation?" Michelle Rodriguez interrupted. "That be okay with you?"

"Yeah, s'long as you get your facts straight."

She shook her head, still smirking. "Anyway, Weaver, that's what, four times the hourly pay?—shut up, Tom, don't even—and then *another* double pay for working in Antarctica in the freakin' *winter*."

"I got *no* idea what that's gonna be like," Stripe, the team leader, said. For the first time, he looked like some of the blood had drained from his face. "Working in Antarctica in the winter is gonna be like working on the goddamn *moon*. Except the moon doesn't have eighty-knot winds to knock you over and kill you. And the moon has sunlight—"

"Yeah, but at six times the wage," Tom interrupted again before Stripe could completely freak out the rest of us—or Tom himself, for that matter. "And, like I said, we get a pretty solid hourly wage in the first place. Hell, with this job, we're making more than professors or even *real* doctors back in civilization."

I tried to make an impressed whistle, but it came out like a blue jay being choked to death. "How can they afford to pay you so much for a scientific expedition?"

"*Scientific?*" Suntan said, then whipped a look at Ash and the other Air Force officers just out of earshot. She continued in a stage whisper,

"This ain't a scientific expedition, Doc—this is a *military* operation. And that means government money, not the nickels and dimes scientific missions pay out from their measly grants. And *that* means they can pay whatever it will take to get us on board. They don't give a rat's ass about how much anything costs. I mean, whatever they're paying for drilling muscle, they got to be paying you big brains a lot more."

I must have looked flabbergasted, because Michelle Rodriguez interpreted my reaction quite accurately and added, "Listen, tip for ya: I don't know what they're paying you guys, but tell 'em you want a lot more or you ain't getting off the plane."

They all laughed, but, seeing my continued expression of confusion and distress, the suddenly disturbed Ski Mask said incredulously: "Wait a second—Weaver, you were kidnapped, for real? I thought you were kidding."

I shook my head in embarrassment. "*Nope.*"

"Man, that ain't *legal*!" Michelle Rodriguez shouted. "They have to—"

"Secure that talk, all of you," Colonel Ash snapped.

Where the hell did he come from? The man moved like a cat. "Weaver, you complaining about your pay?"

"I didn't know hostages were paid at all."

"I will roundhouse kick you in the throat if you say that word again." The colonel's iron gaze left no doubt that he would do it, too. "Join me over here, if you would, Professor."

I gave a small wave to the icenecks, trying to look grateful—because I was, very much so—for their sharing so much information with me. It made things a tiny bit clearer, but I was still as much in the dark as if I were bobbing on the lightless antipodean waves below us. I turned around and there was Ash, right in my face.

"I am going to whisper in your ear."

What? "Um, okay."

Ash leaned in and said so only I could hear, "Upon completion of this mission, you and your colleagues will each be paid *two million dollars*. Tax-free. All right?"

I waited, unsure how—or if—I was supposed to respond.

"In addition, an equal amount in research funds will be provided to each of your respective departments at each of your respective universities."

"Wow, this *is* a government operation." I attempted a laugh to show Ash how my sardonic tone wasn't, in fact, meant to be sardonic. I failed.

"Damn straight, it is, Weaver. You're going to see and spend time among things other scientists would kill their *families* for, just to catch a *glimpse*. All that and we're paying you extortionate rates for your cooperation and know-how. All right?"

"But you—"

"You weren't kidnapped or abducted, Professor. You were *drafted* for purposes of national security. You'll notice we're all Americans here, except for a few who aren't. The *Giorgio* carries the personnel, and all the equipment we're bringing is on the *Tsoukalos* fifteen miles behind us."

I blinked and instinctively looked around. What he said was correct, as, by definition, tautologies tended to be. But something was weird even within this sphere of weirdness. "If this expedition is so all—well, mostly—red-blooded American, then what's with the Greek airplane names?"

Ash closed his eyes and, I was sure, counted to at least three. "They're *code names*, for Chrissakes. Damn it, Weaver, I hope you're less dense on the ground than you are in the air."

He stalked away, condensation steaming from his mouth as he breathed. Like a bull.

And I happened to be wearing a red parka.

I sighed and noted that I had met just about everyone except the pilots, who could be excused from socializing since they were probably a bit busy keeping us aloft. There was nothing now but waiting. And *fear*—so much fear that, instead of being excited about seeing the first alien artifacts ever discovered, I worried that I might never see the daylight world again.

THE OTHER-MIND: YUTANI

Professor of Theoretical Fluid Dynamics and Paxton Chair of Meteorology Wai-Lon Yutani wasn't sure why he felt compelled to touch the sleek metal alien slate when Colonel Ash opened the armored case and showed it to him. But he didn't care about why—he just wanted to lay his hands on it.

This was a different slate from the one Ash had convinced Weaver to touch; its tablet's arcane markings and mysterious sheen were too tempting for Yutani to resist, not to mention that Ash specifically instructed him that he should "feel free" to run his fingers across it if he "thought it might help" facilitate a closer examination. Yutani didn't understand why one had to be lying down on a cot in the infirmary for this, but Ash had told him it was necessary in case Yutani swooned when he touched the artifact, which was mostly true.

Yutani obliged, reaching out in wonder at seeing—and being about to touch—something created by an extraterrestrial race. He wasn't an exobiologist, or any kind of biologist, for that matter. But still, like astronomers and exoscience enthusiasts, as a meteorologist he spent a lot of his time gazing up at the sky. What's more, the shifting colors of the shiny slate looked like rainbows on an oily puddle, mesmerizing him and drawing him in.

The instant his fingers made contact with the slate, the close walls of Criminy Station vanished, he was standing up, and he was looking up at the sky, his view dominated by unmistakable whirling lateral jet streams and swirling storms, one huge and red. He was looking out at the planet Jupiter.

He looked down and saw that he was in some kind of spacesuit—no, it was more like a wet suit outfitted with a (78% nitrogen: 21% oxygen?) breathing apparatus. He was standing in front of a meters-wide hole in the ice kept open by something that looked like a tall ship's short cannon, but enormous: the blue energy beam it shot down the hole in the ice was as big—*exactly* as big—as the tunnel it created in the ice.

Yutani found it hard to peel his own mind away from this other mind—this other-mind— but needed to remember … *something*. He knew who he was and how he had gotten here (if "because I touched a space platter" could count as an explanation without charges of begging the question), but he felt unmoored from the mind of Wai-Lon Yutani. Memories of the past, thoughts about the future, all were gone for the nonce.

At that moment, the alien happened to gaze in the direction of the giant laser short-cannon thing, directing Yutani's attention there. Yutani focused on the apparatus with its etchings … Goldsmith … someone called Goldsmith—etchings that, yes, Yutani remembered now, the linguist Goldsmith went wild for, getting in trouble with the man in charge. *Ash*. Ash was furious because he was in charge of …

God, it was *right there*. What was Ash in charge of? Yutani strained to recall what Ash or he himself or *any* of them (*them*?) were doing back on Earth … in Antarctica …

That did it—everything clicked and his mind finally adjusted, and he found himself looking at a much larger version of the energy beam that held open the tunnel in the West Antarctic Ice Sheet.

The meteorologist had been born in Bakersfield, California, and hadn't visited Japan since he was six years old, but from somewhere in his memory came an awestruck "*shanti rarenai*," which meant "incredible" *and* "amazing."

Yutani had always taken great pleasure in examining the weather systems of other worlds as detailed in the images of Earth's robotic probes. Thus, he knew exactly where he was, based on Jupiter bearing down on him from above as well as from standing on a thick icy surface over a liquid sea (knowledge easily accessed, surprisingly, from the other-mind). He was on Europa, the giant Galilean moon of Jupiter. He knew, then, that he stood over an ocean which lay at least sixty miles beneath the ice where he was standing.

And he saw now that he wasn't here by himself or, rather, *as* himself. It took him about ninety seconds to realize that his mind now

38

inhabited another body, one which the original resident's mind continued to inhabit as well. In fact, after a few minutes of trying to move "his" muscles rather than fall in with what the body's owner was doing, he understood that the other-mind he heard talking with his fellows was the full-time occupant of this body.

But no, he saw, they weren't talking at all—they were communicating *telepathically*., Yutani worked this out within minutes, figuring that touching the slate somehow put him in telepathic contact with this extraterrestrial.

What aided his conclusion was the realization that he was looking *through compound eyes* at a team of bipeds standing on Europa. It should have been difficult or even impossible for a human mind to be able to see anything through what were, essentially, the eyes of a household fly.

But see he could. He chalked it up to tapping into the "raw data feed," as it were, of the perceptions of the alien whose body he was sharing. Whatever the mechanism, Yutani came to a tentative conclusion that he could see because the alien could see, and he figured out the bizarre mental "sounds" sent telepathically from other-mind to mind to mind in the group because the alien could understand them.

Some of the beings were reminiscent of Earth reptiles or mammals; the rest were *definitely-not-earthlike* things on two legs. Yutani had no frame of reference for these aliens, and the other-mind didn't think about what they were—thus, the scientist reasoned, this team must have worked together for some time.

But *why* were they on Europa? For that matter, why was *he* there? Was he some kind of spirit (the idea of which was metaphysical bull puckey, but he had to make hypotheses before testing the situation) inside another body getting ready to spelunk into a tunnel like the one they made on Earth, but on steroids?

It didn't matter why: the aliens each entered the energy beam and dropped out of sight. Yutani's (phantom) stomach twisted at the thought of—

the hunt

—jumping down that endless hole. But the alien he was inside must have been fine with it, because the other-mind was more excited than scared, more thinking of riches—

chaos

—than any danger he might encounter against the [unintelligible-to-Yutani name] in the paralyzingly frigid waters below. Although the alien name meant nothing to the visiting meteorologist, the other-mind flashed an image of something in the dark water, something thick and long like a rugose hair viewed under a microscope, with head features reminiscent of a Chinese dragon. But it wasn't a Europan version of some enormous and wrinkled eel; it had paddles for legs, like a manatee's.

And this *was* an evolutionary adaptation, Yutani felt sure, the creature gradually developing from a land-dwelling creature into something that returned to the sea. Or, alternately, perhaps it was a sea animal with a serendipitous adaptation that would serve it well if it ever needed to walk on land.

Except … how could its ancestors ever have lived on *land*? The "land" of Jupiter's moon was *ice*. There was nothing here that any creature could consume for food. There wasn't even an atmosphere, for God's sake!

The other-mind turned its thoughts to hopping into the endless tunnel—well, not *endless*—but at only 13 percent of Earth's gravity, it would take an object about six minutes to fall sixty miles. Yutani knew that he had no numbers for gravity and acceleration here; it was the other-mind that knew this, and as long as his alien knew something, Yutani knew it, too.

The aliens falling through the ice tunnel would splash into the inner Europan sea at roughly one thousand miles per hour which would vaporize damn near anything, let alone any *living* thing, no matter how hardy the being was. Yutani could feel himself wanting to freak out, trapped inside this alien on a suicide mission—but he was a scientist, and he thought the situation through logically instead of panicking.

His alien must have felt uneasy about the drop, but not scared, exactly, or even necessarily anxious; just an uneasiness like one feels when walking around in the dark. None of the other extraterrestrials, regardless of their species, seemed to him or his alien to be apprehensive about the dive, either. So, as far as his alien's mind and body were concerned, there was no reason to feel nervous, let alone freak out.

As real feeling as this experience was, as much as he felt he was truly residing inside the body of the other-mind, in fact he was *not* physically here. He knew this intellectually, although his every lizard-brain instinct was to flee rather than plunge into the pitch-black and freezing Europan ocean and die upon impact. *I know this to be true*, he reminded himself. *I exist in this "other-mind" only intellectually, in thought-being.*

He was truly glad right then that he created and studied theoretical models of fluid dynamics for a living. He had to separate himself, when "living inside" the simulations, from what he knew was "really" happening. If he posited a dynamic system where storm fronts moved east to west—which he had done as one of the first models he created in graduate school, as did most of his fellow students—then he studied the effects of weather traveling retrograde on Planet Earth. What was "real" was perfectly irrelevant inside the simulation.

A part of him knew his physical body still existed elsewhere, despite currently experiencing sensations of being inside this body falling—

1.315 meters per second per second

—but his corporeal body was … where? He couldn't remember, and it would take too much of his attention to work through the tendrils of connected bits of memory back to where he was before his mind was here. It didn't matter where his body was, anyway—it was operating, or else he wouldn't have a self-construct to wonder if it was still operating. He was 100 percent a materialist, but here he had to agree with Descartes: *I'm still thinking; therefore, I must still be.*

He was falling faster now, and faster, the blue beam surrounding him all the way down. Below him—he could hear through his *feet*—something scraped hard against the walls of the ice tunnel. Then another, separate scraping, and then something shot powerfully out of his alien body's backpack unit into the tunnel wall and *dragged*, gouging out the ice with a horrendous scraping sound that made his feet ring. It slowed him down, all right, reducing his velocity perfectly to drop him into the water's surface no faster than if he had leapt from a kid's diving board into a pool back on Earth.

Although Yutani knew enough about fluid dynamics to fill a textbook—one he had, in fact, already written—he was perplexed: a hole and tunnel of that size being bored through the ice should have produced a veritable geyser of pressurized water that would have shot out the hole like a pressure jet. That water would boil entirely away immediately upon forcing itself into the wisp-thin "atmosphere" of Europa, but under that much pressure it would definitely stay agitated enough to make it as a liquid up through the sixty miles of ice tunnel. His question was *why* did that not happen? Such pressure should have kept anyone, any*thing* from being able to drop into the hole until the entire massive subterranean ocean had been drained upward and boiled away by the vacuum of space

He wasn't a particle physicist, but he did enjoy following the mathematics. That said, his limited knowledge of alien space–laser beam hoodoo allowed him to chalk up the weirdness to that semi-magical technology. The tunnel was open. The water didn't follow the rules of fluid dynamics.

He searched the other-mind as well. His host either didn't know or didn't care enough about the short cannon holding open the hole to devote any time or effort into finding out how it worked. Yutani's host was a hunter of some kind, and they were … *ice fishing* was the only term that came to mind, a bit more specific than the other-mind's *melee hunt*. What the hell did that even mean?

The alien dropped into the frigid water and immediately moved out of the way of the opening to avoid being hit by his compatriots coming down after him. Yutani knew the water was deathly cold, but neither his mind nor the other-mind really *felt* it as cold. True, they were standing on an airless moon with a surface temperature of minus 315 degrees without discomfort, so the water's freezing point of 32°F was, comparatively, like a hot tub—but even with the thermal environment down there leaching away body heat, the other-mind registered no discomfort. And since Yutani's mind was tapped into the alien's sensory system, he didn't register any discomfort either.

He was a scholar of meteorology, so he would leave the explanation of the energy beam to his physicist colleagues. And he wasn't a biologist, so he would also leave open the question of: *How the hell do they not freeze or have their (compound) eyes explode in the vacuum of space?* He was in the Europan sea with the other-mind, however, and that meant water, and that meant he was now in his element ... so to speak.

It was pitch black in the vast ocean, but after a few seconds the alien switched on a light attached to its backpack unit, and the murk was illuminated for at least a few feet. He could see his fellow—

hunters

—aliens floating near him, but that was all. There was no flotsam in the water, no organic matter drifting about, as in the deeps of Earth's oceans. It was all disorienting as hell, but he soon found that the more he let go of Yutani-mind and just *observed*, the other-mind took care of the business of thinking and reacting and doing. Yutani realized he could learn much more, maybe *everything*, if he stopped wondering and struggling to stay separate. If he just stopped his ... *everything*. He took a deep breath, or at least made the mental formations that went along with taking a deep breath when one was still in one's own body, and released himself fully into the other-mind. The alien's thoughts became Yutani's thoughts; the actions governed by the other-mind became *his* actions.

His alien mind-spoke to the others: *Harpoons at the ready!*

All eight of them reached back and withdrew what the other-mind meant by "harpoon": a telescoping rod not resembling what Yutani would have thought of as a harpoon, this capped with a sucker that looked like the bell of a plunger. If Yutani had kept his mind's presence within the other-mind, he would have wondered if they were going to glom onto the eel-thing and somehow drag it up sixty miles to the surface. He also would have asked what in hell they were doing this for—food? Strange to travel light-years through space to Earth's solar system to get protein to eat. The eel-thing was huge, but certainly not so huge that space aliens would—

Goddamnit! his mind cried. Yutani had seeped back in, thinking. He hadn't read one word of Dogen—or even Alan Watts—but he knew his judging mind had to vanish in surrender to the other-mind if he was going to *learn*. And *learning* was what he had devoted his life to. He concentrated and pressed his mind into nothingness, which allowed the other-mind to take him wherever it chose.

Harpoons out, his alien and its fellows switched something on that made his feet tingle. He couldn't quite make out what had happened, but the other-mind knew perfectly, of course. The backpack units were now emitting a very long wavelength of electromagnetic radiation. The aliens knew what Yutani knew: long wavelengths travel much farther in water than shorter ones, especially pure water, like the pure water that right now they were contaminating with their presence.

(When he returned to his own consciousness, Yutani would allow himself to *think* again, and one of the things that came to his mind immediately was the fact he often told his intro students: this is why submarines use long-wavelength sonar instead of the shorter-wavelength radar. But that was in the future. Some vaguely remembered Zen techniques allowed Yutani to keep his mind quiet in the *now* of this experience. The last whisper of his nerd-mind's vanishing presence was *Instant Zen master? So frakkin' weird.*)

The hunters were sending out EM radiation at a wavelength far below that of the visible spectrum. On the lower end of the visible spectrum is red, and on the other end is violet. Just above the visible spectrum is ultraviolet and other high-energy electromagnetic sources; just below is infrared. They wore special "night-vision" goggles to detect and translate invisible (to human eyes) heat signatures into a green glow that falls within our visible spectrum. Most of the electromagnetic spectrum is unavailable to unaided human eyes, which evolved under a yellow sun smack dab in the middle of the visible spectrum. We see what was most efficient for our ancestors to see: the photons given off by our solar system's star.

In other words, infrared is invisible for a reason.

Yutani could only imagine how these hunters evolved, because, looking through the alien's compound eyes, he could *see* the much longer sonar waves (which were even farther from human sensory experience) bouncing off an object ahead. He barely thought this, since he had surrendered for now to the other-mind. This alien's race had either evolved under a Krypton red sun or was using special optical technology (like infrared goggles for humans) to see the photons once they returned from …

From whatever that thing—

apex predator

—was in front of them. Yutani could feel it click in the other-mind that this was what they were hunting here under the ice on Europa. It—

ice serpent

—made a sweeping turn, the red light illuminating both its tremendous length and its—even to a bug with compound eyes—disturbing ugliness. Yutani had, of course, never seen anything like this, but neither had his alien: Yutani could feel the other-mind wanting to shrink away from the ice serpent even as it sent out and received mentally gleeful exclamations of how they had hit just the right spot and how they were going to be [*wealthy? satisfied? appreciated?* The thought from the other-mind had no exact corresponding concept in English] and other things that were outside of Yutani's conceptual understanding and thus were heard by him as alien-language gibberish.

Seeing the beast, the hunters swam toward it.

Seeing the hunters, the beast turned and swam toward them.

The alien and his fellows raised their plunger-headed weapons and let fly. A dozen projectiles swept through the water and stuck themselves against the ice serpent's flank and head.

More cheering inside the other-mind, both its own and the entire party's. All they had to do now was—

shock pain terror chaos melee

—something attacked the hunter just to his left side, and by the time Yutani's host could even turn its head to see what was going on, the other hunter had been swallowed whole by a bigger—*much* bigger—ice serpent, which swept up two more of them as it sailed through their group.

Yutani found that telepathic screaming creates sympathetic psionic vibrations that are far more horrible than human screaming. He tried to stay calm and not panic—it didn't really matter if he stayed calm or not, since he wasn't calling the shots here. His flickering mental presence wondered if his alien being killed meant that Yutani's mind would die like the other-mind probably would.

That did not help with keeping calm.

What *did* help was that the other-mind was cool and collected as the other hunters looked like they were freaking out. Although he heard multiple beings screaming inside the shared telepathy of the group, all of their movements and miens matched that of his alien: dispassionate, cool, methodical.

Every one of them followed the gigantic ice serpent—they had the paddle feet the other-mind had imaged, so it was definitely a member of the target species—with their reloaded plunger guns. The smaller creature was docile in the presence of its alpha, moving slowly and probably unconsciously through the water, like sharks that never sleep.

The bigger one wasn't docile, but it made circles now around the whole hunting party instead of straight-on attacking. Could it understand that these aliens had weapons? That they had subdued its fellow predator and planned to do the same to it?

It was *thinking*. This alien race, of which he was temporarily a member, was either naturally telepathic or, again, had some kind of enhancement to allow it to send and receive mental contents. The other-mind could hear the ice serpent's thoughts—fuzzily, and going in and out—none of the hunters could understand the content of the serpent's psionic transmissions; it was just noise to them and to Yutani ... but it was thinking *something*.

Whatever it was thinking, it was a predator's thoughts. Whatever it was planning, it was a predator's plan, probably to eat what had so graciously dropped into its demesne from above. The static and garbled psionic emissions were increasing in magnitude—it was getting ready to strike.

A barked order came through Yutani's other-mind as well as the minds of the other hunters; it was idiomatic, so there was no making a translation, but the way his alien and the rest held their plunger-rifles forward, toward the middle of their circle where the stunned ice serpent still floated, indicated something was about to happen and Yutani was going to watch it happen—watch it through the eyes of his alien, whether he wanted to or not.

As if cued by the brandishing of the stun-weapons, the titanic eel-monster rushed *past* the perimeter of the circle, unhinged its jaw like a snake, and bit the smaller and drifting monster right in half. The smaller creature's middle to the end of its body was in the giant one's mouth, and then it just closed its mouth and separated the littler ice serpent in two. Its mouth opened again to suck down the remaining half—it must have just shoved the back half right down its gullet. At the exact moment of the ice serpent's commitment to swallowing down the rest of its meal, the hunter who was in charge made a movement with his hand and shot out an order—

bigger chaos

—that must have been the extraterrestrial equivalent of *Let him have it, boys!* because, even in the dim sonar-red illumination of the backpacks, Yutani could see a dozen plunger-tipped projectiles launch at the momentarily distracted gargantuan predator. They struck the giant as every hunter reloaded and shot again. There had to be sparks or something visible coming from the plungers' point of contact—but Yutani recalled that he was seeing something outside the human visible spectrum; maybe short-wavelength, high-energy electric sparks were outside of these aliens' visible spectrum. (Or at least the technology some were using to see now ... like his insect-eyed alien, perhaps.)

The giant ice serpent finished swallowing his second mouthful and then ... just ... *stopped.* It was becalmed by the plasmatic overdose and simply hung in the water as if it were waiting to be scooped up by an even bigger monster and just didn't care.

But Yutani's other-mind agreed with the rest of the group that this gargantuan ice serpent was a much better catch—

recruit

—than the smaller one that, only minutes before, had been the biggest ice serpent they'd ever seen. To what purpose the other-mind and its partners—

melee death chaos

—had caught this massive Europan predator was less important for anyone to think about than to think of how they were going to get the ice serpent out to their ship, up through sixty miles of ice tunnel. One of the aliens swam back up toward the entry to the tunnel, fading quickly into the darkness of the frigid waters.

Below, the suckers were arranged into a geometrical pattern, the purpose of which was either unknown to the other-mind or just routine enough that it didn't merit wasting time thinking about. Yutani's lien hovered near the tapering tail of the beast, keeping watch that it didn't spring back into action, which could happen with sudden sensory—

A bubble of light and sound appeared for a second as the hunter who'd gone above set off a signal of some kind—a flare, but the other-mind's thoughts indicated that it was more than just a flare—and then burst.

Untranslatable cursing—and it was *definitely* cursing—sounded through the other-mind and the minds of all the hunters. Yutani couldn't understand what was wrong, but then the massive serpent, galvanized by its sudden rouse into awareness, jerked its mighty tail. In an instant, thing filled Yutani's field of vision.

Then all was dark.

On his cot at Criminy Station, Doctor Yutani opened his eyes.

Colonel Ash and Doctor Vasquez looked down at him. "Where'd you go?" Ash asked before the doctor could even check Yutani's vitals.

The question surprised the meteorologist, who had snapped abruptly into full consciousness as soon as the … dream? *vision*? … ended, with the other-mind being wiped out as it was killed by the alien predator's tail. "How did you—"

"Secure that and tell me where you were just now."

"Europa."

Ash's mouth twitched a smile, but the colonel beat it down. "*Jupiter's moon* Europa?"

"Yes, sir. At first on the surface and then under the ice, in the sea."

The smile returned to stay on Ash's face as he exclaimed, to no one in particular, "Hot damn!"

03.35: WILSON AIRSTRIP

There is no place to actually *land* a plane in Antarctica in winter. This is, in part, because no scientific fieldwork can be carried out in the darkness and extreme cold of an Antarctic winter, and if it can't be done completely inside, it isn't getting done until spring—thus, 99.9 percent of the time, an airstrip isn't needed during the winter. However, a more fundamental reason was that Wilson Airstrip was the only accessible landing strip on the entire continent; and while it could be kept flat, cleared of lumps of ice and snow during the other seasons, in winter it couldn't be trusted to remain thus long enough for an airplane to safely land on it. There's no way of telling before it's too late to commit to a landing if it's still flat like a runway needs to be, or littered with snow blown into lumps by the wind, or strewn with big pieces of ice. So, there was another confidence-instilling fact about this mission—this landing could very well be deadly.

I knew that our secret expedition would be a big, *big* deal for science (and any technology that arose from that science) and probably was funded out the ying-yang with "dark money" and such. However, it surprised me when Stripe told me that both of the C17s flying on this expedition were designed and built specifically for operating in the unfathomable cold we were flying through on the way to our imminent doom on the landing strip. (That last part reflects my dread, not Stripe's words.)

The aircraft were built with as little "extra" weight as possible; hence, our spartan surroundings inside the plane. Parts that were usually composed of aircraft-grade steel were here, incredibly, fashioned from much-lighter aluminum.

"Aluminum?" I said, incredulously. "Like Coke cans you can crumple by making a fist?"

Stripe raised an eyebrow. He knew a soft academic when he saw one, even if the scientist in question was under layer after layer of protective clothing.

"I mean, I can *dent* the heck out of one just using my fist! Anyway, aluminum doesn't seem like much of—"

"I hear ya, Professor. Check this out: it's *nano-altered* aluminum that phase shifts—sorry, you know what temperature phase shifts are, right? Like for water, it's solid if the temp is 32 degrees or under—"

"American arrogance!" the Kiwi shouted, and the rest of them laughed.

"Fine, fine—water is solid at zero Celsius and below, then it becomes liquid between 1 to 99 degrees, and then gas at any temperature above that. That's what a *phase shift* is." He made sure I got it and restarted his explanation of the nanotech phase-changing aluminum: "The melting point of aluminum is something like 1,200 degrees—that's Fahrenheit, I don't know the other—which would be *unusual* in field conditions on Earth."

"To say the least."

"Right? Anyway, that's its liquid phase. It doesn't change to gas until something like 2,500 degrees. So, the solid phase of aluminum is anything below 1,200 Fahrenheit, and that's why most people never see it as anything but solid. But it's no more or less aluminum when it's a gas or a liquid."

I let out a laugh and said, "That kind of blows my mind, Str—um, Scott."

"If that blows your mind, check this out—nanotech aluminum goes through a kind of fourth phase change. You guys, scientists or whoever, created this special metal so that, at about 80 degrees below zero, its atoms organize suddenly into a honeycomb structure that won't be dented in any air crash possible on Earth. Problem is, the passengers will still be shredded into pulled pork. Complete with the red barbeque sauce."

"Lovely."

"Heh. Man up, Professor! What I'm saying is the metal this plane is built out of won't turn brittle until the temperature drops to *270 below*. You're not gonna hit that unless you're in goddamn outer space. So, for any use other than space capsules or something, the nanotech structure of the aluminum makes it *stronger* the colder it gets. There is some seriously amazing *shiznatch* on this trip."

I shared an incredulous laugh with Stripe at the lengths the government had gone to and the money it had spent just to get us down to the South Pole in winter. Then I said, "How the hell does it keep the fuel, the hydraulics, *everything* from freezing up? I'm an exobiologist, and lots of our research is done in Antarctica to get ready for Mars or to go back to the moon—but it's *always* in the summer. I've read time and time again that they can't fly in or walk anywhere in the winter down there, because in July or August, it's literally *more dangerous than walking on the moon.*"

Stripe shook his head in amusement, and the icenecks who were listening, trying to occupy themselves during the twelve-hour flight, all nodded knowingly. "Yep. I talked with Buzz Aldrin about this once—he was actually there with us on the ice for some Mars publicity stuff, but in summer, obviously. But he said the same thing. He said that *getting* to the moon is insanely dangerous. You're sitting at the tippy top of a Saturn V rocket, which is basically explosives stacked higher than the Statue of Liberty." He smiled at the idea. "But *walking* all day on the moon is easier than trying to take ten steps in an Antarctic howler. That's because the moon doesn't have any wind to knock you down and never let you get up and then you die. I'll never forget what he said then, though. He said, 'Here, there—either way, it's just weird as hell.'"

I enjoyed the shared laugh, but I brought discussion back to the crazy airplane. "Okay, so the metal won't shatter, but what about everything else? How can this thing's systems keep operating when it's 80 below, no matter how cold-proof the airframe is?"

Michelle Rodriguez came over. "It's crazy, man. Even the best, most custom jet fuel is gonna freeze at 50 below. Hydraulic fluid? It goes solid and clogs the lines at 60 below. The higher a plane flies, the colder that son of a bitch gets, even in summer. And in winter? Forget it."

I allowed time for her to get to some explanation before I said, "*Forget it?* Aren't we flying there right now, in winter?"

"Yep. Land in about an hour."

"So ..."

ANOMALY

She laughed. "Getting the plane *there*, they use something called 'prist'—like 30 percent kerosene mixed in with the regular fuel. They don't skimp on that stuff. Keeps the gas lines unclogged so they won't freeze up mid-flight, which would be *bad*, man. Like Buddy Holly bad. Their fuel lines froze up at 40 below. We're at least 60 frickin' degrees colder than that outside this thing right now."

Ski Mask and Big John joined our little circle now. Suntan and Pinkie remained seated, but they were listening, and to great amusement.

Ski Mask jumped in: "That ain't even the weirdest thing about this plane, Professor. Any fool can put some fancy antifreeze in the fuel, but this thing, this *giant* plane? That's not gonna work. So, this plane is completely, no joke, one-hundred-percent mechanical. The only computers on this thing are brought on for navigation and pilot stuff. And those mega-laptops? They're so protected they'd still work fine if they got strapped to the *outside* of this thing."

"What does that mean, 'mechanical'? Just no built-in computers? I mean, nobody had computers sixty years ago, and there were lots of airplanes in the sky."

Suntan's eyes crinkled as she smiled at the professor who apparently held a PhD in cluelessness. "Doc, you have any idea how much computers do to keep regular planes flying?"

"Not really, no." I was sure I was about to find out that I didn't.

"There's this thing called 'fly-by-wire.' Everything the pilot does is captured and made digital to go into the computer. Pilots don't do anything when it comes to actually making the jets operate, the wing flaps go up and down, none of that. It's the computers—they are told what the pilot is doing and then decide if they think that's a good idea. If the human and the computer agree like usual, the computer moves the flaps, speeds the plane up or slows it down, puts out the landing gear—like I said, everything. Really, the pilot is just talking to the computer, and it's the computer that's talking to the plane. It works great, except when it doesn't."

I waited for more, her bait dangling, until I said, "What happens when it doesn't?"

"The computer ignores the pilot," Pinkie said, startling me a bit by seeming to suddenly materialize right next to me. "Well, not so much 'ignores' as 'overrides.' See, the regular airplane computers they have now know if the pilot's making a mistake or going too high or too low or whatever. There isn't time to have a nice, long chat about it with the stupid human—the computer just blocks the 'fly-by-wire' commands and does what it thinks needs to be done to keep the bird in the air."

"Another by-product of the Apollo missions," Stripe said. "Just like digital broadcasting and Tang and those moon flags that can stay open forever."

"These must be amazing pilots to fly with no real computers assisting them," I said, "That is, you said navigation and communications are done by those 'mega-laptops.' But checking the pilot's every action and making sure it falls within safe parameters—isn't that vital for a plane of this size?"

Big John nodded. "It's absolutely required, my man. For anything bigger than a Twin Otter, you ain't doing that without fly-by-wire."

I was confused. "But, then ... how can *this* plane do it?"

Stripe pointed at some braids of heavily insulated–looking wires running down the length of the cargo plane on both sides, against the bulkhead. "Those wires? Not digital or fiber optics. They just send electrical impulses that control mechanical servos and flaps and everything else that needs controlling. Each wire goes to a particular motor or what-have-you and powers it directly. The motors don't need much to keep them going, except what they call 'moon grease.' It won't freeze up in *space*, which is why NASA developed it—"

"You and Buzz pickin' out curtains together or what?" Michelle Rodriguez said with a laugh that all of our little group echoed.

Stripe smiled widely at her teasing but continued right where he left off: "It won't freeze up in space is why NASA created it in the '60s, and it made it to military aircraft in the '70s, then was cleared for commercial flights taking a polar route. Stuff's too damn expensive to use anywhere except where it's absolutely needed, like cold-weather aircraft, space capsules, moon buggies, that 'extreme' stuff. But cost doesn't seem to matter to the colonel and his mission, so our baby is greased six ways from Sunday to fly into this frozen hellhole."

"What about hydraulics? Didn't somebody say something about those freezing, too?"

Michelle Rodriguez said, "Yeah, same as the fuel lines. To handle polar routes, regular planes mix in some additive to keep it flowing. The hydraulics won't work quite as good, but they'll work enough to get you through the cold."

"Um … so this plane uses hydraulics, or doesn't?"

"Nope. We got the direct wiring instead of all that, no relays that could freeze. Flight instructions go right to the motors, no middle man."

After thinking about what piece I was missing—and I was definitely missing something—I said, "I'm still confused. Is there that big of a difference between pilots' movements telling the computer what to do with the plane—the fly-by-wire concept—and what's happening here?"

"Biggest difference is that the computer is *manually* told what motors and servos to activate. It's a lot more complicated in practice than you might think."

"Okay, but … I still don't get how it's *impossible* to fly a plane this big without fly-by-wire, but *this actual plane* is flying with a *manual* system? It sounds a *lot* more complicated for the pilot—surely, he (or she) can't directly operate all of this machinery accurately in the middle of a landing, even if he or she weren't trying to land in the dark on a runway carved out of the ice."

The icenecks traded a series of glances between themselves that would have been funny if we weren't likely to die in the next hour. (I quickly worked out the combinatorial mathematics: in a group of six individuals, there are thirty-two possible combinations of people if you assume that [a] one person can glance at up to five others at one time, and [b] that up to five people can glance at a single person at one time. *Math!*)

Their amused glances made me say in suspicion, "What?"

Stripe put a paw on my shoulder and walked me toward the cockpit. I could hear the others clomping behind us. He asked, "Are you ready to see the greatest thing your tax money can buy?"

I didn't know enough to be anything but as ready as I was going to be. Stripe opened the cockpit door, *cold* air pushing out in a *whoosh*, allowing me to meet the pilots.

My jaw literally dropped open.

There was no one to meet.

There were no pilots.

Instead, there was a chunky, steel-protected computer the size of a sofa ottoman. I knew it was a computer only because it had blinking lights and three braids of at least a hundred wires each leading out of the cockpit, with a few thinner braids that ended with individual wires going to various ports to operate things in the front of the plane, I guessed.

"Whaddya think about that, Professor?"

"I think you icenecks are hazing the new guy." I really did.

"*Ha!* The colonel would throw us right out the rear hatch if we pulled that kind of prank aboard *his mission's* airplane." Stripe stared into space for a second, nearly imperceptibly shaking his head. "That man is intense. He said to me right before I hired on, 'I have no official authority over a civilian, but that won't mean a whole lot if you're dead. Understood?'" His eyes still showed the power of that veiled threat. "You better believe I understood, and *real* well, too."

"You signed on *after* he threatened to kill you?"

"Professor, you joined this expedition against your will—I didn't know a thing about that until my crew and I boarded this plane. We sure as hell would've *un*boarded it like rats on a sinking ship if Ash had told us about the, what do they call them, yeah, about the *renditions* before we were in the air." It was hard to tell with him in that oversized parka, but he seemed to have to shrug off a shiver at the memory. "Anyway, there was an awkward moment there between the colonel and me, believe it. I was wavering, more or less, about signing on for this thing. Then I thought how any one of us could cause the death of every other person down there at almost any time. And *then* I thought of all that hazardous-duty pay, triple time, and realized he was in just as much danger as the rest of us."

I nodded and then snapped out of it: "But the *pilots!* Where the hell are the *pilots*? No jokes—what's going on here?"

"Professor, there aren't but two or three people on the planet—one of 'em's a woman, by the bye—who could even *theoretically* land this aircraft in the middle of winter down there. Even then, from what the Air Force guys told me, there'd be only a thirty or forty percent chance of making it anyway. None of the three superpilots were willing to take those odds for *any* amount of money." Stripe laughed as he looked at my still-completely-stunned expression. "And can you guess what would happen if the colonel and his friends shanghaied a couple of pilots?"

I smiled widely. "They'd make some serious changes to the flight plan."

"*Exactamundo*. Also, flying-by-wire isn't possible at 100 below, anyway. Can't rely on hydraulics in that kind of environment—one part of the line freezing would send everything into chaos until the pilot was able to switch stuff over to other systems or something. But your chances of landing safely without proper hydraulics on Wilson Airstrip, dark as the second before Creation and just as chaotic? Only a Vegas bookie out of his mind would lay you even 100-to-1 on that."

"Wait, so you're saying that this landing is too treacherous for even the best pilots on Earth to attempt, and so science fiction–advanced aeronautic technology was suddenly available?"

"After they got refused by the three flyboys—I mean fly*people*, I guess—the colonel and his gang found a solution to the pilot problem. The government must've had this tech all ready to go."

"Well, *that* sure doesn't sound suspi—"

"*Suspicious*, Doctor Weaver?" the harsh voice of Colonel Ash called from just behind my left shoulder, making me jump. "Of what might you be suspicious? You are part of the most important discovery in the history of civilization. Should we wait until summer, let the Russians get there first? Who knows what weapons Ivan could find in an alien spacecraft? I think it was worth the money to create a pilot with the ability to actually get us on the ground at Wilson."

I desperately stuttered something apologetic-sounding.

"Are you suspicious of American technological and scientific know-how? Or of the United States of America being the one nation on Earth that will pull out all stops for the protection of its citizenry?" He said it amicably, or at least as amicably as anything else I'd heard him say. "Speaking of which, boys, time to strap in. Our descent has begun."

I felt panic rising in my throat.

Colonel Ash rested a hand on my shoulder and said, "Don't worry, Weaver. With our fully digital friend flying this fully analog aircraft, our chances of survival shoot up to fifty percent! *Ha*." With that and in no apparent rush, he perambulated to his curtained area, presumably to "strap in."

I knew I had to do the same, especially now that I could feel the plane slowing as it began its descent. Somewhere down there—we were well past the icy shores of Antarctica—was Wilson Airstrip. But I couldn't tear my eyes away from the light-festooned box that would, without worry or passion, either get us down safely or else liquify our squishy selves while its airframe survived.

A direct crash into the ground was only one way the computer could bring our lives to an untidy end. There was also the specter of something big and solid and invisible lurking in the middle of the lightless landing strip—a block of ice, a piece of debris from the last autumn flight out, a dead seal—that would probably flip the plane at 150 mph. That way, if we didn't die immediately, we'd just be trapped inside as fire consumed the plane, a point of light and warmth soon to be overpowered by the singular dark horror of the Antarctic night.

I would've preferred smashing into the ice sheet and being killed quickly if given the choice between that and hanging in the air from my belt restraints, living just long enough to reach the pinnacle of agony and burn to death. That experience was definitely *not* on my "bucket list."

That said, I shook hands with Stripe, then he and his crew moved to their area of the cargo hold and buckled themselves in. I went back to Egghead Central and did the same.

"Christ, Weaver, what the hell did they show you?" the already strapped-in Goldsmith said with a nervous smile. "Are the pilots drunk, or what?"

I pulled my harness over my head and secured it, dread permeating every nerve in my body. "Worse than that," I said as calmly as possible. "Our pilot is a computer."

Doctor Hurt let out a little laugh. "Right. I don't think they can fly this kind of rig without the help of computers. Seriously—have you guys ever heard of flying-by-wi—"

"I don't mean that, Sue. I mean *we have no pilot*. There is just a big, square, blinky A.I. thing that's been our plane's only pilot the whole time."

"An android?" Yutani scoffed. "No offense, but that is what I call in the classroom environment 'complete bullshoot.'"

I felt as helpless here as I had when I saw the computer in the cockpit. As helpless as I had when I realized I had been kidnapped. As helpless as I had felt through this whole damned nightmare. "Not a robot—it's some supercomputer. Go up there and see for yourself."

Yutani moved to unbuckle his harness, but Colonel Ash appeared out of the shadows like Nosferatu himself. "Keep those restraints in place, please."

We all kept those restraints *very* the hell in place, even tightened them, under Ash's glare.

"Our pilot is the most sophisticated computer in the world, not to mention the best at operating Air Force aircraft in the entire ranks of military or civilian pilots. It is not human, of course, so its artificial intelligence neural net technology is entirely devoted to flying this plane in *any* environment, probably into Hell itself."

Ash let that linger, and I was sure I wasn't the only one to think: *Isn't that our destination?*

"All right, Scott, secure that curtain. You all have more to think about than a computer in the cockpit." He clapped his hands to get everyone's attention and shouted, "Buckle in, people! This will be one hell of a bumpy landing."

If it's a landing at all, I thought. *More like a crash.*

There was no one Ash could look at sternly or yell at regarding the landing of this mutant aircraft, so he must have remained silent and seated, fingers perhaps intertwined, waiting to see if he would be leading this epochal expedition or dying mangled in the cargo jet's flaming wreckage.

The A.I. didn't give us the local time, because there was no such thing as "local time" here; and it didn't read out the weather conditions at our destination, presumably because a computer voice telling us "It's Condition One and a balmy 120 below out" could inspire vital personnel (in the form of the five eggheads) to refuse to leave the plane.

I had heard the term "Condition One weather" several times during this twelve-hour flight, and I knew it meant "very, very bad weather," but a *minimum* wind speed of 63 mph? Coupled with a *minimum* wind chill of minus 100 degrees that would, within seconds, frostbite the flesh right off your face? Also, you'd be lost and your body wouldn't be found until spring because visibility in a Condition One storm is measured not in miles, but in *feet*. (Or whatever that was in meters for the non-American contingent.)

When I was told what Condition One meant, I blurted something that rhymed with *duck hat*.

My interlocutor just shook his head and smiled. "Yep."

One thing I do not care to hear on an airplane is the sound of a wing groaning as it bends toward falling off. That sound hit and we were bumped *hard*. We were swiftly decelerating and the wing was going to shear off completely. The whole science crew screamed and, if not buckled in, would have *leapt* out of our seats and run around in a panic.

"Welcome to Antarctica," Colonel Ash called from his seat on the other side of his curtain.

"WHAT?" I shrieked at the top of my lungs. "A wing is shearing off! We're *crashing*!"

Every person who did not teach at a university laughed their faces blue. Even Ash chuckled, which was just unsettling. "I take it you've never flown on a plane with skis? That sound is the skis sliding on the ground, Weaver. We're safe—"

WHAM

We hit something in front of us, and *hard*. The back of the plane lurched upward as the C17 spun around, centrifugal force pinning all of us to our seats against the walls.

Skis on ice made an even more unsettling sound when an airplane was skidding sideways, apparently. But it seemed like both skis had stayed attached, since the plane wasn't—

RRRRRRRRRRRRRRRRRRRRWHOMP

The horrid rending-metal sound ended with the cargo plane's right side diving into the ice, its ski left behind. I know I let out a strangled scream; I'm sure others were screaming as well, but honestly, I don't remember anything outside of my shutting down in utter terror.

We slid on the ice for ten seconds, half an hour, I didn't know how long, but Reddy Kilowatt at the controls up front at least was able to keep us on the remaining stretch of landing strip. More than that, the computer did something I agree that no human pilot could: it stayed the course forward on the runway as the plane went into a 360-degree spin ending with the plane shuddering to a neck-cracking stop against what I assumed was piled snow and ice at the end of the strip.

But human abilities be damned—we were alive, and the computer had managed to get us to a halt still within the boundaries of the landing strip, the nose of the plane at rest against the ice barrier. We were all canted at a 30-degree angle, but the A.I. was incapable of panic and had dealt with the emergency in a way that even the best human pilot would have been unable to pull off.

Even among these rugged icenecks, experienced soldiers, and black ops fighters, several *whooped* with exultation at our continued existence. I did, too, but stopped myself short as a thought popped into my head and I shouted, "We have to warn the other plane!"

"Already done," came the unruffled voice of our mission commander, visible now since his privacy curtain was hanging off plumb and he was still in his safety restraints at a 30-degree angle to the ground like the rest of us. "Not to worry, Professor. The entire process of our landing is fed in real time to the computer on board the *Tsoukalos*. Now it knows exactly where the obstacles are, based on our pilot's continuous transmission of data."

Yutani spoke up: "But we lost a ski! How are we going to fly back out of here?"

"That's something else you don't have to worry about," Ash said, but it was unclear whether this assurance meant that the ski would be fixed (by whom? with what?) or that we didn't have to worry because we were never meant to return home from the frozen wasteland.

***

By the time he had debriefed Weaver and Yutani, Colonel Ash recognized what was going on and saw how vital this unexpected development might have been to satisfying the ultimate objective of the expedition.

At first, it had seemed too good to be true—the slates somehow hijacked the consciousness of humans, allowing them—forcing them— to *see* through the aliens' eyes and hear their telepathic thoughts. To what end would such things exist, and how could they do what they apparently did? Ash had touched the slates back in Washington, all five of them, had his XSC forensics team test them for any psionic residue, and invited other Above Top Secret clearance military and civilians to examine them as well. They all wore blue gloves strong enough to halt the point of a hypodermic needle, tracing the alien etchings with their fingers as if that might help them understand what they said.

Back in Washington, in terms of the psionic energy XSC detected from them, the alien slates might as well have been used iPads.

Once this mission was in Antarctica, however, it became obvious to Ash that something was definitely going on, and it didn't matter if it were too good to be true—it *was* true. He ordered Bishop and Frost to stand guard in a curtained-off area inside the plane as he opened each of the five custom-padded steel cases containing the slates. The artifacts were made of an iridescent metal blue, with etchings that looked engraved and filled in with some dark fluid.

It was tempting, almost irresistible, to touch the slate in the first case he opened—but that very fact stayed his hand. Ash wasn't given to doing anything—*anything*—in a reckless manner. This was one of the qualities that marked him early in his Air Force career as someone to trust because he didn't give in to bullshit, threats, tricks, *anything*. Even good arguments with evidence didn't earn his immediate concession. He was, above anything else, cautious while still fully committed to achieving even the most abstruse military goals. He shot up the XSC ladder into XSC—into the holiest of the holies, the place where things conspiracy theorists have never even thought of occur with regularity—because of that caution, but also because he was open to ideas that would have been thought insane by anyone outside this undocumented department. He examined questions before answering. He ran worst-case scenarios all the way through in his head, and when computers became advanced enough, he collected Above Top Secret clearance coders to simulate these potential disasters in an exact and even visceral manner.

So he didn't touch the alien slate.

But by God, there in the C17, he craved to answer its strange call, touch it, *hold* it. He shouted "Bishop! Double time!" to make sure a potential witness was there before he could risk the mission or his own life without thinking damn seriously about it first. He had Bishop guarding the cases—not knowing what was going on and definitely not asking—while he conferred with Major Elden in another curtained area.

Elden stood as Ash approached and motioned for him to follow, but he'd been friends with him for many years, so the major could say what he was really thinking to the colonel: "You look like hell. Drinking on the job? Ha."

"Ha," Ash echoed in hilarity, and now both men had hit the very ceiling of their amusement. "No, *thinking* on the job. You should try it. Ha."

"Ha."

"All right, getting serious … there *is* something interesting about the alien slates."

"Other than they're made by aliens?"

"Ha. No, Elden, listen: do we have the psionic test kit?"

"We do, but hell if I know how to use it."

"Your people?"

Elden shook his head. "The XSC psi team is the only place you'll see captains and majors doing actual work, but I'm not one of them. Ha."

"Heh. The SEALs are all Top Secret clearance, but not Above Top Secret, so they won't know any more than the president about these matters." Ash shook his head. "So, we have alien artifacts that are probably *radiating* psionic energy—"

"Even though there was no trace of it back in Washington."

"Exactly. Thus, we have something active going on with these artifacts, something that might be caused by proximity to the anomaly, and we don't have one goddamn person aboard who has the clearance"—he shot a wry look at Elden—"or who's cleared *and* knows how to use the kit that we, for some reason, have on this aircraft."

"Not to make light, sir, but this is definitely a government operation."

"Ha. Good point."

"So … should we examine them, perhaps without gloves in case there's a psi connection?"

"If you want to risk your sanity or possibly lose your life right here and now, be my guest," Ash said, but by the colonel's tone Elden could tell he wasn't being invited—indeed, wouldn't be *permitted*—to do any such thing. "There is a way they can be tested, however. *Other* personnel might be more expendable, not to mention that their insatiable curiosity will make them volunteer to be first in line."

"The scientists?"

"The scientists. We have five artifacts, we have five eggheads."

"What a coincidence," Elden said with a smile.

THE OTHER-MIND: HURT

Doctor Susan Hurt, PhD in evolutionary biology with a focus on allometry, lay upon the cot where Doctor Vasquez and Colonel Ash had earlier put Weaver and Yutani before having them make contact with the alien slate. "What's the cot for?" she asked once she was already lying down on it. She had paid for much of her education with G.I. grants she got after five years in the Air Force, so she didn't question following a legal order—well, technically a *request*—from a colonel. Additionally, she had never been to Antarctica, in summer *or* winter, so she needed to listen about most everything to those more seasoned than she. Being asked to lie down on a cot barely seemed strange at this point, after the landing and the horrors of making it to Criminy Station.

Doctor Vasquez said, "You are the third member of the science team who has agreed to this little experiment, and there was some swooning. We just prefer to play it safe."

"Sounds about right to me."

Ash lifted another steel case and opened it for Hurt as he had done for the others. "Do you know what this is?"

"I'm not saying it's aliens ... but it's aliens, isn't it?"

The jest was lost on Ash, who spent little time on the Internet and none at all checking out "memes." He nodded and said, "We believe this to be an artifact from the very alien race responsible for the giant anomaly half a mile below us."

"How the heck did you get *that*?" she marveled, lifting herself up to her elbows to get a better look. "It's iridescent ... does it have some kind of coating on it to produce ... do you hear that? Like a wavering musical note, almost like a song. Do you hear that?"

"Yes," Ash and Vasquez said in unison.

"I don't anthropomorphize inanimate objects ..."

"Okay …" Ash said, patiently.

"… but it, uh, it *wants* me to touch it. Do you guys feel that, too?"

"Yes," the colonel and the M.D. said together.

"Is it okay to touch it?" Hurt asked, her hand already raised to reach out for it.

Ash would lie about anything to anyone he needed to in order to keep XSC's secrets and personnel safe. But if he didn't need to, he wouldn't. In this case, he didn't need to. He said, "We'd like your scientific insight into what this *is*, exactly. Touching it may help you understand more."

Hurt took that as a yes and touched—

Mars

—the tablet.

She was no longer in Antarctica. She was no longer lying on a cot. She was no longer alone inside her mind. She knew where she was, although it didn't seem strange to her that she was suddenly standing on another *planet*. In fact, she felt only excitement, anticipation, *thrill* at where she was right then.

It wasn't cold. Not just warmer than at the south pole of Earth; no, here it felt about 55 degrees Fahrenheit on the surface, warmer than Australia in July. Did Mars get that warm?

There was wind sending up wisps of red dust, but nothing like those Antarctic Condition One blasts that almost killed them all getting from the plane to the winter outpost. (Of course, the icenecks had to get the outpost—Criminy Station—set up from parts on the second cargo jet before anyone could seek shelter inside it.) No, here the small yellow disc of the sun was shining its best above them. The sky itself was a butterscotch shade of brown. The ground was rocky and its soil full of iron—she could tell because it was red, oxidized like the steel of an old car. The soil here was *rusted*.

COMMENCE

Hurt almost yelped at the sudden loud command inside her mind. She had almost casually accepted appearing on Mars, watching the dust devils, thinking about the sand, the sun, the temperature … but now she realized no outside intelligence was inside *her* mind.

No, *she* was an intelligence residing in this other-mind. This host mind.

An *alien* mind with its body on Mars, one of almost a dozen other aliens, all bipeds but otherwise a myriad crew of disparate species wearing hard-shelled backpack units with strange dishes, lights, and sensors on them. There was a slippery-skinned thing that looked like a walking salamander; a green splay-footed thing with suckers on the ends of its fingers; a hirsute ten-foot-tall creature; and on and on.

Her host body happened to look down, and Hurt saw elongated digits—not *fingers*, as such—and enormous bear-like claws that retracted when the body needed to use its hands for something other than … shredding and killing? She had no idea, of course, especially when the voices going back and forth through the other-mind (and thus her mind as well) seemed to be exchanging orders and reports as if they were on a battlefield instead of standing in the Martian desert.

All of these thoughts inside Doctor Hurt's head passed in a flash, completed by the end of the word that made her shriek inside, the word her mind had automatically translated as *commence*.

That was definitely a battlefield word, or maybe something from a high-energy physics lab. Evolutionary biologists tended not to need that word, unless they were proctoring exams. Things moved—appropriately enough—slowly in the evo-devo world. But *commence*—

She didn't know if the other-mind was hearing it or feeling it, but a *rumble* came from almost directly behind her alien, and it turned around, clawed feet inside big boots. The machine was *massive*, Hurt thought, but the other-mind didn't seem to be overly impressed by its size, mentally referencing it only as *the tool*.

"The tool" resembled a stout Roto-Rooter tanker truck, although this one hovered a few feet off the ground and sported a huge "horn" at the front that rotated, then shot apart as a gaping pentadactyl mouth before slamming back together as the horn again. Its antigrav pressure crushed rocks and ground sand just like such a vehicle with tires would have done. It had no cab in front for someone to drive it, so Hurt assumed— and accepted, as with the fact that she was presently a member of a group of telepathic aliens from all over the stellar neighborhood—that it was operating via a psionic connection with one of the aliens. It also could just have had an A.I. guiding it along. It didn't matter—why was she always into such minutiae? she was on *Mars*, for god's sake—but what did matter was what the aliens—

pirates bedlam

—were trying to do with it.

Hurt found that, if she stopped her own chattering mind, she could explore the other-mind and find out as much as she could about these space-faring operatives—

rapine pandemonium

—like, where did they come from? What sorts of environments would produce this variety of alien species, ones that were similar in standing upright and possessing apparent sentience, not to mention what she would call telepathy? Also, how was she in the mind of one of these creatures, and why just this one? And it seemed she was merely an observer, unable to control the alien body or, for that matter, influence or even be detected by the other-mind in this being—was that accurate?

She remembered—it seemed impossibly long ago now—that she had touched that shimmering metal tablet, the alien artifact, immediately before appearing inside this alien's head. The natural conclusion was that touching the slate *caused* this projection of her consciousness. However, that was less than rigorous, and she made sure she wasn't falling into the fallacy of *post hoc ergo propter hoc*—one thing coming after another didn't mean that the first *caused* the second. But it was the only hypothesis she could put forth right then, so she focused her thoughts with that in mind.

How did establishing a physical connection with a physical object create a purely mental state of being, such as she seemed to occupy in this creature's mind? And *why* would this happen—was there a purpose? She couldn't answer those questions at present, but a good scientist uncovers more questions in the attempt to answer others. She collected data, not just on the slate's effect on her consciousness but also on the physical characteristics of the others in the group. Three of them were those gecko-like creatures; one was the alien generally reminiscent of a slimy-skinned salamander but that didn't really look like any Earth species; and then there was the one in which she resided, which brought nothing to mind so much as a hulking bear, bigger than any of the others, except the other of the same species in the group. The rest of the aliens were not in her ability to describe accurately in words at the moment, but she noted what each looked like, how it walked, whether it wore a sort of electronic skullcap (which she bet was to induce telepathy in those species lacking the natural ability), everything. They all walked on two legs—did this imply bipedalism was a common co-evolution with sentience among species, on Earth and on these creatures' home worlds?

Also: They all wore a breathing apparatus, but how were they enduring an essentially atmosphere-free environment, even if it was the temperature of a nice spring day? And why—

The other-mind interrupted her train of thought: *Prepare for melee!*

What the hell did that mean? Hurt wondered and then sought the source of the thought, leaving her thinking mind behind as she crawled into the other-mind. There was a stream there, a connection linking the word she understood as *melee* with … she needed her host to think the word again so she could—

MELEE

—a dozen telepathic voices shouted at once, and the hovering tanker truck shot forward.

Her consciousness caught ahold of the concept the aliens conveyed by *melee*, which wasn't far off the English denotation and connotation of the word.

But it was more. So much more. It wasn't just a riot, not just violence for its own sake, not just cruelty and insanity unleashed … it was all of those, and *more*.

Hurt couldn't make sense of most of the semantic connections of *melee* in the other-mind, but she saw memories … red-sky worlds teeming with shiny black crab-creatures that ate and destroyed and reproduced again and again and again until anything coherent or purposeful was dispersed, made into death and meaninglessness.

The flashing images of the other-mind's *melee* rarely showed any bipedal creatures other than those in the alien cities that were panicking and screaming and ultimately being ripped apart by the black monsters. The predators also rendered the strange-looking alien forests completely bare of life, like locusts, except that locusts ate what they destroyed—she didn't see one bit of their destruction disappear into their maws for sustenance.

There was no point that Hurt could see or glean from what she saw. But she *was* seeing it, so unless it was visual imagination on the part of the other-mind, what was most likely was that it was the human equivalent of visual and auditory memory. The vistas of horror she witnessed were viewed from a high vantage point, like that of a helicopter ferrying tourists inside the Grand Canyon.

This alien just *watched*. The ruination of an entire world—the images shifted from one area of utter destruction to another, all signs showing them to be of cities on that same planet with the red sky streaked with yellow cirrus-type clouds.

No, she saw now … not the destruction of an entire world. Of entire *worlds*.

She was aware that she was jumping to conclusions by assuming this group of aliens—

FEED

—she gasped as the shock and thrill of a thousand orgasms shot through the other-mind, wracking it with pleasure, the overpowering sensation not sexual but instead like a first taste of opium touching the tongue multiplied by the number of atoms in the universe—

The memory vanished, but her alien shivered in pleasure and anticipation and shouted to the rest of the group's minds:

GET MANY

ALL WE NEED IS ONE

TO ARMS

DON'T LET THEM SEE YOU

The group ran around the behemoth tanker, falling behind as the hovertruck shot forth at astonishing speed toward the outcropping of red rock. Even through the dust its antigrav kicked up, Hurt could see through her alien's eyes when the massive vehicle slammed into it, making the rock explode in spectacular fashion.

Her alien was biggest—along with its fellow species member, the other bear-like extraterrestrial—and the both of them reached the crash site first, running on longer and more powerful legs than the others.

Hurt hypothesized that her alien's species must have been predators, hunters, or perhaps even prey, judging by the sheer power of their legs. Whichever, they were served well by it here—as soon as they got to the scene of destruction, her alien immediately inspected the "horn" of the amazingly still-intact machine. The other-mind sent the thought *closed* to the other bear-like alien.

Closed? it sent back. *Or closed open closed?*

No se, the other-mind responded, making Hurt mentally "laugh out loud," if that was a thing. She didn't care—she wasn't a linguist à la Doctor Goldsmith back in Antarctica—she was just highly amused to hear the other-mind "speak" in Spanish. She had taken Spanish back in college, and "*no se*" was one of the only things she remembered from it. The "auto-translator" or whatever was making her able to understand the telepathic transmissions must have just picked that out from her memory. That was pretty funny.

However, she had to pay attention now. The way the other-mind was thinking and feeling, it mattered if the horn was *open closed open* or merely *closed*. She didn't know the function of the machine, so she would have no idea what was preferable unless her alien (or any of the others) specifically thought about the difference between them.

What they *were* thinking, or at least how they were interpreting their own bodily chemicals as they did their jobs in such a situation, was *DANGER*. Or maybe *FRIGHT* or just *CAUTION*. It was the expression of a chemical bath of emotion (or like one, to be precise; these weren't humans), not a word.

But that wasn't the only thought leaking out telepathically from each member of the group as it approached the point of impact. There was also something strong that she interpreted—again, not in words—as adrenaline rush of *MOUNTAINTOP* or *GOLD* or *BIRTHDAY*, none of which made sense to her in this immediate context. She guessed that life with any kind of sentience sufficient to create a calendar would have the concept of "birthday," even if it wasn't something noted or celebrated in their societies.

But this chemical rush she felt just before verbal thoughts formed was definitely evocative of the feeling one would experience of walking into a surprise birthday party, even one you had known was being planned. *Mountaintop, gold, birthday …*

Joy. The aliens were feeling *joy* even as they prepared themselves for *danger* inside.

Yes, there was an *inside*. The rock structure was hollow.

As her alien stepped inside, Hurt could see that the floor of the structure was packed with chitinous balls about a meter in diameter, some of them dusted or disturbed with rubble from the truck's impact. They looked to her like giant coconuts, but the other-mind made a different association. Judging by the mental chatter of the alien's compatriots, Hurt concluded that all of them did, too, and whatever that association was, they were *not* happy about it. Their minds ultimately let out a shout,

[*UNTRANSLATABLE EPITHET*]

and, as one, they began poking at the giant coconuts, but to no effect. The things looked organic to Hurt's borrowed eyes, if not actually *alive*. Some of the group kicked at them, others sat on them, anything to get some kind of reaction from the things. Hurt could feel, as well as "hear," the other-mind remember something vital and call out to the group

TANKER!

That got their attention. Those who were sitting sprang up; those who were standing raced to the squat tanker truck, but no one touched it. Instead, they waited in anxiety and anticipation for the gecko-like alien to come to the truck. It moved like a leader, swinging those horn-shaped boots, and within the other-mind and all the minds present, evoked equal parts respect and fear.

And here it came, carrying something that looked to Hurt like a driver, that golf club with a flat face: black grip, silver shaft, and black head. She imagined it was rubber or some other shock-absorbing, or perhaps electro-insulating, substance.

The former was on the mark. The aliens between the gecko and the tanker "made a hole" for the leader (captain?), who walked directly to the metal of the tank and put its foot against it.

It smells with its feet, Hurt noted from inside her alien, who had stayed in place while others flocked to the truck, *like a fly.* God knew she had worked with enough fruit flies to recognize the phenomenon, but this was the first time she was seeing it in an animal—and a sentient, bipedal animal to boot. Since she had no context of the environment the creature had evolved in, she had no hypotheses other than the most tautological: it lived in an environment where its ancestors were better at reproduction than competing beings were *because they could smell with their feet.*

Keep that Nobel Prize warm for me, she thought, and if she had control of a head right then, she would have been ruefully shaking it at her *genius* conclusion.

The gecko carefully tapped the golf club–like tool against the metal—and a deafening

SHREEEEEEEEEEEEEEEEEEEEEEEEEEEEEEEEEEEEEEEEEEE

came from inside the truck. Every single alien, including the gecko and her host, recoiled hard at the spine-shredding sound of fury that was the response to the captain's taps. The leader, in fact, hopped a few times, shaking his feet like they were in pain.

It hears through its feet, too? Holy sh—

SHREEE SHREEE SHREEEEEEEEEEEEEEEEEEEEE

She could *feel* the excitement but also unease from the telepathic aliens as well as those wearing the electronic skullcaps. It wasn't enough of a thought to translate into a word—it was a *sensation* within every alien body and mind, including her own mind separate from the other-mind.

The sound of chaos, she thought. *These are agents of chaos, of melee violence.* Her thoughts rang true to her, especially considering the balance of anxiety and exhilaration transmitted from every alien—

pirate

—present. The gecko captain had either overcome or sublimated the pain in its foot-ears, because now he sent out a psychic cry of victory—

weapon secured

All of the hunters, including Hurt's, gave a telepathic cheer. She was still pondering the significance of the sounds within the tanker when a new *SCREEEEE* sounded from inside the hollow rock. All jumped to attention at the new shriek, and the captain sent out

TO ARMS

KEEP THE [UNTRANSLATABLE EPITHET] OPEN

DO NOT TURN YOUR BACKS ON THEM

and each hunter reached into its pack and pulled out a foot-long metal tube from its pack. Hurt watched in fascination as her alien whipped its tube to telescope it into something that resembled a rifle. She could only observe, not communicate, let alone act, so she observed: those coconut things *were* creatures, and now one had unfurled itself and was speeding toward her host.

Unfurled, the things looked like scraped potato wedges, but with eight deadly sharp–looking razor limbs jutting from the inside and leading to a hungry-looking maw.

In order to move, they rolled, throwing their curved tops forward and down, their crescent moon–like bodies repeating the process to roll toward their target lumpily, like an uneven tire going down a hill.

Her alien pointed its weapon at the rapidly approaching monsters and squeezed off a shot. A *pop* sounded, the release of energy striking the creature on its chitinous side, which seemed immune to damage. When the bolt hit it, however, it furled up almost instantaneously into the coconut shape and rolled inertly to a halt several yards in front of Hurt's alien.

The other-mind cursed at itself, and in its racing self-incriminations, Hurt saw that shooting the hard-shelled things would cause damage only if their inside concavity was struck. Otherwise, they would sense danger and roll themselves up into those impregnable coconuts, and that would be that until they decided to unfurl again to attack.

Her alien was trying to decide whether it should bang on the tanker to elicit another of the shrieks that had gotten the creatures to come out to play a moment before when—

AIEEEEEEEEEEEEEEE

—came through telepathically, right into the hunters' auditory centers.

Her alien turned to see the other bear-like creature calling out in agony as the creature her mind had instantly christened a "Ginsu Ball" first grabbed Bear 2 with its legs and then slashed right through its body, chopping it into four bloody sections. The sharp-toothed maw then opened wide and the Ginsu Ball used its appendages to start shoving down each gory slice of unfortunate hunter.

It was not a way the other-mind cared to die.

The alien swung its rifle around and blasted the Ginsu just as the creature was stuffing the third section of its cohort into its gullet. The creature was already committed to finishing his bite before it could get its razor arms away from its mouth, so Hurt's alien let loose with a massive bolt of electric current and shot it in its sensitive interior before the Ginsu could roll itself into a protective ball again.

The electricity galvanized the creature, making it stretch open, a half-chewed slice of Bear 2 sliding from its maw. The thing fell over onto its chitinous back, limbs retracted and harmless, and it stayed open. Was it dead? She couldn't tell, her alien's eyes not bothering to look at the Ginsu once it had been taken down. What she did, see, however, was a glassy *bulb* sunk into the creature's wet interior musculature. Inside the bulb, a stream of plasma continually danced. The weapon must have been meant to paralyze it, not kill it. Hurt had no idea why her alien chose to stun it instead of killing the horrible thing—the other-mind didn't think anything else about it, and so she could glean no further insight.

She'd had enough insight, actually, and wanted to leave this … hallucination? memory? dream? … and return to Criminy Station, where she knew her physical body remained. If she died here on Mars, killed by a Ginsu Ball, would she die back in Antarctica? Or—hell, was she already dead?

Whatever her ontological and metaphysical state, her consciousness remained on the Red Planet, now watching as the ten hunters became nine, then eight, slashed into mouthfuls for the monsters to stuff into their mouths. It looked enormously difficult for any of the aliens to get a shot off while the beasts were rolling—the bulb had to be let loose at exactly the right time to slip in between the end of one rolling exoskeleton and the beginning of another.

But the gecko-alien continued ordering the hunters where they needed to be, shouting to the other telepaths *SHOOT* or *TURN* or *RUN*. It commanded them by their untranslatable names, and Hurt saw it was like a radar screen that needed to be refreshed constantly in order to keep everything in motion as it needed to be that round. She used Greek letters to stand for each different—

terrorist melee pirate

—hunter, amazed at the precision of the Captain [ALPHA]'s orders in real time on the battle, their names called and updated, always in order:

[*BETA*] *BEHIND YOU* go vertical on that rock remember they can't climb turn around FIRE

[*GAMMA*] *get under the tanker FIRE*

[*DELTA*] *get your back against the rock let it come to you FIRE*

[*EPSILON*] *fall on your back let it get above you FIRE*

[*ZETA*] *get under the transport now FIRE you have to FIRE now—NO!* [*untranslatable expletive*]

SOLDIERS [*THETA*] *IS DOWN*

[*KAPPA*] *IS DOWN*

[*IOTA*] *IS DOWN*

[*ETA*] *yours is closing up bang on the tanker it's opening FIRE*

[*LAMBDA*] *we have enough scare the rest FIRE*

SOLDIERS drag [GINSU BALLS] *to the transport GO GO GO*

All of the aliens, including her host [ETA], immediately brought out a pike from a loop in the rear of their protective gear and skewered their locked-in-position catch. They each dragged the creatures up a ramp into the transport, bulbs still with strong plasma bolts going and keeping the things open.

The other-mind noted that they *had* to keep them open if they were to program them, because once one of them curled into that hairy ball, there was no way to get them open that wouldn't kill the thing. The other-mind believed it could feel the predators' fury, and it hoped to keep it stayed in a state of fury and violence until they let it out.

Let it out? Hurt didn't know what to think of that. Why would they "let out" something so aggressive and horrible? Certainly, the translation didn't mean it would be some kind of pet. The other-mind didn't try to picture what it was thinking about—which meant it was nothing out of the ordinary to it. Meaning the alien in which she was living did this, if not all the time, then with considerable frequency.

But *why?* She didn't expect to really understand an extraterrestrial's intentions, even if something did automatically translate its speech into

English and allow her to understand its telepathic communication. What she wondered was—

Holy crap.

Their rugged little transport rode its cushion of antigrav over a rise in the Martian landscape and, sitting there like an entire shining city, was *the ship.*

She had never seen anything made by man—or other sentient beings, obviously—so large and so gleaming and beautiful. Its ethereal blue hull reflected back the red soil as a shiny black, but the tan sky reflected from the ship as a cool blue. She saw no obvious means of propulsion, but she was no engineer. As the group raced over the red sand toward the monolithic beauty, the ship barely appeared to get larger in her alien's field of view—it was *that* big. Miles long, miles wide? She was no physicist, either, but it seemed that a species (or group of them?) with anti-gravity technology could probably move anything they wanted through space at any speed the local gravity situation would allow.

Ha! Maybe I was meant to be a physicist—or an exobiologist like Weaver, whatever the hell that was!

Was she getting giddy? She was, definitely, but why?

She shut off the yammering of her mind to test an idea … and there it was. Her sudden uptick in ebullience was sharing the emotion of the other-mind as it left the scene of carnage and victory behind and approached the alien's home on board the sleek and awe-ful spaceship. She was *so* impressionable, OMG—and made herself laugh inside her mind.

That ship now grew rapidly in front of the aliens the closer they got, and a loud clank was followed by a huge door (*hatch?* she mused) opening at the bottom, underneath the bulk that floated on its antigrav cushion. The other-mind barely thought about the ring of pressure that was exerted under the craft by that mechanism, but thought of it the other-mind did, and it scared the hell out of its mental guest. But the team of disparate creatures Hurt would bet had evolved among different planets and moons worked well together. The telepathic skullcaps many were wearing allowed the whole unit to act *as* a unit, since they could each sense the thoughts of all the others.

This slight bit of anxiety in the middle of their celebratory excitement, for example, was eased almost immediately by the salamander—sal-a-*man*-der? *Ha ha!*—alien, who sent a communication she couldn't interpret to some alien stationed on the ship, hit the gas, and shot through the perimeter as the ship almost imperceptibly dipped for the instant it took for the transport to avoid being flattened.

Anti-gravity! Who could be against it ... except gravity, of course! Ha ha!

Okay, she needed to calm herself. The bear-like alien with whom she was hitching a ride needed to calm itself, but she was responsible for her own mind, no matter that she had just explored Mars and fought a bizarre and heretofore unknown-to-humans Martian—

apex predator

—species and captured them and were bringing them on-board, for what purpose she could only—

riot and laughter

—guess. Maybe it was scientific, but somehow she didn't think so. *Riot* and *melee* and *pirate* didn't seem to her concepts that a group of scientists would keep repeating in the other-mind or, for that matter, the minds of all the others. Maybe they were sample-gatherers for scientist aliens aboard the ship?

It really didn't feel like it. This unit had lost three members in three minutes back there, and not one thought was spared for them beyond accounting for their absence regarding battle strategy. Hurt did notice within her alien's ken that one of the group—she couldn't think of any analogous human species for this one—held three electronic skullcaps. Thus, she concluded, they really *were* like pirates during the age of tall ships, where grief was a waste of time and could be done once they were all on shore, if necessary. Sentiment was for the living, if you really had to have it.

The other-mind had calmed down now, and Hunt remembered the stunned Ginsu Balls in the hold of their transport.

Wait. What happened to the one they trapped inside that abandoned tanker?

She searched the other-mind to see if her alien had noticed what the team did with it, and she found an answer that chilled her right to her disembodied bones: *They did nothing.*

The hunters didn't do anything with the trapped predator. It couldn't be easily extracted from the tanker once trapped, so they left it behind. They left it to die of starvation in panic and darkness. And not one of them gave a Martian rat's ass about it.

Melee. Riot. A thousand shocks of orgasmic ecstasy at the thought of "letting out" the ravenous predators. They *were* like pirates, but the treasure they sought wasn't gold and it wasn't adventure for adventure's sake. *No*, Hurt thought as they rolled up into the ship and the hatch closed behind them, *they're sadists.* That earlier bright explosion of pure pleasure—which she, being human, felt as a sexual orgasm—had to be different for each separately evolved species. But she would make no mistake: It was the promise of that eruption of rapture inspiring the aliens to do what they did.

But how did that *feed* them? Surely, even in outer-space economics, someone or something had to be footing the bill for this ship and the equipment and everything else. Only by following this agent's wishes could the pirates experience that transcendent bliss, only a taste of which blew the doors off what Hurt thought was her highest level of euphoria. With her human mind, she literally couldn't imagine what these hunters received in return for the delivery of these alien monsters.

But her human mind tried anyway. She reached into the other-mind and just came across the promise of this intense pleasure, the feeling—which very nearly overwhelmed her and sent her into a paroxysm of—but—

What the hell is that? Hurt was seeing inside the other-mind something closely related to the ecstasy it had experienced before and desperately wanted to experience again. The view was from orbit down at a planet, green and lush, with land masses spread about breathtaking lavender seas. As in the ways of memories, the other-mind now looked out upon the landscape from viewscreens deep inside the ship. An order came through into the minds of the crew, which included dozens of aliens in every configuration of flesh and scales and fur and microtubules and many, many things she couldn't identify even provisionally, so different were they from anything on Earth.

The landscape upon which her alien and the others gazed looked tranquil, indeed: some bipedal hominid-type beings in clothing performed different tasks in what Hurt saw as an equivalent to the medieval period on Earth. In the distance was a large city going all the way up a large hill. Some of the beings looked frightened by the presence of the enormous ship and ran away; others seemed in excited thrall and approached it. Still others kept their distance, standing utterly still, watching with what looked like a mixture of curiosity and extreme caution.

She herself felt the scene as fascinating—had there been similar evolutionary pressures to Earth that produced these life forms?—but the other-mind was absolutely *thrilling* with anticipation. For what, she couldn't tell—

The entire crew roared—literally, in some cases—as that loud *clank* resounded through the ship. She guessed the hatch they came in through was opening again. But why?

She was still puzzling, down in the memory of the other-mind, when the screams of the now-fleeing hominids were overpowered by the furious, maniacal shrieks of a hundred creatures from darkest nightmare hurling themselves out of the ship and after the bipedal beings ... but not just them.

She saw the Ginsu Balls doing the open roll they had just done in the attack on the—

chaos joy

—band of alien hunters. And she saw too many other species to get her head around, some of them attacking and ripping apart any animal in sight, some launching themselves into the blue-leafed trees and devouring anything that seemed edible and—to Doctor Hurt—plenty that *didn't* seem edible.

Within its memory, she felt the other-mind's full-body immersion into utter bliss. The screams coming in through the audio feed made the alien's body shake, and as it watched the carnage, the chaos, the melee of mindless evil violence on the video, the other-mind reached the peak and stayed there for what seemed like forever, finally using its mouth to let out a sublime scream-moan, the reward—

***

"*JESUS CHRIST!*" Hurt screamed as she returned with a crash to her body back in Antarctica, practically levitating off the table as she heard the sadistic *evil* cry of boundless pleasure of the other-mind as it echoed again and again and again in her own mind.

"*Doctor Hurt! You're all right!*" shouted a woman—Vasquez, the medical doctor—simultaneous with a man who she could barely remember was the Air Force Colonel. "*Susan! Doctor Hurt!*"

Her eyes were clamped shut and she shook her head with violence, as if she were trying to jettison the awful sound of the other-mind's climactic glee at the death and horror. *WHY WHY WHY DID SHE SEARCH THE OTHER-MIND NO NOOOOO AIEEEEEEEEEEEEEEEEEEEEEEEEEEEEEEEE*

Hurt couldn't keep up with her own mind running from the other-mind's memory as her consciousness slipped away and her body arched in the rictus of a full-on seizure, her eyes rolling up, her jaw clamping, her mouth foaming, her larynx making inhuman sounds as the air was forced over it from her collapsing lungs.

"It's been *ten seconds*. How—"

"*Hold her arm down!*" Vasquez ordered Colonel Ash, whose face looked stricken and drained of blood. He immediately complied and fought the immense lockjaw resistance of Doctor Hurt's arm to get it flat. But he did it, dammit, sweat pouring off him as he made it immobile long enough for the doctor to finish preparing a hypodermic needle and slide it into a vein.

Ash's arms were shaking—he was shaking everywhere—but he kept Hurt's arm down until every bit of liquid in the hypo had been delivered, then let go. The arm returned immediately to rigidity along with the rest of Hurt's body, but within seconds the biologist's muscles loosened enough for her body to flatten out. Within thirty seconds, Doctor Hurt was letting out only tiny twitches, tears wet on her cheeks. By the time a minute had passed, she was fully out … but, as the monitors showed after Vasquez hooked her up to the EKG, she was alive and going to be all right.

Vasquez slipped down to the floor, the reinforced plastic wall behind her back, and stared at nothing for a moment. Finally, she gazed up at the still ill-looking Colonel and said, "What in God's name are you doing to these people?"

He did his best to compose himself—there *was* a human inside that uniform, after all, Vasquez thought—and said with precision, "*I* am not *doing* anything to them. They are scientists. They wanted to know the facts of what what's going on here. They were told that touching the alien artifact would tell them everything there was to know. In their role as science team members on this mission, they could not refuse their own curiosity."

"Have *you* touched those things?"

"No, ma'am, not since I saw that being near the alien anomaly *activated* them somehow. And I don't plan to touch them again, either. I'm not a scientist, I'm an intelligence gatherer—as you've been right here for, you've seen that I debrief them upon their return to consciousness. This is how I get the facts I need, whether it's from soldiers coming back from a bombing run or these scientists re-emerging from the minds of aliens—they collect the raw data, I synthesize and analyze it. I make it useful for what we are trying to accomplish here."

Vasquez didn't feel it within her professional rights to treat Ash's statements with disdain or rudeness. But after making sure she was cool-headed enough to speak in a productive manner, she said, "Colonel, what *are* you trying to accomplish here?"

"*We*, Doctor. *We* are trying to understand how and why a 100-mile-long *alien spacecraft* landed or crashed in Antarctica 150 million years ago. The continent was rapidly dropping in temperature in that period, but the production of these immense ice sheets continued millions of years after that."

"Trying to understand it? So urgently that these scientists were *kidnapped* and all of us brought here with, what, a 20 percent chance of everyone making it out alive?"

Ash's eyes narrowed a bit. "You will tell me how you heard that number. Tell me now."

"I—I can't. It's confidenti—"

The Colonel's hand clamped onto the smaller woman's forearm and he yanked her up from the floor and twisted the arm behind her.

"*What in the—what are you doing?*"

He didn't say a word, simply pushing her as she screamed for help through the Station's kitchen—*toward the double-sealed door to the outside.*

The blood drained from Vasquez's face and extremities—she couldn't even feel the pain in her twisted arm now—as he pushed her into the anteroom where parkas and boots and other survival gear were stored. She wasn't wearing more than a light jacket.

"You're not going to—not going to *murder me! Jesus Christ, Colonel!*"

Ash slammed his hand against the huge red rubber plunger, setting into spinning an emergency-vehicle orange light and triggering a *loud* recorded woman's voice blared "CONDITION ONE USE EXTREME CAUTION CONDITION ONE USE EXTREME CAUTION CONDITION ONE—and the first door, and a few seconds later the second door, slid open.

The chaos of wind and ice outside exploding through the open doorways dropped the temperature in the anteroom 70 degrees in ten seconds and kept it falling. Vasquez screamed in panic and, now, in pain. It would take less than a minute to develop frostbite *inside* the anteroom.

"Tell me—tell me *right now*—where you heard that number, or I *will* push you right out this goddamn door and lock it behind you."

"You can't! You *can't do this!*"

Ash didn't bother to contradict her with words—he just pushed her right out the door.

But he didn't shut it. And he still had ahold of her—he had pushed her forward and made her lean out the door, then yanked her back inside.

She screamed and didn't stop screaming until Ash hit the plunger again to close the doors and turned her around to face him. Then she shook like a woman possessed and vomited against Ash's dress blues. She kept shaking. She felt like she would always be shaking.

"Doctor, look at me," Ash said, taking no more notice of the bile splashed against his uniform than he would a fly landing on it. "*Look ... at ... ME.*"

Vasquez managed to open her ice-encrusted eyelids and focused on her tormentor as best she could. She didn't know if she could speak, but he hadn't told her to, so she didn't care if she could or not. Then her eyes did focus, first on his cold- and anger-reddened face and then on the hands that clutched her by her jacket. Parts of his right hand were white, ice white, whiter and colder than flesh should ever be. His thumb was entirely, shockingly white, and he wasn't using it to help him hold onto her jacket.

"Doctor Vasquez," he said slowly, his eyes twitching, "tell me right now who gave you that number."

"Your hand—you have frostbite—"

"*TELL ME RIGHT NOW!*"

Vasquez squeezed her eyes shut and wept. He would kill her if she pushed him any further, there was no doubt in her mind now. He gave *himself* frostbite—he was going to lose that thumb and possibly half his right hand *and he didn't care*—to get her to talk. She would tell him or she would die. So, she told him.

His eyes first registered incomprehension, then under-standing, then disbelief, and finally the shock of true anger. *This* anger, what Vasquez almost screamed again just seeing in his eyes, made his earlier fury at her seem like mild annoyance.

He released her jacket and she fell to the floor. Then he turned and stomped through the stunned SEALs and icenecks staring at her and those icenecks and scientists further back who remained staring at Doctor Hurt unconscious and tear-streaked on the infirmary cot.

Lieutenant Commander Hicks and Master Chief Petty Officer Ferro helped her to his feet. Ferro asked with gentleness, "What the hell just *happened*?"

Vasquez didn't have a chance to answer before Colonel Ash's heart-stopping but deadly calm roar: "*Captain Davidson, report to the infirmary IMMEDIATELY.*"

Boots slapped against the floor on the other side of the Station. The wall-shaking bellow was not repeated. The personnel standing in the infirmary were all too ready to obey Hicks's command for everyone to retreat to their quarters until specifically summoned. The other SEALs hurried as fast as everyone else. Then Hicks, heart in his throat, double-timed it to his own room—and locked the door.

A few minutes later, all those secured in their quarters heard one set of boots double-timing it to the where they had just been standing. Then came the sound of *two* sets of boots marching across Criminy Station. That sound was followed by the recorded voice repeating "CONDITION ONE USE EXTREME CAUTION ... CONDITION ONE USE EXTREME CAUTION ..."; which was followed by the shudder of the Station as the first and then the second doors to the outside were swept open; which was followed by the sharp *crack* of a pistol shot; which was followed by the scream of "*JESUS CHRIST, JOHN!*" from Captain Davidson; which was immediately followed by a pants-pissingly intense scream of terror, overwhelming at first but quickly overpowered by the pounding and *whooshing* of the ice and wind outside; which was followed by the doors closing again; which was followed by just one set of bootsteps coming toward the personnel quarters; which was followed by a knock and a door opening; which was followed by Colonel Ash speaking in a strained but still bloodlessly calm voice: "Doctor Vasquez, please accompany me back to the infirmary. I require medical attention. And I need you to rouse Doctor Hurt. I believe she has something to share with me."

05:05: THE VEHICLE

There was a reason these six particular "icenecks" were hired on for this expedition: they could assemble a prefab plastic building like the one meant for Criminy Station with their eyes closed and one arm tied behind each of their backs. This was fortunate, since putting together their temporary home, clinic, and research site in Antarctica in July would require that very ability.

Stripe, Suntan, Ski Mask, Pinkie, Michelle Rodriguez, and Big John donned layer after layer after layer to leave the sloping but marginally protective environment of the cargo plane. They had to make it to the expedition's other plane (which had landed perfectly, mining the data from our rough landing to avoid any obstacles) to unload the plastic prefab parts of Criminy Station and get them onto the sledge to be pulled by something called "The Vehicle."

I could hardly imagine what magnitude of beast this vehicle had to be. Stripe told me there were two of them, too—together big enough to accommodate the twenty-four members of this motley crew. Our lot was comprised of six members of the Air Force, six Navy assassins, six impossibly rugged cold-weather drillers, five freaked-out scientists, and one doctor who would do best to keep her amputation saws at the ready.

Once the icenecks were suited up, they fit themselves through the small forward door instead of opening the entire ramp door at the back, the latter of which would have filled our plane with the deadly cold I dreaded. Even opening it for the moment it took to get the six icenecks out the door allowed the wind and blowing ice inside the cargo bay—which was already freezing—to drop the temperature another twenty degrees almost instantaneously.

An hour later, the rest of us were forced to crawl out of the plane and scramble through the hundred-below gauntlet to the Vehicles. They was *monstrous*, looking like a giant tractor crossed with a Sherman tank. It was topped by a large cab that fit all twelve of us in two rows of seats behind a higher-up driver and passenger seat. I couldn't see much up front from my angle, but I assumed now that there was probably a computer driving.

We academics (and one "*real* doctor") had been told to run for the Vehicle on the right, and we climbed inside. Our five fellow passengers were two Navy SEALs, Hicks and Dietrich; one Air Force officer, Major Elden; and two icenecks, my new pal Stripe and the congenial Pinkie.

"Why are all the scientists in one Vehicle?" Hurt said to me. "They could just as easily have split us up, too."

"I'm willing to bet they want all the academics together so no information gets exchanged they don't want exchanged."

A stern, slightly smug voice came from the driver's side: "That's exactly right, Doctor Weaver. Also, it helps us herd you big brains, keep you on task."

Goldsmith scoffed. "It's not like we can just run away."

"Call it practice," Ash said.

THE OTHER-MIND: STANTON

Right that moment, Professor of Geology Harold Stanton was more interested in the composition of the prismatic alien artifact than anything to do with the aliens themselves. Thus, having studied metals and minerals for twenty years, he devoted more consideration as to about lying down on the cot as the Colonel instructed than he did about of touching the slate, putting his hands to the mysterious sample before anyone had the chance to ask him to.

Suddenly, he found himself inside ... or maybe it wasn't sudden ... he found himself inside this double-hulled metal sphere, gazing out at the yellow landscape, as he had been doing for as long as he could remember. Gradually, he recognized ... or was it quickly? Or did he always know? ... his container to be some kind of sphere made of an alloy he didn't have the equipment here to analyze.

Here.

Where was *here?* Who was *he?* Analyze *what* with *what* equipm—

A voice made him jump almost out of his ... skin? No ... his mind was the only thing that startled. His body hadn't reacted at all.

Because it wasn't his body at all. And the voice wasn't being received through his—or whoever's—ears. It came from the very center of his mind. But it had always been this way, hadn't it? Of course, but then why did the loud thought of *check pressure* surprise him so much?

His body was sealed within a kind of protective sac that was suspended by gimbals evenly within the sphere, keeping him upright with the viewport directly before his eyes. He thought "protective" because he knew that the interior of the bathysphere was as cold as could possibly be managed, and the gel suit around him in the very center of the sphere was keeping his body warmed to its natural temperature.

The sphere was chilled, his suit was warm. What did that tell him? Why hadn't he ever pondered this question in his entire life spent in this exact situation?

He could feel buttons at the end of his fingers, the pressing of which rolled the bathysphere in any direction or turned it on its axis perpendicularly to the surface it sat upon. Other than that, Stanton was essentially immobilized, and, to his chagrin, the buttons were wonky, responding randomly to the buttons he pushed. In fact, he felt as if his *fingers* were punching the keys randomly. It was a bit nauseating, actually, since he couldn't see his fingers—or any other part of his body—inside the opaque body pouch. He should have been used to it— *why wasn't he used to it after all this time?*

He had no answers, but he sure as hell followed the voice's instruction to check the pressure of his terrestrial diving bell (or whatever this thing was). He checked the HUD that ringed his view—he must have been wearing some techno-goggles inside the jellied body envelope—and he felt satisfaction that the levels were as they should be. What that meant, he didn't know. Why he should feel satisfaction or any other emotion at this, he didn't know.

He also didn't know where he was other than suspended inside a vigorously temperature-controlled metal ball. He had thought of it several times already as a "bathysphere," the name for the spherical submersibles aquanauts used to explore deep in the ocean. They were perfect spheres because that equalized the calculable-yet-unimaginable pressures unleashed on the underwater craft. They had to be made of metal alloys strong enough to endure *thousands* of pounds per square inch so they didn't implode. but that wouldn't matter if the pressure weren't evenly distributed. A dented bathysphere was no longer a sphere at all, and that meant almost instantaneous death by implosion to any explorer aboard.

Rash judgments were dangerous for one's reputation in the tenure-track academic field of geology. This was perhaps appropriate, since it took million or billions of years in some cases to form the phenomena he studied, but …

What was he on about? The words were intimately familiar, but his mind felt jostled and unready to follow that train of thought—

memory

—out of the immediate moment. But he did know that a bathysphere was needed here—wherever *here* was, it wasn't underwater—to resist the same magnitude of pressure. The smallish window in front of him had to be reinforced to the same degree as the hull, maybe made of transparent aluminum? No. He knew that, by definition, metals can't be transparent, but Stanton loved *Star Trek IV*) His thought flickered: *Wait ... Star Trek IV? What the hell is that?*

He shook it off as the voice inside his head called off seven ... names? ... and followed each with

[untranslatable name] report pressure level

The language he heard, although he could easily understand most of it, was nothing like anything he'd ever heard. Similarly, the symbols visible on the head's-up were nothing he'd ever seen, and he couldn't decipher one bit of it. That said, for some reason he definitely felt confident, intellectually and emotionally, that the levels were—

within optimal range

That was from *his* mind! He would have jumped out of his skin again if he had skin, but by this point "his" eyes weren't looking where he wanted them to look, "his" arms within the semisoft, elastic body-shell weren't moving as he was instructing them to move ... and "his" mind was hearing and thinking thoughts *that were not his.*

However, the "words" he thought matched the emotion he felt: safety in that the pressure levels of the gelid version of a silver-age Iron Man suit—

silver what now?

—were exactly as they should be.

Who was thinking all of this? On one hand, who was it who *knew* the pressure levels were satisfactory? Who was thinking of "Star Trek" and "Iron Man"? And silver is a very soft, ductile and malleable transition metal, atomic number 47—what did its "age" have to do with science fiction or superhero stories?

The end of that musing ripped a hole in the membrane holding back the mind of University of Arizona Professor of Geology Harold Stanton knew exactly who he was and what was happening, because *Star Trek, Iron Man, Star Wars*—these were all part of *Stanton's* mind, his history and experience. He "felt" like himself again, but after a moment the penny dropped.

His mind was not alone in there.

The indecipherable—but apparently translatable—language that spoke of pressure suits was comprehended, and somehow translated into English so Stanton could understand it, was the same mind that understood why the body he was inhabiting was upon the surface of this dreary yellow world was a separate mind, an *other-mind*.

The other-mind seemed permeable, but Stanton had no idea how he knew that. He tested this by (somehow—he couldn't say) *pressing* into the other-mind, taking just a sip of its alien depths.

He pulled back right away and focused on the view through the other-mind's eyes. As he shifted his attention, moving from the other-mind's memories to his own mind again, the professor remembered exactly where his own body was: back in Antarctica at Criminy Station, where he had touched the alien tablet made of some fascinating alloy. Making contact with it using his bare hand had moved his consciousness into the mind of an alien being, presumably one of the species that created the artifacts in the first place.

How did it happen? God only knew. And as his occasional undergrad students would sometimes ask, "Does it matter if we know *how* [some geological feature] happened?" (He really *did* remember who he was now!) But he was here, even if it was only his consciousness peeking through the alien other-mind.

The view through that alien's eyes was at a landscape of despair. Stanton wished he could shut his own "eyes." Before his alien was a dingy yellow-brown sky the color of sulfur, so overcast that not a single contrasting feature was visible except for a patch slightly more yellow than brown, something that Stanton would wager was this planet's host star. But that was it: no individual clouds; and no sign of movement in that miasmic sky, even though his heavy bathysphere probe was almost set into a roll several times by the surface's monstrously dense wind.

On the surface itself were highly porous rocks—another bathysphere with another occupant rolled through the other-mind's field of vision, crushing them into powder. To Stanton, this spoke of prodigious volcanic activity on this nightmare world: flat basalts were the primary feature of this landscape, darkly reflecting the fulvous sky. The soil, even as seen from the height of the viewport, was dark and most certainly was borne of vulcanism as well. Fascinating geography, and revealing, too: he didn't know why or how he was there, but Stanton knew the location of the alien being inside the gel suit and bathysphere, the alien filled with the other-mind and Stanton's own.

He was on Venus.

He was a *geologist* on *Venus*, for Chrissakes.

Once he accepted this—be it a dream or something to do with the extraterrestrial slate he touched, he felt like a kid in a candy store. Ten or so years earlier, he had published a paper regarding the surface topology of the planet. It was a bit of a lark—he had some ideas about how the surface was reformed by its continual volcanic activity, but exogeology wasn't his specialty. That said, every geologist worth his or her salt was often transfixed by space probes' images and measurements of Earth's rocky neighbors. The more data, the better.

Was this why he was peering through the eyes of someone (or something) standing on the surface of the planet Stanton happened to be interested in? He doubted it, but it was enough of a possibility that the geologist found himself wondering if the artifact's psychometry peered into his mind at the same time it had placed his consciousness inside another head.

Being on Venus explained a lot about what was going on. The bathyspheres—there went another one—were, exactly as in deep-sea exploration, used here to resist the instant-death—dealing pressure. Except on Venus, where there were no oceans, it was the crushing atmosphere one needed to be protected from. If memory served, the pressure on anything at the surface was some 90 times that of Earth, which has the third-densest atmosphere (behind Venus and Titan, the latter with 1.5 times Earth's atmospheric pressure) of the "rocky" denizens of our solar system.

Stanton did some quick calculations in his head—or the alien's head, wherever his consciousness had set up shop—and figured the pressure on his bathysphere to be in the neighborhood of 1,300 pounds per square inch, the equivalent of what a submersible would encounter more than *half a mile* under the sea.

Those rocks had better *be pretty damn porous if we're rolling over them*, Stanton thought. *One dent and you'd wouldn't have time to realize there had even been a problem.*

Being on the Venereal (now Venusian, since the earlier word now produced an instant and unseemly connotation) surface also explained why this body was encased in its cooling suit: the planet's average temperature was about 900 degrees Fahrenheit. Famously, that was hot enough to melt lead—but actually, it was hot enough to melt anything 50 percent *denser* than lead.

Venus is really hot was, in a nutshell, what he was thinking.

All right, he was one of two minds inhabiting the body of what Stanton assumed was some species of space alien. He hung from the gimbals that kept him upright, but other than feeling from the inside that the being was bipedal and had digits capable of pressing buttons inside the gel suit, he had no idea what "he" looked like. He had seen five other bathyspheres now, all of them rolling, seemingly aimlessly, on this fascinatingly weird terrain.

find anything

The thought projected from one of the other aliens into this body's other-mind rang in his like a bell, but Stanton couldn't tell if it was a command or a question. In a way, it didn't matter, because no one else— not even the other-mind—could hear his thoughts and thus he couldn't have reported anything even if he had understood the intent behind the thought. He would wait for meaning to come, if it were going to come. The volcanoes took hundreds of millions of years to repaint the entire surface with unending, 1,500-degree magma. The *entire* surface.

Stanton could wait a few minutes to find out what was supposed to be found.

The alien was adept at rolling the bathysphere, turning it in place, stopping it on a dime. But everywhere Stanton looked within the other-mind's field of vision, it was the same: yellowish brown, like the slush in a neglected bus station toilet. The flat and porous rocks were the same in all directions (not that he wouldn't *love* to sample one). There was the swell of a volcano in one direction, but its top was lost to the low-hanging miasma above.

Stanton's other-mind "spoke" to its fellows:

no sign

So, they *were* looking for something, something they couldn't find thus far. Stanton couldn't imagine what the group would be expecting to encounter on this death-world; nothing recognizable as *life* could exist with a sky made of sulfuric acid, of a runaway greenhouse effect so insane it was the same near-1,000—degree temperature at the surface … *everywhere*. Day or night.

Stanton could hardly endure the terror when he thought of being on the night side of Venus. It would be utterly and completely without light. It would be the same horror show, with the same thick sulfurous winds constantly slamming against the bathysphere, but you would be blind.

The aliens must have had some infrared technology or the like, but he realized it wouldn't do any good to be able to see by heat *when everything was the same temperature*. Such tech might allow the cooled bathyspheres to see one another, but that would be it.

He shook it off. The explorers, or whatever this team was comprised of, weren't blind. They were on the day side, looking for something that Stanton had assumed was some kind of living thing. However, he realized the fallacy into which he had fallen: he would expect humans on another planet's surface would be searching for life there. But these were not humans and he had no idea what they were searching for. Asking the others, "Find anything?" (Or was it the imperative, telling them to "find *anything*"?)

The group rolled from plateau to slightly higher plateau, the soft rocks crunching under the metal balls. He could feel the other-mind as both patient and concerned for time. It perplexed him until—

check temperature

—he understood that these telepathic commands were more than just reminders. They were *warnings*. The coolant-gel—filled, form-fitting "suits" kept the individual inside at a survivable temperature, but the interior of the bathyspheres must have been kept as cool as possible against the nightmare heat outside. But the metal couldn't be too thick, or it would be too heavy for one to maneuver.

He had no inkling how he knew this. But know it, he did.

From the mind of the team leader: [*untranslatable*] *temperature report! Temperature re—*

Alien, gargling shrieks sounded inside the other-mind's telepathic link. Something very, very bad was happening, and all Stanton's alien could do was roll to the bathysphere occupied by the alien whose name was called by the team leader. The others did the same, but they had no way to help—there were no mechanical limbs attached to the metal spheres, no way in which anyone could do anything except start screaming in its own mind.

Disassociating from the other-mind's mental and physical perceptions forced upon him, Stanton's own mind dove into his alien's stream of memory to escape. He didn't know what he was doing or how he knew to do it, but it dulled almost to nothingness the horror show unfolding before his alien's eyes as sensory memory blocked it out.

In this memory, the other-mind was still on Venus. Stanton was still mentally piggybacking.

But it felt different.

No other bathyspheres were visible. The rocks and the dreary vistas looked essentially the same as they did in the other-mind's current experience, but not exactly. There was an isotropism at work here, the features almost exactly the same from any viewpoint as the bathysphere turned in place. He had a geologist's understanding of fractals, but this landscape showed signs of scale-invariant, randomly distributed features.

Goddamn if the other-mind wasn't remembering its experience in a simulator. This had to be *training* for the expedition to Venus, the one the aliens were now engaged in.

Stanton supposed that any manned (aliened?) space mission would require, or at least benefit from, repeated simulations and practice, just as astronauts did in Earth's still-nascent program. So this was the simulation of surface conditions on Venus. If he hadn't *just* been there, it would have utterly convinced him. As it was, if he hadn't recognized the few signals that this was a fractally generated landscape, he might still have believed the simulation was real.

Also, the view outside the simulator bathysphere was three-dimensional. Inside the sphere—which Stanton assumed was part of the simulator and real—was three-dimensional as well. Thus, he—or, more precisely, his alien—probably wasn't viewing the interior with any kind of 3-D viewing aid. But he didn't even know how many *eyes* his host possessed, so he was just relying on analogy, which was good for hypothesizing but often bad, indeed, for scientific understanding.

He gazed in wonder as the alien practiced turning on pointe, the rocks and soil beneath the bathysphere crunching. Stanton could feel it vibrating through the wires of the gimbals keeping his alien upright.

The bathysphere moved forward, then stopped, then again turned on a vertical axis perpendicular to the simulated surface. He was almost certain now that his summation had been correct: the landscape *was* simulated … but also real. The ground the simulation sphere rolled on was generated randomly within preset fractal parameters as needed when the bathysphere turned or moved. It was like the "kinetic sand" that kids molded into different shapes that kept their new form until it was shaped anew. This, obviously, was on a much more sophisticated level and the molding was done by someone unknown, probably an AI. However, now that his alien was moving the sphere around this kinetic landscape, Stanton knew without a doubt that this stuff was all "real" in that it was three-dimensional (at least) materials used to simulate moving on the surface of the hellish planet.

He knew because when the bathysphere turned in place with any real speed, centrifugal force pulled on him. The gimbals worked mightily to keep the sphere's occupant in place, but they couldn't eliminate the pull of centrifugal force. It was the same with straight-line inertia and momentum. This thing was moving. Wherever this simulation was taking place—inside a spaceship or back on the home planet or somewhere else—it felt exactly like the trainee was operating on the planet itself.

A voice within the memory within the other-mind resounded:

[untranslatable] *where are they*

The other-mind didn't respond except to wheel the bathysphere around in place, its eyes fixed on each inch of the landscape as it passed the window. There was nothing in particular that seemed to be the "they" that outside mind was referring to. Stanton could feel his host's tension as it sent back the thought—

I don't see anything

—to its trainer, who responded—

go blue

—and his alien simultaneously pressed two buttons, one with its left appendage and the other with its right. This deactivated a series of color filters in the tech-goggles; first lost was everything yellow—which, since it was the light in which most of what he could see out the window, turned almost everything outside to black. Then the alien shut down the filters for green, then blue, then deep blue, then violet … and then *ultraviolet*.

Outside the bathysphere was utter darkness. *Why did they turn off their filters?*

It was beyond bizarre. Stanton was no biologist, but he was a polymath, and he had casually studied both the physics and the physiology of color reception. It took him only a few moments to work out that this being, whatever it was, had evolved under a star putting out a spectrum of electromagnetic radiation centered on the "near ultraviolet," 350 nm or so. Just as Earth creatures evolved with the light of our yellow sun at the center of our visible spectrum, so must have his alien, but with the invisible-to-humans ultraviolet wavelengths as the dominant "color." Censuring himself for once again expositing on something that was not his specialty, Stanton made the analogy that such a being could see, unaided, into "Ultraviolet C"—almost to x-rays—at one end and into our visible "green" at the other.

Therefore, he concluded by assuming an analogy, this alien couldn't see wavelengths of what humans call "yellow" without special equipment. The predominant, perhaps the *only*, color on Venus is that dirty yellow. This alien—and perhaps all of the team in the other bathyspheres at that moment—couldn't see anything with unaided eyes: not the sky, not the ground, not even the sun, since the massively thick carbon-dioxide-and-sulfur atmosphere of Venus completely absorbs ultraviolet light.

Distantly, Stanton wondered how he could know all of this. He had an interest in color theory and such—and even in Venus, of course—but to know what EM was blocked by another planet's atmosphere? That seemed impossible. As in, *he* didn't know this information.

It was the *alien* who did. And Stanton was deep inside the other-mind's memory, using the host's experience and knowledge to form his own understanding. He could see nothing but blackness except for the bathysphere's instrumentation, which must have emitted its displays in the ultraviolet.

Then came a telepathic command—

blue light now

—and his alien flipped a switch with its right appendage. This instantly threw a broad expanse of illumination, making everything visible wherever the light reached in front of the sphere.

Stanton marveled. The aliens—or at least *his* alien—could see best at ultraviolet wavelengths. The Venusian atmosphere blocked ultraviolet radiation more completely than a pair of thousand-dollar sunglasses, rendering the aliens utterly blind. The filters they used to see in the dingy yellow of Venus didn't allow them to simultaneously see in their natural

—just as the "ground" began shaking. Venus didn't have earthquakes, Stanton knew, because it didn't have the equivalent of Earth's tectonic plates. (Everything was melted and boiled together there—he *did* know that.) Maybe it was a volcano erupting. Whatever it was, it was less like an earthquake and more like the crunching sound the bathyspheres made when rolling magnified ten times.

Something was coming.

Stanton felt the other-mind's sudden tension, even fear, and kept his own mind calm by reminding himself that this was just a simulation, and even if it were "real," *he* wasn't really there. He knew his body was actually unconscious on the cot inside Criminy Station.

But even though he *knew* that to be true, this abstract knowledge didn't help at all once the creatures began leaching their way out of the holes in the surface's porous rocks. Some of them had already oozed out before the ultraviolet light was turned on.

They were horrible, lacking shape as they squeezed themselves from the holes, but it got worse: the things took on a teardrop shape, a man-sized blob of shiny, sinew-threaded organic material. It had no eyes, no external features of any kind.

But apparently, that didn't matter. The creature—

acid blob

—sensed the presence of the bathysphere and immediately undulated toward it. Its movement was in the fashion of a tank tread, small rocks and soil sticking to it as it extravasated into a flat glob of creeping horror.

This made the other-mind want to scream inside the simulation and made Stanton wish he could travel further into his alien's mind and get away from *this* the same way he had gotten away from the present moment when—

POP

—he found himself returned to the other-mind in the present, or in whatever slice of the past this was all taking place. Only an instant had passed in the real time of this world, so he had only put off witnessing the horror, not escaped from it.

All six of the bathyspheres on the surface of Venus were clustered together now, five of them arranged so each alien could look through its own viewport at the malfunctioning probe, with Stanton's alien at an angle allowing it to see inside. Stanton didn't know if anyone was going to be able to *do* anything for the—

withdraw now

Hey, Stanton thought with absurd pride, *that's* my *alien talking!* After a few seconds watching his and the other metal balls roll back a few yards, his next thought was *Why did it say that?*

He found out soon enough. The other-mind had a plan, and Stanton know knew that plan, and it made him wonder what kind of mercenaries or pirates they really were. A thought from another alien's mind came into the other-mind—

all recording toward [untranslatable name, but Stanton assumed it was the name of the alien in distress they were all watching]

Stanton, again absurdly, felt disappointed that the leadership of the group seemed to be distributed among them, not his alien's alone. Maybe this was because their official leader was the one inside the malfunctioning bathysphere? He dipped into the other-mind for just a moment, but he didn't detect any information about the hierarchy of these agents of chaos.

Chaos? Where did that come from? What the hell did that even mean? It didn't matter, but it made Stanton uneasy: Why were they "recording" this? For further training, like what he had seen in the memory of the other-mind? Or—and in one fleeting thought the other-mind confirmed his odd intuition—was it to celebrate chaos and death and pain? What in the hell *were* these things?

He felt his alien tap a couple of buttons which must have started the recording mechanism, because after that, it was still. Everything and everyone stood as still as possible, the only movement the rocking of the spheres as their cybernetic feedback gyroscopes worked to keep them upright in the nightmarishly dense wind.

The other-mind, Stanton's mind, and every other alien's mind recoiled from the telepathic scream of the suddenly flailing and doomed occupant of the failing Venusian probe.

Another mental voice—his alien's again—"shouted" over the shrieking—

unlink from [the unfortunate bathysphere pilot's name] followed by

do not stop recording for [a different name, one that resembled the phonemes of "Blatt," so that became the name in Stanton's heuristic perception]

—and the horrifying sounds cut off.

Stanton had only an instant to think *why would Blatt want this?* Maybe training, but it felt like something much more akin to … *excitement.*

Stanton's alien could still *see* what was happening inside, and Stanton could feel in the other-mind some kind of arousal, what in humans would be an "adrenaline rush" but, of course, most likely related to a different chemical mechanism.

What was happening inside was that without its life-support temperature control, the bathysphere's metal shell was heating like something thrown into the sun. The interior of the probe was more than 300°F even with the coolant working properly, which was one reason why they all were covered in these gelatinous bodysuits, which warded off the lower-but-still-lethal oven-like heat.

Stanton knew, without consciously remembering learning it, that the interiors of the bathyspheres were almost-complete vacuums. This was because heat convection, like the transmission of concussive sound waves, can't occur without some kind of medium. Therefore, only infrared radiation from the rapidly escalating temperature of the hull could heat up the interior.

The infrared radiation must have been intense indeed, because the screaming and writhing figure inside the formerly cooling suit was being baked alive, which had to be a mercilessly slow and tortuous way to die. At least until—

BOOM

In an instant, too fast for his alien to see the movement, the bathysphere imploded, the metal shell crumpling into a slim crescent like an arced section of coconut shell, barely three-dimensional. The violent concussions released were so loud that the vibrations conveyed through the howling atmosphere carried through his alien's bathysphere shell and down the wires suspending it. His alien reflexively recoiled, and the other-mind buzzed at the shock.

The doomed probe's occupant was crushed so quickly, he couldn't have had time to realize what was happening apart from the unremitting, spiraling, merciless roasting. Dead in an instant from the first, slightest melting of the hull, which created an imbalance of the uncountable tons of atmospheric pressure.

Stanton couldn't understand the epithets coming from the other-mind, as well as all the others as the telepathic link was re-established, but his own thought was *Venus is an unforgiving bitch.*

The other-mind felt disappointment that its fellow didn't suffer longer. "Blatt" would have oozed with voyeuristic bliss, and that ooze would make Stanton's alien transcendent with awful pleasure.

Stanton felt sick as he experienced the other-mind's excitement at the thought of—*gah!*—consuming the ejected glandular waste product of the thing's enjoyment of prolonged, deathly anguish. The whatever-these-were essentially lapped up the onanistic sweat of an obese, eyeless being Stanton could see in disturbing clarity through the other-mind's anticipation.

Blatt looked like a super-sized pile of excrement. Inside that revolting body was a mind, if it could even be called a mind—it literally lived off the energy of telepathic vibrations. It had no mouth, so its brain or whatever housed its sensory experience consumed the kinetic energy of broadcast thought. (He couldn't imagine what the physics would be on that, and he didn't want to.)

This is really specific knowledge, Stanton thought. *Why is the other-mind thinking about this particular thing right now? You're on Venus! Hell, why are we even here?*

After the collapsed bathysphere's crescent lay still but for the rocking of the wind, rapid-fire telepathic shouts burst into the other-mind. His alien whirled around to see—

acid blob

acid blob

where

go blue

GO BLUE

—where their quarry was, the yellow-brown scene fading quickly into blackness from the suit's infra-yellow filter being shut off and allowing the ultraviolet light to be seen by the eyes that naturally included it in its visual spectrum. Since not a single photon of that EM frequency could penetrate the Venusian atmosphere, each alien's bathysphere shined a broad ultraviolet beam to illuminate its immediate environment.

The soil and rocks and even the particulate matter being hurled around by the wind were once again visible, looking exactly like what humans would see if they shined a powerful flashlight onto a pitch-black landscape on Earth.

That is, pitch-black to the human eye. The dingy yellow vista of Venus looked utterly Stygian to his alien's eyes, apparently. But now he could see, through the other-mind, the blackness of this world as it appeared to these aliens. None of the sun's ultraviolet could get through the clouds, and nothing on the planet gave off such radiation. (Stanton was amused by the thought that you couldn't get sunburned on Venus if you walked around naked all day, even though you would be crushed and baked to death in seconds.)

The high-frequency beams shining out from behind the viewport bounced off the features of the landscape and showed the loofa-like rocks and volcanic soil in an eerie blue light. Stanton was mesmerized by the way the other-mind perceived color, reminding himself that he knew from very recent experience that infrared goggles transformed invisibly low-frequency heat signatures into a shimmering, monochromatic green.

The other-mind sent a thought to its remaining fellows, but he couldn't understand what it meant, even though he understood that it represented a series of numbers, three sets of two separated by a pause between each:

2, 3 ... 0,3 ... 0,9.

It was immediately clear what the numbers meant—three-dimensional coordinates of some kind—when all five bathy-spheres concentrated their UV spotlight on the same rock. It didn't look different to Stanton than any of the other thousands of rocks in the area, looking like a strangely geometrical ocean sponge due to the holes running through it at all angles.

The other-mind thought it was different, however, and he felt his alien's digits pressing a short series of buttons, and something *loud* happened. Only the tiniest vibrations made it through the guide wires, but their intensity was visible outside even if it couldn't be heard inside the vacuum of the bathysphere.

It was a sonic weapon of some kind, Stanton guessed, and every probe was aiming its own at that same rock. Sonic waves would have to be strong as hell to make a dent in the dense, sulfur-laden wind; that was probably why every weapon was blasting at the same medium-sized rock. The reinforced concussion waves created one "super-wave" at the crests and nothing at all at the troughs, making each super-wave punch the target even harder as the rock rebounded into it.

It didn't take long for the porous stone to crumble, and it took Stanton a moment to notice the liquid oozing from the holes and center of the ruined rock. *Jesus Christ*, his mind muttered in terror, *that's the goddamn acid blob from the simulator*. He wanted out of this other-mind, out of Venus, out of seeing the simulator's terrible sight again, but in reality ... or whatever this was.

It gradually pooled on the soil, visible only because it was nauseatingly oleaginous, darkly reflecting the blue light as a puddle of ichor would: mostly black, but with shifting reflections from its surface. The other-mind spoke up—

found one

—and in seconds the other bathyspheres turned their spotlights away from the disintegrated rock and its molasses-like discharge and onto the rocks near the newly crumbled home of the acid blob. One target shook and crumbled, the another nearby, the cycle repeating again and again. Stanton couldn't see if the newly busted stones leaked whatever the hell that blobby liquid was, but his alien's gaze remained fixed on what had come out of its own targeted rock. The sight was terrible … and familiar.

After emptying entirely onto the surface, the blob shifted, then slid toward his alien's bathysphere.

It was *alive*.

The blob, which Stanton estimated, as best he could without any real reference points to measure it by since he didn't know the *size* of anything there, to be about one square foot wide. It looked to be a couple of inches thick, but the blue light revealed only the barest details, and those only from the shifting shine from its black body. He could see a lot less than what was shown in the simulation. He didn't know which was worse: seeing all of it, or seeing almost nothing as it approached.

The thing was fascinating, Stanton thought, even as he could practically feel a horripilating shiver spreading over his prone body back at Criminy Station. The shape bunched and undulated, moving toward his bathysphere.

It didn't really have a shape. Or, rather, it could be any shape, like a flattened blob of mercury inching its way across a petri dish, and probably just as deadly.

SPLAT

A black shape *had been hurled* smack against the viewport. His alien jerked in reflex, just as Stanton would have if he were in control of a body.

He thought for a moment that something liquid had been thrown against the viewport by the wind and that the heavy wind was keeping it smeared to the window; but he knew it was one of the acid blobs.

Stanton looked closer through his alien's eyes at the blob smearing itself off of the window, sliding to one side.

SPLAT

Now there was another one, inching onto the glass. Now was another one, and another.

Sound couldn't travel through the vacuum inside the bathysphere, but Stanton's mind provided the soundtrack as the *splats* increased in force and number. The other-mind transmitted—

[Untranslatable] *majority covered*

—and was acknowledged by the other aliens checking in with their status—

[Untranslatable 2] *majority covered*

[Untranslatable 3] *majority covered*

[Untranslatable 4] *majority covered*

[Untranslatable 5] ...

The other-mind spiked in ... anticipation? Of *what?* Its thoughts rang through all minds in the group—

status [Untranslatable 5] *NOW*

All that came back was that alien's gibbering. It couldn't be translated, of course, but Stanton knew panic when he heard it. So could all of them, apparently, since each bathysphere turned and fixed its light on the panicking alien's bathysphere.

It was covered, *slathered* with the black creatures, and the other-mind agreed with its fellows that they needed to record this for *Him.*

The buttons inside the gel glove were pushed for the recording mechanism. But Stanton could feel anxiety mixed with the excitement because something bad was going to happen to this alien, and if they didn't hurry and—

ship contact made

coordinates transmitted

hurry [untranslatable epithet]

—get off the surface *very* soon, that same bad something was going to happen to the rest of them.

All recorders were on the distressed alien's sphere; it was completely concealed by layers of acid blobs, and Stanton's alien felt more fear now than excitement. But it calmed itself with a surprisingly human-sounding mantra:

All for Blatt.

We need, He needs.

We give, He gives.

and for an instant Stanton saw the other-mind's image of the pleasure-lactating shite-pile called *Blatt* waiting for its next meal. And he felt the other-mind's rush at the thought of what Blatt would give them as it was fed the chaos of this moment, the suffering and imminent death.

BOOM

The attacked bathysphere imploded exactly as the hull-compromised one did earlier. The acid blobs remained stuck to it. Some of the things were surely crushed within the buckles of the shell when it lost its integrity, but ... they weren't dead: they oozed out of tiny cracks in the metal and squirmed toward Stanton's alien's bathysphere.

The soothing mantra stopped as melee panic seized the other-mind. They were going to cover this one next, secreting the acid that breached the hull of the other sphere a moment earlier. In fact—

[untranslatable]

—the blob on the viewport was pissing acid onto the transparent material. Stanton could see it sizzling as it ate away at the window. The same thing was happening all over the probe, the other-mind was sure. In seconds, enough of some part of the shell would be eaten away, causing an imbalance of pressure, and *BOOM* he would be no more.

No forever

Stanton understood the words, but their meaning—which coincided perfectly with the feelings of dread and sadness—escaped him. There was no pause in the thought for a "comma," so Stanton parsed it to mean that there would be "no forever." Did these aliens live indefinitely until some catastrophe happened to kill them?

Was this to be his alien's catastrophe, probe eaten away at by acid blobs and then death by implosion? Stanton wanted out of the other-mind, and *now*. He mentally squeezed his eyes shut to force himself out of this dream-state, concentrated on getting back to Kansas ...

... and nothing happened.

His alien was freaking out now, his mind hearing the telepathic screams of the occupants of the other three surviving bathyspheres and sending out its own cry—

ship [untranslatable epithet] *ship SHIP*

CLANK

The unmistakable sound of metal making contact with the hull of his alien's sphere resounded through the cables. Through the almost complete layer of blobs covering the viewport, Stanton could see large, tethered suction cups—which must have housed powerful magnets—come down into the top of one of the other bathyspheres, then two, then all three—

BOOM

That last bathysphere imploded even as the other three were yanked so hard and fast that the rigid gimbal wires supporting Stanton's alien stretched almost to the floor of the probe, up away from the surface into the atmosphere, out of crushing depth. Consciousness was lost almost immediately, but not before the geologist understood that the aliens *wanted* the blobs to cover the spheres. They would be taken aboard and used to spread pain and chaos for their shite-pile's sheer sadistic pleasure.

The other-mind went dark.

***

Doctor Stanton opened his eyes, disoriented but otherwise feeling all right.

"It didn't work," Doctor Vasquez said. "He wasn't out fifteen seconds."

Colonel Ash inspected Stanton's expression and said to him, "It *did* work, didn't it? Where did you go?"

Stanton's mouth was dry, but he hadn't noticed it until Vasquez brought him a beaker of water. He had a sip and that lubricated his throat enough for him to speak. He said, "Venus."

Ash damn near smiled. "*Venus?*"

"I was inside the mind of an alien. They were …"

"Hunting?"

Stanton blinked at him. "Well, *yes*. The tablet, the artifact, transported me there." He paused. "You knew that was going to happen."

Ash shook his head and said, "I didn't know, exactly, where your mind was going to go, but the others—"

"Others?"

"Interrupting is bad form, Professor."

Stanton swallowed hard, remembering the extreme prejudice with which Captain Davidson was dispatched. "Please excuse me, Colonel."

"All right. Several others have experienced transference into a member of a hunting party, one at the Saturn system, one at Jupiter's, and then on the surface of Mars. Now you observed a group hunting on Venus, is that right?"

"They seem to have skipped a planet," Stanton said, sitting up on the cot.

"Could be. One scientist waits in the wings to commune with the final artifact. I doubt there's life to be hunted on Mercury—but I would have doubted there was anything on Venus or Mars, too. Hell, before Goldsmith made the first contact, I didn't know enough about the slates to form doubt about what they could do. This is all extremely valuable intelligence you scientists are providing to this expedition."

"This is why you forced us to come here."

Ash saw no reason to be disingenuous. He nodded.

"Why not have some of your Air Force people touch them? Or the SEALs? Or the icenecks? Or *you*, for that matter? What did you need academics for?"

"Allow me to answer that question with a question, Professor: What were your aliens hunting there on Venus?"

"They were ... acid blobs. That's what the other-mind called them. Translated, of course."

"Of course. Now please describe these creatures to Doctor Vasquez and myself."

Stanton shot a glance at Vasquez, who leaned against the counter of the infirmary and gave him an "it's all right" nod and smile. This tamped down his anxiety at Ash's briefing; that's probably why the Colonel had her there during the—

interrogation

—debriefing. "They were hard to see in the ultraviolet beams, but they got ... *closer*. They were mostly black, like a pool of oil, but definitely *alive*."

Like Socrates gleaning Menos' innate geometrical knowledge through highly leading questions, Ash simply nodded and stated more than asked, "How can something live on the surface of Venus? Isn't it something like 900 degrees? That and the atmospheric pressure baked and crushed two Russian landers, each in less than two hours. Surely, life as we know it is impossible there."

"Life *as we know it*, yes. But these "acid blobs"—their physiology is utterly different than that of Earth life. The only similarity is perhaps to that of extremophiles like tubeworms at the bottom of the ocean, feeding off the sulfur at the hydrothermal vents … which are also about 900 degrees Fahrenheit, come to think of it.

"But these things are even stranger than tubeworms, Colonel. They reside inside of porous rocks on the surface—all the rocks on Venus are like an anthill, riddled with holes and tunnels and quite fragile, since they're probably weakly lithified sediments or volcanic tuff—"

"Professor."

"Ah, sorry—geologist here. Anyway, these acid blob creatures live inside the porous rock, which can exist in such high pressure because it's essentially 'filled' with that same high-pressure sulfuric air. It's as on Earth, where the 14 pounds per square inch of atmospheric pressure are balanced by the same air pressure within the human body."

"Okay for the rocks, but how can these acid blobs survive? They wouldn't be protected from the pressure and heat even if they're hiding inside a Swiss-cheese rock."

"I think *hiding* is the key term there, Colonel. The blobs aren't hiding from the air pressure and heat—there must be some kind of danger, possibly a predator as highly adapted to the Venusian environment as their prey. Or it could protect them from predation by larger acid blobs."

"All right, they don't get eaten. But how in the heck do they *live* there in the first place?"

"Remember that liquid cannot be compressed; or, to be more accurate, it takes an *enormous* amount of pressure to significantly compress a liquid. The pressure at the bottom of the Marianas Trench in the Pacific is something like 1,000 times that at the surface. The pressure on the surface of Venus is only—ha, '*only*'—90 times that of sea level on Earth. Enough to crush us, certainly, and enough to render iron-encased space probes inoperable, but not nearly enough to compress a liquid to any meaningful degree."

"So, these things are *liquid* life?"

"That's what I take from the evidence of the alien's experience. I would venture that they are nourished by the predominant sulfur or carbon dioxide in the Venusian atmosphere. I don't know how that consumption would work, since I couldn't detect any mouth on them, or, indeed, any opening at all. They didn't have eyes as such, no anus, just a highly oleaginous—that is, *shiny*—surface. They were the size of a common stingray, and much the same shape.

"It would be my guess that the blob creatures evolved to be largely unaffected by the atmospheric pressure on Venus in the same way marine animals like the fangfish adapted to the even-higher pressure of the deep ocean on Earth. The fangfish and tubeworms and all other creatures living that deep rely on the same thing us at the surface do: they balance the pressure outside their bodies by filling themselves with water with the same pressure. Venus has no oceans, no water of any kind, so these acid blobs, it would seem to me, followed an evolutionary track that favored survival in the planet's crushing atmosphere by, essentially, becoming a liquid that *can't* be injuriously compressed.

"I have a lot more to ask you—I need every bit of data you collected before we go down the hole—but right now please answer me this: why were the alien hunters after these things? What would be the advantage of taking them rather than killing them?"

"This—wait a second. How did you know they were hunting? And that they didn't kill the acid blobs? They *did* take them with them, up to … well, I assume some kind of mothership, as in the movies. But how could you know that?"

"I don't like questions," Ash said flatly, but loosened up and gave Stanton a shrug, "but I guess it's only fair. Goldsmith, Yutani, Hurt—all of them went before you, and all of them saw from inside the mind of one alien that the unit was hunting one kind of alpha predator or another. Now, if you please: why, do you think, would these alien blobs be valuable to bring back to the, as you say, the mothership? Why not kill them? In fact, why go through the pain in the ass to get to the surface of Venus to find and hunt them in the first place?"

Stanton chewed on this for a moment. "The entire environment of Venus is highly acidic. The bathyspheres themselves must have been specially treated to resist sulfuric and carbonic acid—"

"Bathyspheres? Like in deep-sea exploration?"

"Exactly. In any case, the acid blobs must have some interior musculature, because they would leap into the wind and be carried to where they could attack these intruders, to attack *us* in the hunting party. They stuck to the exterior of the bathysphere and oozed acid—this substance must have been more corrosive than even carbonic acid, because it immediately started eating through the hull.

"In my opinion, these acid blobs, once collected and their abilities neutralized on board a controlled environment like a spaceship, could be used as weapons. Like liquid, they would probably not change in form or function in lower-pressure surroundings. Anything they attacked would be either killed or *wish* it were killed from the oozing of acid the blobs seem to release under stress. I don't know what the purpose of aliens using such a weapon would be—to inflict great pain and suffering unto death, I suppose, but if they just wanted to kill things, I'm sure they would already possess advanced weaponry to that end. No, I believe that the aliens would go to the life-endangering trouble of collecting these specimens only if they had intentions that bordered on the barbarous. The production of *suffering in itself* would appear to be their main vector."

"Astounding," Ash said, and gave a wry smile. "See, Professor? *That* is why we sent in scientists."

07:05: CRIMINY STATION

It seemed impossible, but just one hour later, we arrived at what Stripe told me was "the spot."

It would have been hard for me to believe that a 25-mile drive could be completed so quickly in complete darkness and Condition One weather if I hadn't been there myself. Driving 25 mph on some Alabama dirt road ... in the woods ... at high noon would be borderline suicidal; but in The Vehicle, which was as tall as an African elephant and twice as wide, it was downright *homicidal*.

It seemed like Ash had a sixth sense about where there would be trouble, like a thin layer of ice with snow on it hiding the crevasse below. The ice would immediately collapse and drop us to our deaths. Or there could be huge ice boulders we wouldn't see until it was too late to avoid crashing into them. But the Colonel kept us moving fast, making sudden course corrections that I had to assume were evasive actions.

"There's a strong radar hooked into the front of this thing, lets me know what's under the area in front of us," Ash said, anticipating the questions we lab coat–wearing professional worriers were formulating about the zigging and zagging of The Vehicle. "There was also advance recon of this entire epicenter of the gravitational anomaly. The ice on the way to the Anomaly from our landing site was scraped flat to allow for faster transport in this very Vehicle. Some of the path couldn't be terraformed like that in such a short time, thus my weaving around them."

All of us in the back exchanged surprised glances. There had been people here already to create paths in the ice? In the *winter?* "Sir," Goldsmith the geologist said with an impressive show of deference, "are we permitted to know how long ago this 'recon' took place?"

"Of course. It was done one week before our arrival. Used one of the very cargo planes we just flew here. We needed them to level the ice for a runway, to begin with. And now all we have to do is follow the path they made to get right to where we need to drill down to the Anomaly."

A week ago? That meant they had personnel in position to get started drilling—why didn't they?

Then the answer came to me: they didn't have *us* yet. This was *not* a scientific expedition, but they waited until their scientists were identified and abducted. We "eggheads" must have been vital to the mission, although just the icenecks and the military could probably have gotten down to the Anomaly in the first place. But they needed us to the point where there would be no mission without us. What I couldn't figure out was *why*.

On the sledge behind us and the other Vehicle were the snap-together parts of what would become "Criminy Station," our base, shelter, and laboratory. The icenecks were the ones who would snap it together, using gear (I assumed) that wouldn't freeze in the amount of time it took to lift the pieces off the sledges and onto their bit of the building. They would be doing this in the light coming from the Vehicles' flood lights but otherwise in the dark and hundred-below winds and its projectiles of ice.

The tank treads eased us to a stop from what was a breakneck pace in Antarctica, even something as huge as The Vehicle being rocked by the gales. I wanted to ask how this machine even operated in the ice-planet conditions, but I knew the answer would be some technological explanation that possessed one key component in common with the cargo planes and the rest of the tech I had been told about:

Like the man said: *I don't want to say it's aliens ... but yeah, it's aliens.*

***

When we were finally called to make the 100-yard dash from the relatively warm confines of the running Vehicle—it had to be running constantly because its enormous tires had to be constantly moving on the ice lest the treads freeze irretrievably to the ground. Moving the thing back and forth over the same twenty-foot stretch sounded like the most boring assignments one could have; but when the signal came that the building was ready 90 minutes later, one of the airmen, Bishop, snapped a salute at Colonel Ash and replaced him in the driver's seat. I assumed Airman Frost (a name for which had taken a lot of ribbing this entire journey) would remain behind the wheel of the other Vehicle.

Before exiting to trade places with Ash, Bishop pulled from his duty bag a coil of rope and put it into my hands. He said to all of us, "Everybody needs to hold this rope and loop it around your wrist like this," and showed how he twisted his hand to make his wrist the center and keep itself free to wrap his fingers to hold on to the untwisted length, making it very secure. "All right?"

The military types shouted as one "*All right!*" and the rest of us kind of murmured the same. It was most certainly *not* "all right," but it was as all right as this situation was likely to allow.

We got our ropes fastened correctly—a small value of "correctly," I admit—wrapped around our wrists and grasped in our hands with a yard's length of rope between each of us. Ten people in the back of a monster-tank-truck thing, coiled together. Stripe had the first position and said, "Everybody zipped up, tucked into your layers, both sets of gloves on, goggles on? Anything you expose to this wind for more than ten seconds is going to get frost-bit."

I wondered how the icenecks had done everything they needed to in the conditions. Don't tell me: aliens again?

I didn't get a chance to formulate the question, irrelevant at the moment as it was, before Stripe yelled "*Let's go!*" He led us down to the ground through some kind of protective tube attached to the cab of The Vehicle, then pulled us through the insulated four feet of clearance, all of us crouching as we speed-walked. And we weren't even as tall as Stripe, whose back must have been screaming as we did our best to zip through to the end of the tunnel, which was latched onto an open hatch, our first look at Criminy Station.

***

Inside was a kitchenette, the other side of which led into the infirmary. (Maybe because the doctor might need boiling water for instruments?) There were six sleeping quarters to accommodate our entire contingent, four bunks to a room.

It occurred to me that I had not been told the expected duration of this little expedition. Would we be here long enough to need a kitchenette? Or beds to sleep in? As I wondered this, I realized that I was famished and would gladly push others out of the way to get at food right then. Also, after I had come back to consciousness on the plane, there were still hours upon hours of travel to get here into our double-wide—and I wanted rest more than I wanted food, which was saying something for me.

We got both, eating in two shifts the food heated up by the icenecks I knew as Michelle Rodriquez and Big John. Canned spaghetti with meatballs was more welcome right that moment as a 14-ounce porterhouse steak with a baked potato on the side. The bunch of us ate a *lot*, as did those in the second shift—but by the time they were done eating, most of us first-shifters were unmoving in our bunks, all of our protective layers still in place, having shed only the outer pair of gloves and our boots.

It felt like hours in that bunk, dead to the world, but it was only about 45 minutes later when Lieutenant McCall entered and nudged me awake, doing his best not to disturb my roommates. "Colonel Ash needs to see you in the infirmary."

"The infirmary? Is someone sick?" Hell, was *I* sick?

"No, everything is fine—he just needs your professional expertise to help him work out some of the mission points."

There's few ways to get an academic out of bed than to tell him his opinion is vital to something. I nodded and thanked the lieutenant, then started peeling off my layers now that the building was heated and I was drenched in sweat.

I wondered what could be up in the infirmary. I wasn't a medical doctor; that was Vasquez. But an exobiologist's opinion was sought, and maybe the infirmary was the most secure place at Criminy Station. The truth was that I had no idea what Ash wanted me for, but when I stepped through the kitchenette into the infirmary, Ash was already there, seated, holding on his lap an intimidating-looking steel briefcase as he awaited my arrival.

THE OTHER-MIND: GOLDSMITH

"Professor Goldsmith, I thank you for coming," Colonel Ash said.

One corner of Goldsmith's mouth curled up into a gallows-humor smirk. He said, "Considering I live about fifty feet away, it wasn't too much of a burden."

"Ha," Colonel Ash said.

Doctor Vasquez motioned to the infirmary cot. "If you'll just lie down here, Professor ..."

Goldsmith didn't lie on the cot; in fact, he didn't move at all except to cross his arms. His smirk had vanished. "I don't believe I will, thank you."

Ash's face registered mild surprise. He said, "Is that another joke? A lot of time and money has been spent bringing you here—"

"I'm sorry if my kidnapping was inconvenient for you." His sarcasm floated around the room like a cabbage fart. "I would never have signed up for it if I had known. Oh, wait—I *didn't* sign up for it."

"You're right," Ash said in a voice that sounded suspiciously conciliatory, "we didn't ask you, and for that I apologize. I am a government employee placed in charge of an unprecedented, unsafe, and *literally* unbelievable operation involving two branches of the United States military, the best ice-drillers in the world, and five scientists at the very top of their fields. Asking you would risk your refusal, of course, and if you refused, you would be in possession of Above Top Secret information. That would not be pleasant for you."

Goldsmith blinked, but his defiant expression remained otherwise unchanged. "Meaning the United States government would have me killed."

"*What?* Ha. You've seen too many Bourne movies, Professor." Ash leaned against the infirmary counter. "*Meaning* that you would be placed under close black ops support surveillance twenty-four hours a day. The NSA would attain a classified court order for your home and cellular phones to be tapped. Agents would examine every scrap of garbage you put on the curb *or* kept in your home. We would be inside your home when you were there and sometimes when you weren't, mostly the latter. We would use a rolling set of search warrants from an NSA court judge, so it would all be 100 percent legal.

"Your computer would be outfitted with tracking software in a way that you would never be able to discover. Your person would be subject to search and seizure if the NSA found probable cause for the CIA to suspect you of espionage—and, believe me, they have a very liberal definition of 'probable cause' and a very unpleasant regimen of punishments for espionage. If you were deemed a risk through your own behavior, or because our intelligence indicated foreign agents or journalists were trying to contact you, then you would be remanded to an undisclosed detention facility.

"Every one of these acts of protection of classified intelligence would remain in place until this expedition is deemed completed and the declassified files ordered opened to the public."

Goldsmith's arms had fallen uncrossed to his sides. His eyes felt like they were going to roll up into his head. He opened his trembling mouth to speak: "And h-how long would that be?"

Ash didn't smile and he didn't frown as he said, "The default amount of time for any classified information to be declassified—this is unless the Powers That Be decide to release this information to the press and public, of course—is ten years. Legally, classified material can sit for twenty-five years before a formal declassification review. It can remain classified for *seventy-five years* without requiring special permission for a continuance of its status. And, believe me, if we've kept information secret for that long, it's going to stay kept."

"So, a life sentence just for knowing something. You're threatening me with prosecution for what is, essentially, thought crime."

"I'm not threatening you with anything, Professor—you are *here*. We successfully pressed you into service. We did it for specific reasons, the main one dependent on your cooperation by lying down on *the goddamn cot*."

"And if I don't?"

"Well … you can imagine how sensitive the intelligence will be about whatever we find here. We already know it is an extraterrestrial spacecraft 190 miles long and 95 miles wide. That's *28,000 square miles*, two thousand bigger than the state of Maryland.

"God only knows what's inside that ship, Goldsmith. Whatever it is, one thing is certain: there are treasure troves of data, including what we expect to be a great deal of written *language*. No other language expert on Earth has seen these—*no one* has seen these markings with the background to make any sense of them. This treasure is *yours* for the taking. This could easily lead to a Nobel Prize in linguistics."

"There is no Nobel for—"

"Get on the goddamned cot, Professor. Time is short."

"What does assuming a supine position have to do with what is inside the anomaly? It seems all one does by lying down is risk being immobilized for waterboarding or sodium pentothal injection."

"Ha. You *have* watched too many Bourne movies. Trust me—"

"I prefer not to."

Ash looked like he might explode again and this time drag Goldsmith outside to die. But he didn't; instead he nodded and picked up the last case. "All right, forget the cot. Doctor Vasquez, please attend to our friend here, keep him from hurting himself if he faints."

She took a position behind Goldsmith, disliking this whole operation immensely. Besides, if the professor knew anything about fainting, he would know that people fall *forward*, not backward like in the movies, and he would become justifiably suspicious.

Ash opened the case in front of the linguist, revealing the iridescent metal tablet nestled inside its protective gray foam. "Do you know what this is?"

Goldsmith could feel his breath quicken and a wave of horripilation race over his body. He did his best to remain aloof, but he couldn't deny the mesmerizing power of the inscribed alien artifact. *O, just to study its relative symbol frequency!* His head nodded yes, but for all Goldsmith noticed his own movements, they might as well have done by a third party.

"Ah, you *do* know," Ash said, a smile of complete non-surprise on his face.

"Yes … I, um … my colleagues mentioned these … these *things*. Artifacts."

"I assume this was immediately after their experiences, as soon as they returned to the common area? Against my direct orders, as I'm sure they also told you." Ash seemed *just* amused enough by the behavior of his guinea pigs to put Goldsmith at ease about being tossed to die next to Captain Davidson. "It's all right—I know that you folks thrive by sharing information."

Folks? The ease he had just felt evaporated at the incongruously non-military word. Goldsmith said, "I was told that touching the tablet somehow induces an experience of oneness with an alien in a hunting group of some sort. Their stories differed in the aliens' morphology, but the hunters were at Mars, Venus, Jupiter, and Saturn. Where will *this* tablet take me?"

"That is a mystery that only you can resolve."

"Surely any human coming into contact with this artifact would have the same experience. You don't need me to risk—"

"All right, forget it. I'm tired of telling scientists why they're so important to this mission. But you must admit you feel the … *psionic waves* even without touching it."

Vasquez met Ash's eyes and knew not to say anything contradictory, but … "psionic waves"? She wanted to say <<*estas lleno de mierda*>>. She didn't even speak Spanish (but her best friend in high school did) and she could pick up on the stink of pseudoscience.

"Can you feel it?" Ash said to Goldsmith, proffering the open case. "It's almost like the meaning *radiates* from the inscription. You don't have to *touch* it. Just feel the air"

Goldsmith admitted he thought he *could* feel a buzz or something from the tablet's direction. He carefully extended his hand, palm out, to get a better read on any—

Ash shoved the case forward, shoving the flat face of the slate against Goldsmith's palm before the linguist's reflexes could yank his hand away—

—and he was on Earth.

Not Mercury or Pluto or Neptune—*Earth*.

At least, he was pretty sure it was Earth. It definitely wasn't blazing Mercury or a frozen outer planet. The gravity was right to be Earth's; the yellow sun; the blue sky streaked with white clouds. It was hot—not Death Valley hot, but close. He stood on flatland, no mountains visible, with lush trees … his guess was that his alien was standing somewhere on the African savanna.

Or had been. Or would be. If Goldsmith could have understood the writings on the tablet before being forced inside it, maybe he would have been able to glean a clue of *when* this other-mind had experienced this scene. Or, quite possibly, time progressing as an arrow was irrelevant in this ghostly existence. Or maybe it was all times at once, time a purely spatial dimension inside the slate, and thus he had always been there.

That doesn't make any sense. "All times at once" was literally incoherent. And how could he *always* have been there, anyway? That begged the question of *how* he had gotten there in the first place, unless he had *always* been there, like a ghost, disembodied but eternal.

Goldsmith wondered if the others had always been where they went as well. They wore breathing apparatuses, as did he, so their green scales must have been protective enough to …

Whoa, wait a minute. He wasn't disembodied at all. He felt like he had a body, just a different body from what he'd been walking around in for the previous sixty years.

An *alien* body.

Goddamn you, Ash. Goldsmith now adjusted his mental schemata to allow understanding of what was happening with this, as Weaver and the rest called it, "hunting party." This is what a skilled research linguist did if he (or *she*, or *they* if the individual in question self-identifies as agender and uses "they" to signify their non-binary gender status in a language lacking neutral personal pronouns; Goldsmith was always *very* careful to show respect to any non-normative students or faculty lest his tenure come under fire for being some kind of "-ist") wanted to really *absorb* a language. The assumptions one made often became—

herd approaching

—even though he had been told there was telepathic communication in each of his fellow scientists' experiences, not to mention that his consciousness was within an alien "other-mind," he still started at the loud thought inside his—or whomever's—head.

But it was fascinating, especially as the other alien hunters responded to the thought with their own broadcast telepathic messages. He heard the (to human ears) gibberish being trucked back and forth (using "psionic waves"? Was that a thing?), but he could understand the meaning in English!

He considered it further, paying attention to the alien phonemes and also to his own mind's reception of its meaning—it wasn't a translation into English or any other tongue. He heard the thoughts as his alien heard them, and understood in the exact same way Goldsmith understood. The *meaning* was what came through, the putting into words an action of each alien's mind, including his.

It dawned on him through closer observation that almost every alien's telepathic language was different from that of its compatriots. The sounds of the "speech" were different. This hunting party was made up of beings from different worlds, he felt sure. The telepathic transceivers on each alien's head (including "his," he was sure) broadcast semantic meaning along with the actual syntax of whatever language the transmitting alien used while thinking.

For example, the first thought that he "heard" was:

power up

While he knew the meaning of "power up" in English, it was highly unlikely the "speaking" alien's thought corresponded exactly to the video game concept. That said, what the hunters now did—lifting their odd weapons up in front of them and "activating" them for use—was exactly what an English speaker (most likely Caucasian, under 30 years old, and male) would mean by "powering up."

What he had come to regard as "his alien" lifted its weapon and powered it up as well. It looked like the railgun that Weaver described in his odd adventures on Titan. Did that mean "big game," such as Weaver's Titan Gilas? Goldsmith presumed that railguns would be ineffective at helping them capture—but not immediately kill—something like the Venus blobs, so he prepared himself for something *big*. The others told him about the Titan Gilas, the Jovian moon's Ice Serpents, the Mars Ginsu Balls, the Venus Blobs. If these aliens were collecting apex predators from every life-supporting world in the solar system, what would they want to take from Earth? A lion or tiger? (He immediately corrected himself by noting that lions were indeed found in Africa, but tigers were not.) A hippopotamus, which killed more humans each year than all other animals combined? If Ice Serpents were taken from Europa's ocean, then perhaps a shark or a cone snail, the latter being the deadliest creature on Earth?

He had no idea. Earth's apex predators were awfully unimpressive compared to the—

silence

The gecko-looking alien thought, and added

stop

it is near

It was near? A herd of something? Nothing Goldsmith could see through his alien's eyes indicated anything was around that could be construed as a predator, or any animal, really, let alone a herd of them. Nothing that would fit the aliens' bill, something to strike terror and cause a near-unlimited amount of pain and death. "Melee chaos" predators as they were described by his colleagues—whatever *that* meant, exactly.

There were a few groves of trees, some within 50 yards or so and some further off, all disturbingly opaque. If something were near, it would have to be behind or hidden within the little pockets of trees. A telepathic impulse sounded in the other-mind:

go red

Almost immediately, Goldsmith's alien moved a slider (toward red, he would assume, trying to keep the alien word in his memory to write down later) and the view from behind the alien's seamless goggles quickly transitioned from familiar Earth colors (if, indeed, this were the Earth) to red. Goldsmith had a curious mind despite his "full professor" tenure status, and some of the knowledge he had osmosed in physics lectures for the non-mathematically gifted came in handy now.

According to Stanton's account, the aliens on Venus could see in the high-ultraviolet and so the lowest frequency of electromagnetic waves they could see with their natural eye-analogs was somewhere in the yellow-green area of humans' visible EM spectrum. Thus, even though they weren't evolved to see under Earth's yellow sun, the aliens could see perfectly clearly because of the ultraviolet radiation flowing from it. (This wasn't possible on Venus, as Stanton had expounded, because the thick carbon-dioxide atmosphere blocked EV most efficiently. Hence they needed the UV lamps to see the oil-puddle creatures.)

On what was undoubtedly Earth, however, natural UV from the sun was as good to the aliens as yellow light is to humans.

But the command from the other-mind had said *go red* (Goldsmith filed that one away, already envisioning a paper on the imperative form in his alien's language). The goggle filter color changed from the UV-to-yellow spectrum to what Goldsmith would judge to be the red of one half of those old-school anaglyph 3D glasses. The scene was now made up entirely on shades of red, the other colors being absorbed by the goggles.

His alien scanned the area, as did the other lizard-men, bear-men, and the rest of the less-describable breathing-apparatus—wearing bipeds. The other-mind—which seemed to be in charge of the seven other aliens and transmitted its orders to them through the electronic skullcaps—sent an interrogative to them—

???

—and all checked in to say that they saw nothing remarkable in this red light. Even still, the gecko alien with its hearing organs in its feet repeated

near

The other-mind acknowledged, then transmitted

go red more

Goldsmith didn't immediately grasp how the goggles could "go" any more red, but the English syntax formed from the alien telepathy "language" fascinated him. Were the sender's messaged thoughts simplified into some kind of Chomsky-esque "deep structure"? If so, he reasoned quickly, this broken-down proto-language was what was actually transmitted to the other members of the hunting party. The receivers' telepathy skullcaps would then take the proto-blocks and "unpack" them into the receiver's mind in its own language, with rough syntax but crystal-clear semantic content.

Goldsmith hypothesized that any attempts at complex communication through this system was likely to be as incoherent as the results of using (then-nascent) Google Translate to go from one language to another and back. One of his graduate students once wrote an entire dissertation examining this phenomenon in Chinese (his first language) and English (his second language, one in which he was perfectly fluent), with the results amusing even as they were insightful and relevant to natural language processing, machine learning, and cultural "loading" of meaning into allusive networks of idiomatic expressions that didn't translate well at all. Google used this research to greatly improve their translation algorithms, and that graduate student now earned income an order of magnitude greater than Goldsmith's, something of which he was quite proud.

Lost in his own mind's chattering, he hardly noticed that his alien's goggles had shifted the scene from bright red to what humans called "infrared," which Goldsmith saw as the alien saw was converted into the ultraviolet light they could see by, the same way infrared was translated to green in the human team's goggles back in Antarctica.

Goldsmith assumed that the other alien's goggles were set to view the same scene as the other-mind's goggles, but adjusted to work with whatever light that constituted those beings' visual spectrum.

In the violet-translated infrared light, the trees themselves were almost invisible. There were eight groves in a rough circle about half a mile in diameter around the hunting party. But in the distant groves, one within or behind each was a tremendous glowing heat source in the unmistakable shape of what Goldsmith—no paleobiologist, he—identified as the famous Tyrannosaurus Rex.

I guess that answers the whole "cold-blooded or hot-blooded" debate, Goldsmith thought. His mind turned immediately inward to consider with whom he could co-author a paper with on the subject. Obviously an eminent paleobiologist, one who could incorporate Goldsmith's firsthand knowledge—

in the trees

The other-mind didn't seem particularly disconcerted by a *dinosaur* in the African Savanna. In fact, it mentally counted off the number of dense but discrete inhabited groves of trees that, Goldsmith realized, didn't resemble any trees he'd ever seen in real life or in photos of the continent's grassy plains.

He was definitely on Earth. But he now strongly believed that his alien's "recorded" experience accessible through the metal tablet wasn't from the present, or even the near past. His son (now grown and in graduate school himself, studying paleontology, of all things, meaning Goldsmith would never get a break from dinosaur talk) had, through sheer repetition, emblazoned in his father's mind that Tyrannosaurus went extinct some 65 million years ago, wiped out along with 80 percent of life on Earth (and all of the dinosaurs) when the Chicxulub meteor struck. So, if this group of alien hunters *were* on Earth, it was the Earth of at least as far back as the Cenozoic Period, not the current Anthropocene.

That meant what he was seeing happened at least 65 million years ago, probably much more.

Goldsmith's mind reeled. If he could have picked any time in Earth's history to visit, it would have been 3,500 BCE or so, when Proto-Indo-European was spoken on the Pontic—Caspian steppes of Eastern Europe. There existed no written record of this language, but—

Pay attention, goddamnit!

His mind's admonition shook Goldsmith back to the present … past? *That would be an interesting linguistic conundrum*, he thought, followed by a second lashing: *You're worse than a daydreaming undergrad!*

Goldsmith's career-furthering thoughts vanished as his alien shifted its gaze from the relatively distant dinosaurs half a mile off to the smaller copse of wide bushes just the length of a football field from them. There were glowing heat signals from within that as well, but multiple and smaller.

There were murderous giant lizards in the tree clusters and god knew what hiding in the bushes, but none of the hunting party lay low or otherwise tried to hide themselves from being seen in the misleadingly inhabited area. That probably meant they *wanted* to be seen. They *wanted* the Tyrannosauruses (from τύραννος + σαῦρος, Ancient Greek for "tyrant" and "lizard," respectively—"τύραννος" also meaning "king," which explained its later tacked-on Latin taxonomy of "rex") to see them and come after them.

He could sense from the other-mind that it was easier to have the apex predators attack than to try to chase them down—

[Untranslatable name] *rouse them*

—one of the alien hunters, this one looking like an upright bear wearing a breathing apparatus, stomped intentionally loudly the 150 feet or so to the bushes and swung its huge paw-hands through it, claws extended.

Immediately, a handful of hen-sized, scaled and feathered creatures ran out of the bushes, some running on two legs, others leaping and using their proto-wings to glide a few feet, then leaping again upon landing. It looked like the thing was hopping, and not very fast. (Goldsmith's son would know what these things were called, but they usually just talked about larger beasts and when and where they lived.)

stop all

No sooner had the hen-creatures been flushed out of their protective thicket than the massive dinosaurs lurking inside the scattered tree groves exploded into action. They didn't all leave their hiding places at the same time, but the first one running tripped the signal for them all to bust out and run.

Directly at the alien hunters, who, Goldsmith noticed, remained stock-still (now he understood the other-mind's command to *stop all*) as the hen-things ran and hopped in circles, not wanting to get near the hunters and not wanting to get run toward the *Tyrannosauruses reges* racing in from the semicircle of their hunting blinds. The lack of net progress in any direction despite their panicked running around meant that the small animals made themselves highly visible between the motionless aliens and the approaching dinosaurs. Goldsmith remembered his son being fascinated with the idea that some huge predators of the Cretaceous Period couldn't detect something standing still, most likely because anything it was hunting or being hunted by would be in motion. (Evolution was nothing if not parsimonious in its distribution of sensory abilities. Apparently, it would have been too "expensive" in terms of brain resources to allow the T. Rex the capacity to see both moving and stationary creatures.)

Goldsmith could feel and thus shared the other-mind's tension as the beasts rushed directly toward the hunting party. However, since he was spared the necessity of—or ability to—take any action himself, he took the moment to examine the dinosaurs that would reach the hen-dinos in roughly thirty seconds. The main thing he noticed, something that took him entirely by surprise, was that the predators sported a crest protruding from just above their eyes. It looked like a prehistoric version of a Spanish comb, the kind that *mujeres españolas* displayed in their hair on special occasions. This told Goldsmith immediately that these were *not* Tyrannosauruses, but instead an even more rapacious theropod known as *Rhiasaurus.*

His son had talked about the Rhiasaurus, which formerly bore (and still did, officially) the name *Cryolophosaurus* because it lived in Antarctica. However, this name was rarely used anymore—even less than its moniker *Elvisaurus* used due to its pompadour-like crest—because when Rhiasaurus lived there, Antarctica was still part of Gondwana along with what would become Australia.

This memory or projection of whatever the tablet had sent him into was at least 200 million years old. He was in Antarctica. If he had to wager, he'd bet that this whole scene was happening very close to what eventually became Wilkes Land.

To the Anomaly.

To 200 million years ago, when the climate of Gondwana was warm, even tropical. It was the time and location of the undisputed rule of *Rhiasaurus*, thus renamed from *Cryolophosaurus* ("cold lizard") because of the presence of running water on the ancient and warm proto-continent, as the attached Australia-Antarctica was during the Early Jurassic Period.

Goldsmith remembered all of this during a series of public lecture his son once gave at his university (and which he attended as a proud visiting papa) called "Jurassic Jive: Myths and Truths in Dinosaur Lore." In this talk, he learned that *Tyrannosaurus* lived not during the Jurassic Period but instead the much-later Cretaceous Period, that time of biodiversity that ended abruptly with the catastrophic meteor strike of 65 million years ago. It was during this lecture, in fact, that his son described the T. rex-like predator now known as *Rhiasaurus.* (He was glad he could remember *how* he had picked up enough information to so quickly distinguish between the flat-headed Tyrannosaurus and the crested Rhiasaurus.)

Goldsmith could feel the rising tension in the other-mind as the massive predator theropods shook the ground with their hungry race to get to the prey first. It was a particular tension, however, one that was tinged with excitement and anticipation of … sex? No, not exactly—more like anticipation of ecstasy at the end. The more the other-mind's adrenaline analogue tensed the alien's body, readying it for a fight and tantalized by picturing the very specific fruits awaiting the hunters should they prove victorious.

hold

thought the other-mind, and if Goldsmith could have physically snickered with the thought of *Alien Braveheart*, he would have. His wife was right—not only do men act like children and laugh at *very mature* humor, but they like it that way.

The leader in the dinosaur race was only 60 feet away and moving fast—50 feet now— and the hens were going bananas, ultimately remembering where they were hiding and running back to their protective bush.

Forty feet.

hold

Thirty.

hold

Twenty. The other-mind was as focused as an electron microscope and just as still.

hold

Goldsmith's alien shot a glance to his left and his right, the other-mind noting that one hunter was positioned on each side, ten feet back from the rest of the aliens and holding their wide-mouthed weapons at the ready

hold

They held.

hold

The lumbering giants knew exactly where the hens had gone, and leaned their snouts low to consume the hens and probably the bushes as well in one motion. The pack was upon them now for the hunting party to stop them without being crushed by their sheer momentum as they scooped up their prey where they saw them move last.

The behemoths coming at them were fast as hell and if $F = ma$ were still the law of the land through a window into the Antarctica of 160 million years ago, the hunters would be smeared into unidentifiable stains on the grass.

Yutani had shared with Goldsmith and the other academics about his experience being ejected from the other-mind when his host was apparently violently killed by the tail of a Europan Ice Serpent. In seconds, he expected, he would be jerked out of the past and into the present on the cot back at the station.

NOW

A neon purple energy beam seemed to jump into the five feet separating the hunters and the dinosaurs, shot down from a point above that Goldsmith's alien glanced at while its compatriots let out a cheer within, below, and above the frequencies of concussive waves humans hear as sound.

But they were definitely celebrating, as well they should: the immobilized Rhiasauruses were lifted from the grassy Antarctic plain, the half-dozen creatures gaining speed as they gained altitude. They disappeared into the sky, to what Goldsmith knew had to the giant mothership that in the future would become the ice-buried gravitational anomaly.

Seconds later, the alien containing the other-mind containing Goldsmith's consciousness was hurled off its feet in a cone of purple light.

***

Goldsmith opened his eyes and noted Vasquez taking his pulse and blood pressure while Colonel Ash's face hovered with an expression much more expectant about what the linguist could tell him than concerned about the human just returned from the mind of an extraterrestrial being.

But he was honest with himself—if the person came back alive, he wouldn't worry about the human as much as the information he had brought back. Vasquez finished her check of his vitals, smiled down at Goldsmith, and gave Ash a thumb's-up.

"Professor Goldsmith, welcome back—*what did you see?*"

At least he welcomed me back, Goldsmith thought, and decided, as an internationally recognized member of the worldwide scientific community, that he would annoy Colonel Ash. This was also because he was an incorrigible tweaker of noses. "How did the order go?"

"'The order'? What order?"

"You know, Weaver was on Titan, Yutani was on Europa …"

"That's not important right now—"

"It's important to *me*, Colonel. A scientist needs context in which to understand that which he sees, let alone to explain those observations to other parties." Goldsmith smiled. "So, please, *do* proceed."

The Colonel pulled a face as he stood up and spoke in an annoyed monotone. "Professor Weaver entered an other-mind on Titan, the largest moon on Saturn. Doctor Yutani found his consciousness displaced to the surface of one of the largest bodies in the Solar System, Jupiter's moon Europa."

"So, the other-mind in question moved one planet toward the interior. Were they traveling from the most distant from the sun to the closest, or just randomly to whatever planet came up next."

"Doctor Golds—"

"I suppose they'd encounter whatever outer planets were on the aliens' side of the sun. Like Neptune may be the furthest planet out, but it could be on the opposite side of the sun and so in fact became the *furthest* away—"

"All right, enough nonsense. What did you see inside the other-mind?"

"Humor me for just one more moment, Colonel. Who went where next?"

Ash sighed in, yes, further annoyance. "Next was Professor Hurt, on the surface of Mars. Followed by—"

"Something another planet closer—"

"*Airman Frost*," Ash grunted from behind clenched teeth, just barely maintaining a civil tone.

Frost reported within ten seconds. "Sir."

"Your sidearm, please."

Vasquez, Goldsmith, and most of all the young Air Force member turned their heads to stare at the Colonel, who had his hand out to receive the weapon. Frost removed the pistol and placed the butt into Ash's open palm.

Ash immediately—and loudly—slid a load into the chamber. He then brought it down and placed the mouth of the pistol against Goldsmith's left knee. "May I continue, Professor?"

The suddenly not-so-amused linguist couldn't move his mouth to form words or wave his arms to indicate to Ash that they just move on, since his attempt at humor as ill-advised and not funny and *oh my god please don't shoot me*. He just nodded, eyes round like two frightened hubcaps.

Calmly, *very* calmly, Ash pressed the muzzle harder against Goldsmith's precious, pain-receptor—rich kneecap, making the academic squirm and grunt in pain without a bullet ever having to leave the gun. (He would never tell Goldsmith about leaving the safety on, but as much as he wanted to maim this asshole, he would need him able to walk when they commenced exploration of the spacecraft.

He could still hurt the smug bastard, though, and did, pressing harder as he finished the list: "Yes, so another planet closer to the sun. However, they skipped Earth, and Stanton spent some exciting time on the surface of Venus."

"Venus?"

"Yes, indeed. The hunters were ingenious in defying the heat and pressure." He held the gun painfully under the kneecap and pushed up until both the anterior cruciate ligament holding the joint together and Goldsmith himself screamed. He removed the pistol and handed it back to Airman Frost, who looked almost green. "Thank you, airman. That's all for now."

Frost saluted and got the hell out of the room.

"Now, I would *really* like to know where *you* were during your half-second journey into the tablet. Oh, and *tell me what you saw*."

Goldsmith swallowed in time to avoid throwing up and croaked, "Earth. I was on Earth from 160 million years ago."

It was Ash's turned to be stunned. He said, "How do you know it was Earth, especially if it was supposedly so long ago?"

"I knew because I could tell I was in Antarctica. On *Earth's* Antarctica before it broke off and settled at the planet's southern axis of rotation. It was quite green and lush."

"Professor," Ash said with a once-again—rising tone of impatience. "Then *how* did you *know* it was *Antarctica?*"

"I knew because the dinosaurs there were *Rhiasaurus*, the bigger and angrier cousin of *Tyrannosaurus Rex*. My son was a huge—"

"The aliens were hunting … *dinosaurs*."

"Yes, sir. Well, they were more *baiting* them to run into a tractor beam. I saw one of the monsters five feet in front of my face, and it definitely thought that it was *they* who were doing the hunting in this little episode. But so do fish before they swallow the worm, I suppose."

"They captured the dinosaurs with an energy beam, and hauled them into the sky to the mothership."

"That's what I saw, Colonel. Can I go now?"

"Sure, you can go—just come back on the double with your gear on and head out to the tunnel."

"Tunnel?"

"Yes, indeed. It goes all the way to our gravitational anomaly. There might be some interesting reading for you down there. At least, that's the hope."

13.16: TUNNEL

It was bone-achingly cold down there, even in our gear. Being that deep inside a bubble of air trapped when the ice formed 34 million years ago, of course it would be soul-chillingly cold, but still ... the environment was nothing like the misery at the surface. At least there was no wind underneath the surface.

The nearly blinding lights mounted next to the cam on each SEAL's helmet illuminated the glass-smooth surface of the ancient machine and rendering clear the markings—letters of the aliens' language? Supernatural sigils? a mathematical code? I had no idea—that were etched next to what our military bosses thought was an entry hatch.

My excited breath caught in my throat. An alien spaceship ... alien writing ... and inside, actual *aliens*. (Who were certainly dead at this point, but probably well-preserved enough to study, scan, and autopsy. I was the leading exobiologist in the country, maybe the world—so I would be the one getting the opportunity to see and learn from an extraterrestrial being!) Finally, some hard data to support further speculation!

But only if I survived this suicide mission.

"Doctor Goldsmith," Colonel Ash said in a hushed voice, since any loud percussive vibrations could slam shut the mile-long tunnel the icenecks drilled for us with that impossible technology, "front and center. Can you decipher this?"

Goldsmith, our plump and usually jovial information scientist, stepped up and took a long, close look at the markings before saying, "No."

Ash blinked. "No? Just *no?*"

"Well, not *just* 'no,' of course. One might be able to suss out the general meaning if he had other examples to induct from, examples written on something for which we know its purpose. However, without the help of a living user of this language—if, indeed, it *is* a language—who also can understand human language or an interstellar Rosetta Stone, there's nothing to hang a translation onto. I'm sorry."

"So, what you're saying is that we can't read the instructions. We can't open this thing and get to the aliens aboard without one of the aliens on board telling us how to open it."

"I highly doubt anything is still alive on a spaceship that crashed 200 million years ago," Dr. Hurt said, and since she was the evolutionary biologist among us, we all nodded along with her. (Of course, I had come to that conclusion already and would publish first.)

Well, not *all* of us nodded. Ash barked, "I don't care if the aliens are alive or dead. You know our mission. There may be contents in this machine much more valuable than space aliens to our overall campaign."

Yutani and I shared a look. Ash didn't mean *this* was the entirety of his "campaign." What he meant was … hell, I didn't know, and I didn't believe I *wanted* to know.

"Maybe," Doctor Goldsmith said, "but I advise you not to act on a completely unsupported hypothesis. These markings may be instructions revealing how to enter this spacecraft, but they may, alternately, be a warning not to enter, or simply classification information, like an interstellar license plate. There's a possibility it is a slogan like our *e pluribus unum*. It may even be a visual representation of something meaningful only to this alien society. A human analogue to this might be the images stamped on World War II fighter planes representing that pilot's 'kills.' We have no way of knowing—not without other examples to use for purposes of induction."

Doctor Hurt interjected, "Colonel, we should also consider the possibility that the aliens who created this ship can sense electromagnetic radiation—that is to say, *colors*—outside of what we consider 'the visible spectrum.' They might see in ultraviolet or infrared wavelengths, and so any markings they made on this thing might be visible only within *their* visible spectrum. Other samples would be helpful in order to detect any characters or ideographs other than those humans can see. My point is that this might not be the whole message but rather just the part we can see with eyes evolved for our planet's yellow sun."

I didn't say out loud the Superman reference that pops into my head. I needed to stay focused, for god's sake. My brain was rebelling against this whole adventure into the unknown, even though it could very well result in something I'd searched for my entire career, my whole life.

Ash chewed over the linguist's and the biologist's input, looking down at nothing in particular. The turning and twisting of his thoughts was almost visible. Finally, he took in deep, deep breath and let it out slowly and (I assume) with a new sense of calm.

"Doctor Hurt, Doctor Goldsmith … what if we *did* happen to possess another alien artifact with this kind of chicken scratch on it?"

All the academics stayed perfectly still, like a deer wanting to make sure it hears a predator before it comes after them, waiting for Ash to break the suspense. But it was Goldsmith who spoke up. "It could make all the difference in deciphering any of this ideography."

The Colonel straightened his already ramrod-stiff frame. "We have such an artifact."

"Where?" the linguist asked immediately, no doubt excited as hell for more data. "*Here?*"

Ash nodded. "It's about a mile above us right now. It's the force-field device that's keeping our tunnel open against more tons of ice than any human can comprehend."

"Then let's go up and get it!" I said with real excitement. I looked at the four SEALs who had come down with us but hadn't said a word or moved a muscle since we got there.

"I just told you that it's *holding the tunnel open*, Professor."

"Oh, right, of course." I felt like an idiot.

"But how," Doctor Yutani said—gently, so as not to trigger the Colonel's 'no questions' reaction—"did you figure out how to use such a device? No one could read whatever writing was on it, I assume? Whatever instructions there might be?"

"That is correct. Initial findings hypothesized it was a particle accelerator of some sort. My superiors in this operation agreed with my suggestion that we bring the machine to our highest-security-level physicists for them to try to discover what it was and how it works. They somehow scienced it enough to figure out how it worked. It is officially 'a force-field generator,' although more testing may show—"

"A *force field?* Like in *Star Trek?*" Yutani scoffed. "That's impossible with today's—"

"Do *not* interrupt me again." The Colonel kept his steely eyes on the meteorologist until it was clear his point has been made. "All right, then. The physicists reported that it could generate a particle-beam 'force field' of far more strength than anything physical could possibly provide. They stated in this report that it produced a beam composed of 'quark-gluon plasma.' It broke through a concrete wall when they were testing different ways that they might activate it."

"Holy cow," Stanton, the geologist, marveled. "The pressure exerted by this ice continent is beyond any measurement we can make. And it's being kept open by *a laser beam.*"

Ash nodded. "Those whitecoats were the smartest dumb bastards I have ever heard of. They immediately reported their findings to my bosses," he said, then gave what was undeniably a smile. (Small, but progress is progress.) They also reported that the outer wall of their laboratory was … in disrepair. Heh. In any case, their work was the genesis of this emergency expedition."

Something is not adding up. The government had in their possession an apparent alien artifact *with writing on it,* and, instead of calling in linguists or say, an *exobiologist,* they immediately tested how it could become a top-secret weapon. That wasn't what was bugging me.

"In any case, those top government physicists found at least one function of the device. There might be others. That single function, however, is all we needed for this mission. There is nothing any scientist in any laboratory on Earth has ever conceived of that could create a mile-deep hole in the Antarctic ice sheet and keep it open—nothing on Earth, anyway."

There was an almost-audible *click* in my mind. "These weren't conceived *or* created on Earth."

"Correct."

"So, this particle-beam gluon-quark force field creator is …" I said in wonder, looking at my colleagues, all of whom must have had come to the same conclusion. "… *space-alien technology.*"

"That is correct."

"Wait, sir, if I may," SEALs Lieutenant Commander Hicks said with astonishment. "You're saying we are already in possession of extraterrestrial tech. I thought this mission was to *find* alien technology."

"We do have some. But not enough. And certainly not enough to let the Russians just steal this treasure from right under our noses."

"Understood, sir," Hicks said, looking light-years away from understanding the motivation behind this deadly journey, one that was only going to become more deadly the closer they got to the Anomaly.

"The hole's open. Let's move, people. That tunnel could close at any moment, so we'd best hurry."

That was not comforting. But it didn't matter, did it? We were all going down that hole in the ice, and if any of us didn't follow Ash's instructions, we would surely be left down there, for a few hours, even a day or two, still alive, in the pitch darkness.

"Understood."

14.31: ENTRY

The glass-smooth hatch opened with a *whoosh* of air being released after 200 million years. I couldn't tell if there was any smell to it because of the gear wrapped across my face to keep my nose from falling off from frostbite. I probably wouldn't even notice a smell anyway, so mesmerized was I to be looking *inside* an extraterrestrial vessel. And I was such a tool of academia that I was also mesmerized by a prospective lifetime of journal articles, books, and work *knowing* there's alien life, not just assuming it for hypothetical purposes.

This impossible machine, buried in ice for millions of years, was mine to explore. I was so intensely focused that before I knew what my body was doing, I speed-walked, almost running, toward the open hatch, and rush into the last step, lifting my foot forward to enter—a footstep more epochal than Neil Armstrong's—when Colonel Ash shoves his arm in front of me, clotheslining me to the floor.

"Wait for my instructions, goddamn it!"

He didn't help me up or even acknowledge almost crushing my windpipe. I took a moment to cough and rub my abused neck, then stood back up, a little shaky. Even in pain, I managed to croak, "What, you're going to *beat* us until we submit? That's illegal, even in the military, you *asshole*."

In an instant, Ash balled one hand into a fist of steel and punched my body at full force, right under my ribs, right into my diaphragm.

All the air whooshed out of me as I hit the floor already curled into the fetal position, nearly vomiting in pain. *I can't breathe! Jesus Christ, I couldn't take in a single breath!* After a moment of intense pain and panic, I was able to suck in the smallest amount of air, but I still watched black flowers blooming before my eyes. I was passing out.

Ash motioned to one of the airmen and cocked his head at me. Just before I was going to lose consciousness, Bishop pulled down my face wrap and pressed a plastic oxygen mask over my nose and mouth.

I still couldn't take in much of a breath, but what I was able to get was pure, blessed oxygen. Bishop lifted and placed my gloved hand against the mask and nodded at me to hold it in place myself now. I now watched everything from the floor.

Ash pointed at my pathetic carcass on the floor. "Any complaint, any demand, any *anything* I don't like—will be met with my force and your pain," he said gravely, and every academic's eyes went wide. "The pain Doctor Weaver here is experiencing is *trivial* compared to the *vital* mission we're doing here. You will all follow my instructions to the letter. *Period.* Any questions? Any bitching we need to get out of the way?"

Indeed, there was not.

"I knocked Weaver to the deck because he tried to rush in when he had no instruction or permission to do so. We don't know what's in there, people. We don't know if it's safe."

Safe? Several of the scientists subtly glanced around the pocket of air we were in, the only exit climbing up through 6,000 slippery feet of a manhole-sized ice tunnel that Ash had *just* told us could soon collapse, and I bet that was with, literally, even the smallest hiccup of electricity. None of this was "safe." (But I sure as hell wasn't going to share my opinion.)

"I treat you like I treat the men and women under my command. No better, no worse. We aren't on a training drill here, people. This is the most important thing any of us will ever do. This could very well be the *last* thing we ever do if you Brainiacs don't do *exactly* as I say. Understood?"

Everyone nodded, including me. I had a feeling not one of us understood anything except that we would get the hell beaten out of us— maybe executed—if we didn't act like good little slaves.

"All right, then." He extended a hand to me and helped me up. "No hard feelings, Weaver. I just need you to concentrate on the mission and not do anything hasty. Focus on that every time you feel the pain in your throat and stomach."

I nodded—I would have nodded at him no matter what he said—and pulled the oxygen mask off from my face. I handed it to Airman Bishop. "Thanks."

Bishop smiled and said, "Can't have you dying on us just yet."

"That's certainly reassuring."

"Now, the reason *why* I didn't want Professor Weaver to run right inside the ship is twofold. First, he was not authorized to do so. But the main reason is that we have five highly, *highly* trained professional black ops Navy SEALs locked and loaded down here with us ready to deploy into the ship. They can handle any hostiles and I keep 100 percent of my brain trust."

Automatically and to no purpose at all, each of us academics turned to look at the SEALS, those stock-still, at-attention elite commandos, who all remained exactly where they had stood since they examined the writing with the rest of us and then fell back to await further orders. They looked badass, I had to admit. They made my colleagues and me look like we were carved out of soft butter. I could see the Colonel's point now. And, as I swallowed with deep discomfort, I could feel it in my throat, too.

"Two of our friends here will enter the ship and reconnoiter what's inside. After they return and brief us, we"—I assumed that was a rhetorical *we*—"can decide what the next course of action will be. Does *everyone* understand this?" Ash looked the academics in the eye, and not only us but also the other Air Force officers and airmen. He even checked the understanding of the SEALs. No one made a sound, and he didn't seem to be dissatisfied. He stepped back and addressed the chief of the SEAL detail: "Lieutenant Commander Hicks, please commence your protocol."

And I thought university jargon was pretentious.

Hicks, who was outfitted identically to the other SEAL team members, made some signals with his fingers that I knew from movies means something like *Hey, you. And you. Pay attention. Do the thing.* "Dietrich, Drake, recon the site."

The movies I'd seen got this stuff right, although everything in any movie featuring purported extraterrestrials got every single thing wrong, by physics and biology and cosmology and probably a lot of other stuff, too. I'd spent a lot of time on BadScientist.com helping them correct misconceptions about … everything.

Commander and commandos checked the SEALs' helmet cam and radio connection. All was functioning correctly: I could see the images appear on the boss's Dell Latitude 14 Rugged Extreme. (I recognize the exact make of the laptop because several of the better-funded university geology departments outfit their field workers with one. It's designed to be well-nigh indestructible.)

"All correct," Hicks said after running through the checks of their equipment. "Dietrich, Drake—*go*."

The two SEALs did as instructed, stepping into the alien ship with assault weapons at the ready. Holding their powerful-looking mega submachine guns upright, they double-timed it to the entrance to the ship, checking each other over quickly. Drake went in first, followed closely by Dietrich. Once inside—their first step inside mechanical, not dramatically epochal at all—Drake headed left and Dietrich went right. There were two football fields' worth of spacecraft here and the open hatch was right in the middle, so splitting up made sense to me. However, the comm—the visual and voice radio helmet-cams used to sum up unexpected threats and guide the wearer—almost immediately lost coherence and was shortly nothing but random video pixilation and audio static.

"Dietrich, Drake," Lieutenant Commander Hicks spoke calmly into the mic on his headset, "we're losing the video feed. Can't hear you, either. Can you hear *me?* Check your cameras again—but do *not* remove your helmets. Copy."

The same audio that was going into Hicks's ears was audible to all by the Latitude 14's speakers.

It's just static. Not looking up from his forearm-mounted monitor screen, Hicks reported, "Colonel, our comm radio waves can't penetrate the hull of the ship. We've lost contact with them."

Ash nodded, his eyes on the ship and his mind apparently somewhere else, churning with thought. After a moment watching Hicks and another SEAL struggle with the comm, he said, "But are they all okay in there? Can you tell?"

Hicks shook his head, wearing an expression of embarrassed consternation. "Our telebiometry piggybacks on the comm frequency. But losing the comm temporarily is no reason for concern—"

POP-POP-POP-POP-POP-POP-POP-POP-POP-POP-POP-POP

"*Jesus!*" I yelped and hit the floor in instinctive self-protection. No one needed the comm link to hear the sudden burst of automatic weapons—or to hear the unnerving hiss-shriek of something very angry.

Or to hear the screams.

Hicks yelled into the headset, "Fall back! Dietrich! Drake! Do it *NOW!*"

More screaming, another hiss-shriek, reverberating concussions. If they could hear Hicks—and there was no reason in the world why they would've been able to—then they were either ignoring his order to fall back …

… or they *couldn't* fall back from whatever the hell was happening in there. But in a moment Drake ran past the open hatch as a blur, heading from his side to the one where Dietrich was screaming.

"Hicks," Colonel Ash said calmly.

The Navy Lieutenant Commander looked suddenly ill—but, I thought, this must be something that happens to the commandos all the time, scary situations with loss of communications … right?

A long and horripilating scream reverberated from inside the ship and was abruptly cut off.

"*Hicks.*"

Hicks looked up but didn't acknowledge Ash's call, but instead sets hand signals to two more of the SEALs—Crowe and Hudson—to get the hell in there and—

"*COMMANDER HICKS!*"

Finally, the SEAL commander looked at Ash and says, "I know what I'm doing, Colonel. We *do* have some experience with extreme scenarios. I need to get more of my people in there to take down whatever is—"

"Hicks, I *strongly* advise—"

"Crowe! Hudson! *Go!*" Hicks barked, brushing off whatever strong advice Ash might have wanted to offer.

The two SEALs made sure they were locked and loaded, then stuck themselves to the side of the alien ship like they were trying to sneak up a terrorist holing up in a Mosul apartment building. Amid more gunfire and a human shout of anger, Crowe motioned to Hudson and counted silently *one … two … three!*

They rushed the door—but are almost knocked down by Drake, who rushes out and crashes into them at full speed. Drake's eyes were wild and his uniform and face were awash in blood. Hicks grabbed him by the shoulders and looked him in the eyes. "You're all right, Chief. Where is Dietrich? Report—where is—"

"You gotta shut that hatch. Shut the hatch, sir—*shut the hatch! JESUS CHRIST! SIR, SHUT—*"

He broke off as an unholy gurgling *howl* resounded out of the ship and echoed against our ice bubble. I could see I wasn't not the only one anxiously watching the mouth of the tunnel as the ice shook. I didn't know how much would be enough to collapse our escape route, of course, but I bet it wasn't a whole lot more than this.

Drake, still held at the shoulders by Hicks, grabbed the straps between them that held in place Hicks's Kevlar vest. "Sir," he pleaded, "we have to get out of here." To see one of the toughest black ops soldiers in the United States military reduced to begging for them all to retreat filled me with tendrils of dread that I had to swallow back and try to ignore. I'm not claustrophobic, but the cold, the goddamn unceasing *cold*, already had me on edge before we even descended through the tunnel to get here.

I looked at my hands huge-looking under the heavy layers of gloves. They were trembling. In fact, all of me is shivering, trying desperately to warm up but also reflecting my knee-knocking fear. And now, with the yowling like something in a nightmare and a Navy SEAL completely freaked out, I could barely keep up my own fight against the cold or the enclosed space or imagining the hell-beast that had reduced Drake to tears.

"*Dammit*, Drake, where is Dietrich? Get yourself together and *tell me his location.*"

"He's dead."

"What?" Hicks visibly held back from throttling Drake to shake the details loose. "What happened? What is the hostile? Come on, Drake! I need intel!"

"It … it *squeezed* him. By the time I got"—he pauses at the horrible yowl, which is significantly louder now—"to him, it had him squeezed between its legs. Six legs, like a giant cockroach. Drake was still alive and screaming, so I discharged every round my weapon held into the creature. The legs went slack and Dietrich got loose."

HORRRRRRRRRRRRRRRRRRRRRRRRRRRRRRRRRRLGHHHH

Hicks shook off the ever-louder—thus ever-nearer—gurgling howl of whatever in hell is coming and said slowly and clearly, "Then *where is Dietrich?* You said he was dead, but now you say he was still alive— *where is he, Drake?* I need to know what we're up against. *Report!*"

"There was another one," Drake muttered, catatonic with shock and fear. "It jumped him and its razor legs cut right through him before I could reload. He's dead, sir, he's inside the ship and he is dead."

Hicks patted his commando on the shoulder and said, "Thank you, Drake." Then he turned to Ash and asked with an accusatory tone, "Colonel, how the hell is anything *alive* in there?"

"It doesn't matter *how*, Hicks. All that matters is *what*. As in *what are we doing about this?*"

"No, *how* matters, goddamnit. How many are there roaming in one hundred miles of spaceship? Are these things unkillable? Or are they actually *immortal*, living for 200 million years without food or whatever they consider fresh air? How is there *oxygen* still in there, enough for people to breathe?"

Yes, of course." He thought for a moment, a million SEAL strategies no doubt fighting for supremacy, and something clicked so hard we could all see the light bulb switch on. "I've got it—Crowe, Hudson, Ferro, take up positions at *AYYYYYRGHHHHHHHH*—"

The thing—*what WAS that!?*—launched itself from the hatch ten feet onto Hicks's back. He screamed in shock and pain, then the roach-like squeezed even him even tighter, forcing what was left of his air out over his vocal cords. Then it deployed the blades obscured under its six insect-hairy legs and—

BOOM! The rifle in Colonel Ash's hands—*where the hell did he get that from?*—was pressed up against the thing's side on the same level as its eyes when Ash blasted its chitinous shell into a hundred pieces, shards that drifted slowly to the floor of ice. Hicks fell down but somehow retained his consciousness, shaking like somebody had just filled his rectum with liquid nitrogen.

Killing the alien before it could slice through Hicks was great and all, but the *noise* was literally deafening, forcing hands against ears and immediate checks of the hole in the ceiling. (If we hadn't all had a layer of full-body-including-head insulation and our parka hoods—and the SEALs their hearing protection protection—eardrums would have been ruptured all around. Ash was fine, but I couldn't figure why he had earplugs already in when the attack happened. Or maybe I had an idea but didn't want to think about it.)

Apparently, I was mistaken about the amount of vibration the tunnel could take. And I realized it wouldn't have a chance to get "unstable"— the force field would simply exist in one moment and then lose its integrity the next, collapsing and trapping us all in here forever.

Like *200 million years* forever. I didn't want to be down there for five more minutes, dead *or* alive, let alone eons upon eons. So, like everyone else at that moment, I tried to keep the tunnel open by the sheer force of staring at it.

Doctors Goldsmith and Stanton took the opportunity to projectile-vomit, thoughtfully pointing against the wall of the ice cavity.

Commander Dietrich collected himself and addressed his squad: "Team, report! *Ferro!*"

"Uninjured! Discharged weapon. Target eliminated."

"*Crowe!*"

"Uninjured! Discharged weapon. Target eliminated."

"*Hudson!*"

"Uninjured! Discharged weapon. Target eliminated."

"*Drake!*"

Shakily, Drake muttered, "Uninjured … d-discharged weapon against h-hostile inside ship but did not eliminate target. Discharged again outside ship. Target eliminated."

"You all right, Drake?"

"Uninjured, sir."

"How about inside your head?"

"Focused on the job, sir."

"Keep me posted," Hicks says, then turns to Ash. "One casualty, Colonel. The hostile, um, *grabber* has been rendered inactive."

Doctor Hurt spoke up: "They're called *Ginsu Balls*, Commander. They're from Mars."

"*What?* Who the hell calls them that?"

"The hunters. The aliens."

Dietrich furrowed his brow. "The aliens speak English now?"

Ash stepped in and said, "The sentient aliens, the hunters, use technology that allows them telepathic communication. Doctor Hurt was in the mind encoded somehow within those tablets I showed you." At Dietrich's nod of understanding, Ash showed no particular emotion I could detect. He pointed at me and said crisply, "Weaver! Brief us on this 'Ginsu Ball.' Defense animal, like a guard dog? Or is it a predator roaming the surface of Mars—"

"Actually, they're subterranean," Doctor Hurt interrupted.

"Thank you, Doctor Hurt. It seems our care with the tablets has been well rewarded already." Then he said to me, "Now, Professor Weaver— speculate, if you please. What are we dealing with here? Underground Martians that are deadly as hell, we know that much."

"I, ah—yes," I muttered, everyone staring at me for an answer, any answer at all when Hurt could have described things better than I could since she was actually there—or more "there" than the rest of us. I was, after all, the conscripted exobiologist of this expedition, the one who had speculated more about extraterrestrial evolution, biology, and ecology than anyone else on Earth. This moment was the culmination of my studies, my theorizing, my entire career. This moment was why I was kidnapped and covertly flown 10,000 miles. *This moment.*

"*Weaver*," Ash said with a definite edge in his voice.

I shook myself out of my stupor and figured, if I were going to be thrown into the volcano, I might as well march to the lip as boldly as I could. "Yes, excuse me, Colonel—everyone—I was just trying to figure out how to say this in a way—"

"*Weaver!*"

"Sorry! All right, the closest terrestrial analogue I can think of right now is a giant prehistoric centipede, the, em … gah, I can't quite remember the species …"

Doctor Hurt, our evolutionary biologist who had seen the things in their natural habitat, nodded and said, "Exactly how I would have described it, Professor Weaver—the genus *Arthropleura*, actually an ancestor to centipedes *and* millipedes. It had more than six legs, of course, and, so far as we can tell, lacked any hidden three-foot-long razors in those legs."

"Thank you, Doctor Hurt," Ash said, possibly having asked me for information rather than Hurt because she had already told him *her* information when she returned from the other-mind on Mars. "Now, Professor Weaver, please resume your insights. What do we have here, anything more than a rolling coconut that can slice you into man-steaks?"

Intentionally or not, Doctor Hurt had just bought me enough time to cobble together a plausible answer. I began, "Our sample has been rendered into dust, but I would bet that a DNA sample—if, indeed, such a creature *has* DNA as we do—would show it to be of extraterrestrial origin.   This,   Colonel—colleagues —airmen—SEALs—is undoubtedly the first actual *space alien* mankind has ever encountered."

"That's something, Weaver. Let me ask you, in a more immediate context, how in blazes is an alien—or any living thing—still kicking, still *alive* in a spaceship inside an inescapable, airproof pocket of ice after 200 million years?"

I nodded, chewing over his question. Ash, for all his bluster and authority, was asking the right questions. (And, as any professor knows, fielding coherent *questions* from a class is rarer, and much more satisfying, than getting coherent *answers* from them. Perhaps ironically, it shows a greater depth of understanding, which is what teachers are trying to inspire in the first place. This classroom is horripilating and deadly, but as a graduate student I taught English Composition I, so it's really just a matter of degree.)

"Weaver! Goddammit, Professor, get your head in the game. You're burning up time we don't have."

"Right, yes, sorry. Some of us scientists need to enter the ship—with SEALs, your two airmen, and their weapons protecting us—and see whether there are any more life-forms aboard, hostile or otherwise. If it were up to me, and if it were possible without further endangering anyone, I'd like to see any further specimens more or less intact. Alive would be ideal, of course."

"I agree with Professor Weaver," Ash tells the SEALs as well as his Air Force contingent. "Kill anything about to kill any of us. Otherwise, consider it as standing order that no one go 'rock 'n' roll' on anything. Try to keep them in one piece, dead or alive. Understood?"

The volume and enthusiasm of their "*Yes, sir!*" sent my gaze automatically upward to eyeball the hole in the ceiling again.

"Excellent," he said to the soldiers, then turns to me. "Weaver, grab who you need and let's move."

Oh, god, don't make me do this. I tried to balance the need for expert analysis inside the apparently deadly ship with my equally strong desire to not force any of my colleagues to their deaths. But I man up and ask the group as steadily as I can, "There is information inside there that, literally, no human has ever encountered. Potentially career-making discoveries, maybe even life-changing knowledge. But there are probably more man-eating monster aliens that could kill us as soon as we step inside. So … any volunteers?"

To their everlasting credit, all four of my fellows raise their hands immediately, stretching their arms upwards like Hermione Granger in potions class.

I let out a laugh. "Well, *okay* then! Doctor Hurt?"

She answered crisply, "Evolutionary biology, evo-devo, and of course I've seen those things at first hand. You need me in there."

I laughed again and indicated Doctor Stanton. "You want to get in on some of this?"

"Indeed, I do. I'm a geologist. We're a mile under the surface. It's like living in a core sample. I want to see what created the gravitational anomaly—and *how*, if that's possible."

"Doctor Goldsmith?"

"I'm the only one of us who may be able to decipher the alien markings. Doctor Stanton needs me in there if we're to find out *why* this thing is here. I'm crucial to this … mission? Expedition? Grave robbing? I admit I am, a bit ironically, lost for words for what's happened the last 12 hours. But, because of me, we already know the warning on the side of the ship here and can proceed with caution."

The Colonel's eyes narrowed. "Pardon me?"

Goldsmith's face is one of confusion and fear, and after a moment, he responds, "What? Er—what, sir?"

"How in the hell do you know that the chicken scratch on the ship are some kind of warning?"

"I got very lucky," Goldsmith says, his expression now adding some pride in addition to the confusion and fear. "In my business, luck can often be the deciding factor between successfully sussing out the meaning of a foreign—in this case, *very* foreign—tongue."

Ash glowered at him.

Fear took pride's place as the primary emotion on Goldsmith's face. "Are—are you going to slap me, sir?"

Ash said, with an evenness that was unnerving considering his temper, "I thought you said you needed more samples."

"I—em, I *did*."

"Tell me what I want to know. *Now*."

"I … I don't know what you're asking—"

"For God's sake, man! Where did you get the second sample?" This from Ash's second-in-command, Major Elden, who I hadn't hear speak one word since the moment I woke up on the plane.

"Oh! Yes—I noticed some strange markings on the particle-beam thing and snapped a picture on my phone."

"You snapped a picture on your phone," Ash repeated. "You *snapped a picture* of a highest-level Top Secret piece of intelligence. You *snapped a picture* and thus violated sections 1.4(a), 1.4(c), 1.4(e), 1.4(g), and 1.4(h) of Presidential Executive Order 13526 regarding classified information."

"I was—"

"Just for *snapping that picture*, I could have you put in a Supermax prison—solitary confinement in your cell 23 hours a day, one hour to exercise in a concrete pen—for the next 30 years, Doctor Goldsmith. You would die in prison."

Goldsmith looked like he wished the Colonel *had* chosen to slap him instead of dressing him down. "Sir, if I hadn't taken the photo, we wouldn't know that this ship's markings meant, which was, essentially, *DANGER INSIDE*. I used both data sources, the glyphs on the weapon up there and the ones on the ship down here. Actually, I would appreciate some ... well, *appreciation*. I was thinking only of the success of this mission."

A bit unkindly, I thought: *And the journal publications and best-selling book that would result never entered your mind.*

Ash relented but still fixed Goldsmith with a gimlet eye. "Let's say I accept that. Then why didn't you share this warning translation before a member of the team was killed?"

"Would it have made any difference, Colonel? They went in there with machine guns ... oh, *and they're friggin' Navy SEALs.*"

"That's not your call, Professor," Ash said through a jaw tightened by Goldsmith's insubordinate tone. "If you hold one iota, once goddamn *scintilla*, of information from me again, I will shoot you dead with my own weapon."

(I noticed that Goldsmith's response to Ash wanting to know why he didn't share the translation did not actually get answered. But I knew exactly why he didn't, and it was for reasons other than his improvised confabulations: he intended to publish, and he meant to do it before anyone in our group could beat him to the punch, even though none of the rest of us were linguists. I firmly believed that, had we any Internet access—or a sat-phone signal—down there, he would have emailed or called in a hasty abstract and claim primacy of the discovery to the top-of-his-field publication, *The Journal of Memory and Language*. Once the academic jungle is in your blood, survival via publication becomes your constant obsession.)

"I understand," Goldsmith said. "Nevertheless, it *does* say something like 'DANGER'. Perhaps we should reconsider—"

"Secure that crap," Ash barked. "This is not an *recreational* expedition. We don't get to *reconsider* anything, *pick and choose* what parts we think are worthy and which are too dangerous. There is no 'too dangerous' for us, people—our objectives are for the whole human race."

Goldsmith nodded quickly, obviously wanting like hell to get out of the Colonel's spotlight. But our linguist had to be thinking what everyone else in the ice bubble was thinking: *The human race? What, all of it?*

Ash motioned at us. "The four of you eggheads are hereby ordered to surrender any photographic technology on your person to Airman Bishop."

"*What?*" I found myself yelping like an eighth-grader. "This *absolutely* has got to be fully documented! How are any of us supposed to study what's inside? If there's alien life—I mean, obviously, there *is* alien life—we need to take *as many pictures* as we possibly can!"

My three sheep-like colleagues handed over their smartphones to Bishop without pause, as Goldsmith had. Everyone then looked at me. What if I rebelled? What if I said no? It would probably hurt worse than Ash's clotheslining.

"We got to get a move on, Weaver," the Colonel said wearily. "Just give your phone to Bishop already. *Please.*"

I did as I was told. *B-a-a-a.*

He pointed at Doctor Yutani, the meteorologist. "So? Are you in or are you out?"

"But there's no weather in there."

Ash let out a pre-homicidal sigh and closed his eyes for a moment before saying, "You know, we'd all get along a whole lot better if you people would *just answer my goddamned questions.*"

"Excuse me, Colonel," Yutani said in a small voice. "Yes, sir, I am in."

"There we go. All right, Weaver, I'm glad to see the solidarity in your group." Ash turned to the remaining SEALs. "Commander Hicks, who's going in as the eggheads' security detail?"

"Ferro will lead the team."

At that, Ferro looked to and received confirmation nods from Crowe, Hudson, and Drake. She lingered on Drake slightly longer than the others, perhaps making sure that he could go back into the same place where he saw his brother SEAL sliced into pieces by something that was still inside the ship somewhere, perhaps part of a herd.

Drake gave his chief a single nod. I should have assumed he would be right there with the rest of them—Navy SEALs weren't exactly known for shrinking in the face of potentially violent death.

"All of us, Colonel."

"Excellent," Ash said with a nod of his own, then asked, "Chief, will you need assistance from any of us bluebirds on this?"

"Thank you, sir, but the eggh—*experts* and us SEALs might need your support out here if things go sideways," Ferro said, then shouted to us, "The rest of you poor bastards, let's get in there!"

She arranged us into two lines, one of which would turn left at the hatch and the other right, following the protocol that Drake and Dietrich had followed. Drake assumed the lead of Team Left, with Crowe at the rear. Between them was the "package" being delivered into the ship: biologist Hurt, meteorologist Yutani, and geologist Stanton. Team Right was Hudson up front, Ferro at the back, and Goldsmith and me in the middle with our notebooks and writing implements at the ready.

And, like water through a tap just turned, four trained killers and five tenure-track chalk-pushers flowed into the ship, into something ancient and utterly *other*.

***

There was one long stretch of what I would call a corridor once we entered the ship, one that makes a *T* with the hatch they were able to get open. Team Right—Hudson, Goldsmith, me, and Chief Ferro went to the right, of course; and Drake, Hurt, Stanton, and Petty Officer Crowe took the left. I'm not an architect, much less a spaceship designer, but it immediately struck me as odd that the corridor was not much wider than a human body. Wouldn't this create a tight bottleneck for the crew if there were an emergency?

I guess there *was* an emergency, 200 million years or so ago. No bodies lay in the corridor—maybe the "grabber" had them for a meal. Maybe it had friends, too. Then I slammed the door on my chatty-ass mind: *Stop talking.*

It was a good thing to tell myself. The lights are still on," Goldsmith marveled quietly at the blue glow emanating from recessions in the ceiling, and Ferro's giant gun's barrel pushed forward over my shoulder at the back of the linguist's head. She nudged him with the tip, and when he spun around, the barrel was pointed right at his face. He started so hard I thought he was going to knock over Hudson, who had stopped and turned around in front of Goldsmith.

Ferro's mouth formed the words *"Shut … up."* Her pupils were wide in the soft blue light, making her look as terrifying as her extremely terrifying weapon.

Even partially concealed by his parka hood, Goldsmith instantly drained from indoor-kid regular pale to milk-white. He nodded, barely daring to move his head, and turned back around very, *very*, slowly. Then we started moving again.

Although he would have been better off never opening his mouth in the first place, Goldsmith had made the same observation I did: this ship had been buried here since Antarctica was just getting cold, and the lights and whatever powered the opening of the hatch *were still working*.

Nuclear power could keep things going for a long time, I supposed, but unmaintained? How long of a half-life would the fissionable material need to have?

I allowed myself a (silent) chuckle at my own expense. I'm doing *exactly* what I always warn students, magazine writers, and Nye and Tyson about: I'm thinking like an earthling. I was thinking of this incomprehensibly advanced race as if they were humans living on Earth in our present state of technology. But that is a serious misstep, especially for a tenured exobiologist. The extraterrestrials could have had—in fact, were almost *guaranteed* to have—nuclear-fusion technology, at the very least. Compared to fission, fusion is like shooting bullets instead of throwing them. I scolded myself at my lapse, no matter how "automatic" my assumptions were. I had to be as a camera: recording, archiving data for later analysis. I don't have—*humans* don't have—the context to judge even this spaceship's blue lights, let alone whatever else utterly *alien* was inside this leviathan from space.

The temperature inside the ship was even lower than the ice bubble around it, something that didn't seem possible until I realized that the body heat of a dozen and a half people warmed the air of the ice bubble for very likely the first time since the ship crashed.

At least—and the thought hit me with queasiness and a sudden flash of claustrophobia—I *thought* the ship crashed. That was what makes sense. That was exactly what a human from Planet Earth would judge as making sense. I had to literally shake the thought from my mind. I had enough to be scared to death of right then, and speculating on the circumstances surrounding this spacecraft being there in the first place were enough to freak me out existentially, thanks very much.

Almost as I thought this, Hudson halted on a dime and put his hand up to alert us. Amazingly, neither Doctor Goldsmith nor I stumbled into him or each other.

It took just a second to see why the SEAL stopped. He was at the end of the strange corridor and looking right at where it opens into a larger space. I couldn't see his face, but I could see that his upheld hand was shaking.

Whatever was in front of him, it was making *a Navy SEAL's hands shake.*

Jesus Christ.

"Hudson, report," Ferro whispered this as quiet as a snowflake hitting the ground.

He turned around, *very* slowly, and reports in the same whisper, "N-No hostiles visible, sir. But …"

"But?"

"It's … I can't hardly describe it, Chief. It's … *empty.*"

"Of hostiles?"

"Of everything."

Ferro chewed on this for a short moment. "Lead the way, Hudson. This we gotta see."

He acknowledged the order and executed an about-face, silently and slowly. He took a careful step forward, then another, and another, leading the rest of us into the "empty of everything" space in a straight line, like the corridor is continuing. We all followed him without hesitation. I literally had no idea what else anyone would—or could—do.

I almost walked into Goldsmith, who was shuffling behind Hudson but froze in awe as he beheld the interior of the ship. I nudged him, maybe a little harder than necessary, but I wanted to see this, too.

He moved. I followed him until I looked left and the sight unfolded before *my* eyes.

Mother of God, what am I looking at? What—

From behind, Ferro nudged me. Maybe a little harder than necessary.

I shuffled forward enough to allow her to see as well. She stopped in place, jaw dropped open, but she could stare as long as she wanted with nobody nudging her from behind. "Mother of God," she said in a nearly disembodied whisper. "What *did* this?"

Stretching before us seemed eternity itself.

The vastness of the interior space filled my entire field of vision. Two enormous blue spotlight beams from just in front of us pointed outward into the space, but they faded not very far from where they began. These lights—although giving off no heat I could feel—were massive and their beams obviously intense, so their fading suggested an unfathomable depth. It felt like we had been swallowed by a whale, but a whale whose body stretched beyond our sight, beyond our reason.

Complete silence from Goldsmith and myself and the two SEALs as we tried to take it all in.

After a moment, Goldsmith remarked in awe, "Ha! There *is* weather," recalling Yutani's words as he craned his neck to espy the distant ceiling of the alien spaceship. "Look—clouds."

We looked up, and sure enough, there was a nebulous covering that looked much like Earth clouds reflecting some of the blue light. For research, I had visited the McKinley Climatic Laboratory at Eglin Air Force Base, one of the largest structures in the world, and it showed hints of "clouds" of condensation near the top of its huge and empty space.

But this space was incalculably larger, and the formations reflecting the blue glow from its highest reaches were undeniably *clouds*. I wondered what Yutani on Team Left would think of them—it's possible that more rain fell inside this ship, deep under the ice, than on the Antarctic surface above, which was the driest place on Earth.

Hudson's mouth hung open. "Chief, how are we gonna find anything on this ship? It's a hundred miles long!"

Ferro shook her head slowly, chewing on the scale of what "exploring the ship" was turning out to be. She started to speak, but everyone in the six-person detail heard a horrendous, horripilating, *animal* shriek of fury.

The chief SEAL said in a gallows-humor tone, but one full of dread and without a shred of amusement: "Hudson, I get the feeling that finding them isn't gonna be a problem. They're on their way to *us*."

15.20: ATTACK

And they were.

We could hear the wild, gargling shrieks from whatever predator would be the first out of the gate to kill every one of us. If it was one of the Titan Gilas I had experienced, and it definitely sounded like a bunch of them thundering our way, I knew what to do—but I had no idea how *we* could do it without the railguns the alien hunters had. Those things ripped the bastards apart. I hoped that the machine guns our SEALs carried would do the trick, but a hunk of metal coming at you at just below light speed is far more deadly than even a machine gun's ammo coming at 1,500 feet per second. The rail bullets that shredded the Titan Gilas traveled at nearly *665,000 times* that speed.

An idea hit me: "Ferro," I said as quietly as could be heard. "Do we have any railguns?"

"*Railguns?* Let me check with Buck Rogers … yeah, the answer would be 'negative.'" But she narrowed her eyes a little, considering the question in spite of her remark. "Why? Or do I already know why?"

"When I was hunting Gilas on Titan"—all expedition members had been briefed on the scientists' adventures inside the tablet—"the aliens used railguns to rip apart those things. I don't know if big machine-gun bullets would even slow them down."

"Are they *that* big?"

"They're big, but more than that, they're *stout*, just rampaging balls of hard muscle and teeth. They look a lot like … what's wrong?"

Ferro swallowed hard as she squinted to peer into the darkness ahead. "They're coming in, twelve o'clock. They're still back there in the dark. Coming this way."

She shouted into her radio for Team Right to get their asses to where Team Left was, and get there *now*. There was heavy static on the signal, but Crowe responded in a way that gave the solid impression that, not only had he heard her, he might have started beelining for us double-time before Ferro had even spoken the words.

She seemed to be in "battle mode" now, every one of her movements distinct, even choppy: she scanned the entryway, in which bootsteps were getting louder already, then looked at the wall, and then returned to peering into the darkness. She said in fast, discrete words, "We can't have a wall at our backs. The rest of the unit is coming through that entryway in less than a minute—we can't stand here in front of the hatch. We can't keep moving as we were, either—I don't like the looks of those glowing disks on the floor *at all*."

I hadn't noticed those, but if I had to guess—and I *would* be the one asked to guess, being a *full-time* exobiologist as opposed to the dabblers from other disciplines, no offense—I'd say they were booby traps, being so relatively near the entryway that led from the outer hatch.

But no one asked me to guess. They just took Chief Ferro's words at face value. So, I cleared my throat a little and said, "I'd say those look like booby traps for intruders, being so rela-tively near—"

"Yeah," Ferro said sharply, but also distractedly, as she planned our next move, "I already said they looked bad."

Goldsmith said, "We're going to get crushed."

"*Thank you*, Professor," Ferro snapped. "All hands move forward, away from the wall."

"Into the, um, *darkness?*" Hudson nearly whimpered.

"*Move!*"

We moved perpendicularly from the outer bulkhead, creeping forward. It was still illuminated enough to see one another where we were, but soon that light would be far behind. My body did *not* want to move, and every step I took felt like I had bones made out of rubber.

"Chief, we're almost to you," Dietrich said, his voice clear on the line now. "We're just passing the hatch we entered the ship through … oh, hell … hey, Chief?"

"We have hostiles, Petty Officer—what is it, and tell me *fast*."

"The hatch is shut."

Ferro let out a stream of curses that only Navy personnel who have seen combat—not to mention the Philippines—could possibly muster off the top of their heads. The NATO alphabet lacked official names for some of the sounds she was making.

Hudson, Goldsmith, and I were freaking the hell out at the conniption blasting out from the Chief, more than the fact that we were now locked inside a giant spaceship with god knew how many alpha predators from how many planets collected by the alien hunters. The only predators our "team" had seen were one on each (apparently inhabited) planet. Now that I saw the vastness of the interior of the craft, I realized there could be—almost had to be—many, many more stored here before the ship crashed 160 million years ago.

Crowe and Yutani and Stanton and Hurt and Drake rushed up beside our line marching into the abyss. There was certainly enough room for hundreds or thousands more to spread out along that same line.

We moved farther and farther out of the light and into the vasty dark, the SEALs and the scientists, everyone with weapons, only four who knew how to use them outside what we'd learned from the movies. Also, I was losing my spatial orientation with the encroaching blindness produced by the fading of the floodlights.

"Halt," Ferro called, and we all came to an immediate stop. I don't think any of us wanted to go one foot deeper, so she didn't have to ask twice. "Go to nightscope. And light up your lamps."

I didn't have any idea what that meant, but I watched Hudson when he turned on a powerful flashlight attached to the bottom of his weapon. *Thank god for light*, I almost said out loud. He then removed an item from his gear pack and clipped it onto the top, 180 degrees around the machine gun from the spotlight. He switched it on and I could see green light on his eyes before he placed his right one snugly against the scope, the "nightscope."

They couldn't just say *infrared?* I secured my snark, as Ash would say, and found the "lamp" on the bottom of my own weapon. Then, moving my hand around the weapon, I found—no doubt pre-installed for PhDs—a scope already in place. I switched it on as Hudson had his and looked into the green phosphor glow. We also had in place our earplugs that automatically blocked only those sounds above 90 decibels. Otherwise our hearing would be shredded at the explosion of firepower about to be unleashed.

I muttered, "Still can't see a damned thing. Only now, the damned thing I'm not seeing is a *green* damned thing."

Every one of the SEALs stiffened up at the same second, then crouched, their weapons (and thus their scopes) never wavering from some vanishing point.

Goldsmith and I—as well as Yutani, Stanton, and Hurt, I could see from the lamps on *their* weapons—crouched down as well, with no idea why except that it was good to automatically do whatever the highly trained and lethal commandos next to you were doing.

"I hear them," Goldsmith said in my ear. "It sounds like a stampede of buffalo."

I nodded. Whatever the herd might be, their approach was pants-wettingly unmistakable. The hunters had taken eight of the creatures, but had been millions upon millions of years ago—as long as they were kept alive, whenever they were not in stasis, they must have been multiplying like crazy.

I took another look through my nightscope and could only just detect a brighter green source in the distance, beyond the human visual spectrum at the moment, but coming fast.

There could be a thousand of them, or more. The ship was so vast, with so much space inside for breeding monsters …

"Stay sharp, people!" Ferro barked. "Weaver, Goldsmith—keep those barrels pointed *away* from us and out toward the targets. We don't want to be shot by you guys, and you don't want to accidentally shoot yourselves, either, all right?"

Goldsmith and I mumbled assent. His weapon was shaking. So was mine, dammit. But we would hit the Gilas or we'd hit nothing.

"Lamps off! We don't need to advertise our exact location."

We obeyed the command, but once again we were plunged into soul-sucking darkness.

"Here they come," Hudson said, both eyes open—one on the infrared scope and one looking out on the same scene in darkness. (All the scientists copied her move.) "Permission to fire, Chief?"

She saw them, too, and the same way as Hudson: one eyes with the nightscope infrared, where the shape of the horde could now be seen as a mass of *things* rather than just an amorphous glow in the distance. "Not yet," Ferro said. "We need to spread out and give them less of a target. Crowe, Frost—you take the flanks. Hudson, get the scientists to the bulkhead back near the entrance and *keep them safe*."

Goldsmith's voice sounded whiny as it floated in the darkness: "Against the wall? Didn't you just say we would get *crushed* there?"

"Hudson, get them out of here, already! The Colonel needs them safe, and that wall will be the final place they can reach. Professors, if the SEALs fail here, just *run*. Escape and hide. Eventually the Air Force people are going to come down if we don't come up first."

That was cold comfort for us five civilians about to be smeared against a wall by a herd of space buffaloes on nuclear steroids. But Hudson got his bearings and ran/walked us eggheads what must have been half a mile, to where we had all been taking in the sublime sight of the vast interior of the ship less than an hour before. The two SEALs ordered to the flanks had already disappeared into the darkness on either side before we could see the outer wall, our destination.

The diffuse blue light at the wall was the most beautiful light I had ever seen. Hudson deposited us like kids at daycare and ran back into the darkness again.

"All right," Doctor Stanton said. "Our best bet is to let the professionals do their jobs and for us to hide in the corridor, where the …"

"Gilas," I prompted.

"… where the *Gilas* might not be able to reach us. How big are they, Weaver? Would they get stuck in the corridor we just came through?"

"One might just squeeze into it, but it wouldn't be able to get leverage to move any farther. That'd stop them up right there," I said, motioning at the corridor we just exited from a hundred yards away, but shook my head. "Too bad the hatch is sealed now."

Stanton closed his eyes and let out a huge sigh of resignation. "Another beautiful theory ruined by ugly fact."

I cracked a smile at that, but it fell from my face quickly as I heard Chief Ferro's voice crackling on Hudson's radio: "Give me Weaver. I need Weaver *now*."

I was handed the transceiver and said, like what I think a commando would say, "Go for Weaver."

"Okay, sure," Ferro said. "You never told me how we kill these things."

How would I know? "All I know is that railguns are effective."

"Yeah, those don't exist except in science fiction and futuristic alien-hunter technology. What do we already *have* in our arsenal that—"

"Chief, this is the hunters' ship! It must be in their ... gun storage? Is that the right term?"

"No. You mean they have the weapons on this ship somewhere?"

"They must. Only ... where do we even start to look?"

"If the aliens—*gah! Holy hell*, hostiles approaching, team! Filling the clock from 10 'til 2! People, weapons forward, keep grenades ready to pull and throw. Drake, what do you read for distance? Are they in range?"

"In range, Chief."

"*FIRE!*"

We couldn't see the SEALs a half-mile away until the machine guns started their staccato flashing. The sound took a few seconds to reach us, and when it did, it sounded like cap guns ... but more than that, we heard the little *pops* very starkly. There was no echo and no absorption by structures (that I could see, anyway) wasn't happening. It was listening to a container of Jiffy Pop, but *in space*.

I had let my nightscope (and thus my weapon) down, but now I snapped to attention from my analyzing the qualities of space popcorn sounds and lifted the scope to my eye.

And there they were, hundreds of them, maybe a thousand: the Titan Gilas. They were bigger than the ones I saw inside the tablet, but 100 million years of breeding for size and ferocity would tend to do that.

(An aside while we waited for the Gilas to stampede the front-line SEALs into pancakes and our SEAL back here to be crushed into paste against the wall along with the rest of us: Although I had worked and studied for years to come up with plausible scientific scenarios of what life would be like on other worlds, it hit me forcefully—just like the Gilas were about to do—that I was making assumptions that flew in the face of what I had always considered proven scientific fact:

I knew *for a fact* that a thousand genetically healthy members of a species cannot be bred from just eight individuals, no matter what male/female ratio might be to start. But by stating that, I was assuming there are distinct "males" and "females" in the Titan Gila species. They could be asexual, or they could have three sexes, which would definitely affect the genetic viability of just eight specimens mating and their offspring mating until the current thousand or so monsters made up the millions-of-years-down-the-line generation we were facing now.

I suppose the hunters could also have returned to Titan to round up more of them. As with most things once you start really thinking about them, none of that mattered now. There were a thousand beasts running at top speed, regardless of *why* they were there.

Also, wouldn't animals from Titan need those methane-lake temperatures to live? Did this ship have different environments for its different catches, or were they bred over the eons to operate in the less-cold environment of Earth? It made little sense as I thought about it on the fly, but, once again, reality didn't have much respect for my speculations. What was happening was *definitely* happening, "possible" or not.)

I could see the machine-gun flashes in almost-white flares of brightness on my nightscope. Hot for an instant and then gone, their signal only highlighted the wall of bodies getting brighter, which meant their body heat was being detected more clearly, which meant they were closer every second. And I could see them like this *half a mile away* from where the SEALs were shooting, loading, shooting. To them up there, they must have been within one hundred feet.

"Thirty meters," Drake's voice said from Hudson's radio.

Ha! my disturbingly competitive academic mind shouted. Thirty meters (what the military used) was about 98 feet (what I used) away. Thirty yards would, of course, be 90 feet away—but I didn't say "100 yards," I said "100 *feet.*" Put down a point for the exobiologist, master of all disciplines!

My idiot revelry came to an immediate stop at the fear registering on the voice on the radio now. It was Crowe: "I have twenty meters. Chief, we gotta—"

"Secure that."

"Fifteen meters!" his unsteady voice called out. "*Chief!*"

"Five more seconds, team. Aim for the middle of the line. Three … two … one … *release!*"

The nightscope showed the warm and bright shapes of Ferro in the center and Drake and Crowe from the sides all making the motion of throwing something *hard*. The beasts were upon them—forty feet at most—and their silhouettes were almost as bright as the commandos'. Assuming their temperature was roughly the same as those of humans, there was a just-barely-discernable difference in infrared intensity.

Jesus God, they're dead already.

Flashes so bright that we all recoiled from our night scopes filled our screens with hot-white-green phosphor. Even looking at the pitch-dark scene with just my eyes, I could see the super-grenades going off and I could for a second see the Titan predators illumined.

They were titanic, indeed—now they were the size of actual buffalo and the resemblance was hard to shake. We had no railguns, nothing but bullets … and powerful grenades. Those would definitely spot a buffalo or even a herd of one thousand buffalo. But these just *looked* like those stout and powerful creatures—even the Titan Gilas, the ones I had seen, made their earth-native counterparts seem like weak kittens.

There was one brilliant flash in the middle—that must have been Ferro's weapon—and then came the sound, again without echo and thus very distinct, but unmistakable, explosions: *POMP! POMP! POMP! POMP!*

The next sound we heard was shrieking, but it wasn't from a human.

Taking the chance of looking through our night scopes again—we could see the light of explosions with plain sight, but to actually *see* our SEALs and the Titan Gilas, we still had to rely on the infrared.

The tide of monsters parted around Ferro and the shrieking Gilas only *partially* torn apart by the explosion. There must have been quite a few killed to create a fork like this. The explosions to the flanks did the same, taking out multiple (but not enough) charging predators.

So, concussive weapons could incapacitate and/or kill these Kronian beasts at close range. That was good to know. The scientists had each clipped on a couple of grenades, but we were very explicitly warned that we had them at hand in order to quickly give them to an actual fighting person if that commando used all of his or her own.

(An aside: "Kronian" means a being in the Saturn system. It comes from the Greek name for Saturn, *Kronos*. It is used because "Saturnine" and "Saturnial" already have other definitions describing personality traits. Suck on *that*, Doctor Goldsmith!)

My thought made me crack a half-smile even though we were all guaranteed to die in the next sixty seconds. But the smile died on my face when I saw that the pattern of explosions had channeled every Gila into one relatively narrow stream of killer monsters.

Which was still running right at us. We had less than half a mile between them and us when Hudson, completely out of the blue, ordered us to stomp one foot—*one* foot—down onto the lighted disks.

"Which foot?" Stanton said, completely reading my mind.

"It doesn't matter!" Hudson yelled and instantly saw our academia inability to act or decide. "Okay, fine—*right* foot. *Go!*" I realized it was Hudson's duty to stomp last, once all of us overeducated types had followed his instructions.

Here came the Titans themselves, in both meanings. I shut my eyes tightly and stamped my right foot hard against the disk I was standing on.

When I opened them again, the disk was floating in the air above three alien hunters. I could see the flared ear-feet of the species—or maybe the same individual who had been in stasis—of hunter whose mind I had earlier entered, albeit more than 100 million years ago. The other two were of a different species, probably of an entirely different planet.

They were *alive*. How in the holy hell were the pilots still *alive?* This ship had been buried under the ice as soon as Antarctica's movement to the bottom of the planet created the permafrost that could, apparently, be pierced only by state-of-the-art drilling equipment or an advanced alien civilization's force-field beam.

They sensed immediately that one of their disks had materialized, and after a moment all three looked up and saw me.

They were each holding an iridescent slate, indistinguishable to me from the five slates Colonel Ash had shown us. In the cockpit—if that's what it what it was—I could see there were six discrete grooves no doubt meant for the tablets. An iPhone-style charging port? The incongruous and anachronistic thought amused me.

The one whose mind I had resided in put down the tablet he was holding and selected another from the many floating to one side of the room. He then stamped where he was standing, and a glowing disk raised him in the air and sent him toward me with no more trepidation than one would have staring into an open refrigerator.

He tapped my hand with the tablet before I could pull the hand away—and I was no longer there with the aliens.

Well, that wasn't entirely true—I was still floating above them, but somehow I was also back in the endless space right where I had been standing, our whole little unit about to be buffaloed and flattened against the wall.

But that wasn't all—I could also see the entire vast spaceship, like looking at a 3D blueprint and seeing all places at once. This was something that the aliens possibly used to check on the many, *many* creatures that roamed the vast space of the ship. I wondered if all these predators were separated by some kind of force-field acting as impenetrable fencing.

I didn't have any idea why the calm alien had bestowed this ability on me, but I focused my mind on where my compatriots were, and all the rest I could see shifted into the background and dimmed.

This is what I saw.

***

Hudson, Goldsmith, Hurt, Stanton, and Yutani all were distributed in what seemed to be random positions. Yutani was no more than fifteen miles from the cockpit; Stanton sixty from the cockpit, but eighty from Yutani; Stanton also about eighty miles, but not anywhere near the others; Hurt within one mile of Goldsmith, twenty miles away; and Hudson the SEAL thirty miles or so miles away, in an area just near one of the ship's outer walls.

They all were fighting monsters.

Ferro and Drake remained on the extreme edge of the vast plain, at the end of which was a tremendous inland sea.

The sudden disappearance of the Gila's prey—those who were ordered to stay behind at the wall—caused the Gilas to hit the brakes—but only the front-most line of one hundred or so. However, the hundreds and hundreds of Titan Gilas behind that front row, all of them bred to kill with brute muscle and terrible mass, kept stampeding and shoved the stopping front row forward into the wall. They were forced into the wall full-force, the ones in front crushed to gristle and black blood. A literal wave of destruction spread back through the line of creatures that had fanned out to become a phalanx, shredding the two or three rows—the next-foremost of the stampede—into pieces. Behind them, the wave knocked them down, possibly dead, possibly fatally injured, possibly just injured. But these walls of dead Gilas acted as an actual wall—the Gilas behind them hit hard, the ones behind them less hard, and the ones behind them mostly able to come to a stop, and the rest just stopped and waited.

It was impressive as hell. I had to think that the SEALs already had this worked out—then it hit me that Navy commandos would know how to deal with an angry mob, whether from another country or another planet. Either way, it was *spectacular*. I felt like maybe we would make it through after all—

A man's shout—"*GODDAMNIT TO HELL!*"—and the sound of a machine gun going "rock 'n' roll" on multiple targets—ended any thought of any of us making it anywhere except the afterlife (not that I truck with such metaphysical nonsense). I could hear and see the SEAL who had taken the right flank as he was crushed by monsters flowing right around the ill-placed explosion. His throwing of the grenade wasn't far enough to the side to herd all of the creatures in one direction, and their overflow hit him, then stampeded over him, his powerful bullets causing no more trauma to the Gilas than a mosquito bite would to a human.

Crowe. That was the SEAL under the foot-things of the herd of extraterrestrials. So far I had watched three people die and heard another one being murdered by being thrown out to the elements. Afforded the luxury by my entry into four-dimensional separation from 3-space, I took a moment and bowed my head for him.

Now there was just Ferro and Drake, both tougher-than-nails commandos, but there were *so* many of the Gilas remaining, the mostly uninjured six hundred. Did they have a plan to extract themselves? As far as I could tell from my time in the other-mind on Titan, these things didn't bite or scratch—they just ran into you and you got hit as hard as a freight train, the shock waves turning every organ to jelly. But, as the unfortunate Petty Officer Crowe had just learned, they could also just knock you down and stampede you to death in seconds flat.

"Drake, get to me!" Ferro radioed and set off a flare (which was certainly an unusual and serendipitous piece of kit to carry). "They can't move fast—*go!*"

Without even a second's hesitation, Petty Officer Second Class Drake ran at the herd—and they really were a herd, satisfied waiting behind the rows of stopped or dead creatures. If they were anything like Earth buffalo, they would eventually think to turn around, but nobody would be moving until the final row of Gilas turned around and the rest followed.

Drake took three huge steps and hurled himself into the air, landing on the second Gila in, and deftly used the powerful but dumb aliens as stepping-stones to get to his commander. The monsters were so big and dense that none of them reacted at all to being stepped on, and hard, as Drake ran over their backs.

Once he hopped off the last Gila and landed next to Ferro, they both laughed for a moment and reached into their packs. They took out odd objects fashioned for dark metal, then took less than one minute to assemble them into … what *were* they putting together? When the last of the three pieces were clicked together and their power supplies switched on, I recognized immediately what they had in their hands.

Oh, my God, I thought. *They have railguns.*

How in the hell did they have railguns—and why didn't they use them from the start? I had no idea, but I could smell Colonel Ash all over this. There may have been another alien ship found somewhere—under Lake Vostok in Russia, maybe—and that's where Ash and his team found these. The two SEALs definitely knew how to hold them, and they were—for a moment, to my mind inexplicably—pushing between the boulders of Titan Gilas to the rear of the hundreds of them still alive. The

Gilas didn't seem to be capable of, or perhaps not interested in, moving laterally to kill or eat (or both) Ferro or Drake. Their slipping through—and, once or twice, jumping onto and stepping over the creatures—reminded me of a driver who had abandoned his or her car right in the middle of an insanely backed-up L.A. rush hour, choosing to walk to their destination, the faster choice.

They nimbly made their way through the rows from Ferro's location and reached the back of the herd. The rearmost row was now the nearest to the SEALs, and some of them began turning around with bovine curiosity—and possibly a predator's malice—which would ultimately reorient all the surviving Gilas.

Ferro looked at Drake. "Locked?"

He smiled and said, "Loaded." Then he said, "The Colonel said 'just enough,' right?"

"Good boy! Just enough to make another wall of dead animals. We need to trap most of them between the bulkhead and the first pile of dead." She put her railgun into firing position. "Let's make it happen, you mother—"

Even from my interdimensional point of view, I couldn't hear the rest of Ferro's curse word, because the commandos opened up on the Titan Gilas, the projectiles impacting on them at least 90 percent of *the speed of light.*

The did that machine-gun "rock 'n' roll" on the front line of Gilas. The ammo, whatever it was in a railgun, went right through the first three rows no matter what angle the SEALs shot from. It tore them apart completely in the first row, then killed the second row after having traveled through the dense meat of the first row. Ripping through the creatures slowed the projectile down to merely 100 percent deadly, and the third row behind them were either killed or wounded so badly that they just fell over and stayed there. Some of the Gilas had hunkered down like cats with their wounds, but they wouldn't be getting up again.

This made a thick wall of the dead that sealed off the unharmed alien predators. This wouldn't have been possible if the area near the rear bulkhead were as open as the main interior of the ship. But it wasn't, and the Gilas were well and truly trapped. They didn't seem to mind terribly and most did that "cat blob" sitting as they waited for an opportunity to move freely again.

Ferro and Drake clapped their hands together, their fingers wrapped around each other's hands. Then they did some kind of Navy SEAL brostein secret celebratory handshake, took a huge breath of relief, and began disassembling the railguns. The weapons didn't even look warm. As a gadget lover, I found that fascinating—but so would every gun aficionado in the world.

"So glad the smart guys got away," Drake said as they stored the railguns back into their packs and picked up their machine guns. "We would've had to get out the alien guns and start shooting anyway, Ash be damned."

"The scientists can't know about this. I wasn't briefed that there was some kind of transporter mechanism, but thank god there was—we *need* those guys."

"May I speak candidly, Chief?"

She laughed. "*What?* Of course!"

"I'm concerned about this mission."

"I believe that to be an uncontroversial statement, Drake. We just saw Crowe—may he rest in peace—get trampled to bloody mush. I'm concerned, too."

"Yes, Chief," he said, "but dying isn't the thing I'm worried about."

"Whoa. Okay, I'll bite—what is?"

"Why is this ship here? Why is it full of killer extraterrestrial animals? What were the aliens transporting them for?" He paused, was reassured by Ferro's look of interest, and continued, "And *why does Colonel Ash want so many of them alive?*"

Ferro chewed this over and said, "I don't know, I don't know, I don't know, and I do not know."

Drake laughed. "Do you think these smart guys know? Have they even been briefed?"

"That was not shared with me, but I think that they never would have left Criminy Station if they had any idea what Ash's goal was here." She shook her head slowly and thoughtfully. "They're not military, so they could have been given at least *that* choice, choose not to come down. But hell, if I had known, *I* never would have gotten on the plane in Tierra del

Fuego in the first place. They have plenty of SEALs other than me. But orders are orders."

Drake considered all of that, then said, "So, Chief, what's next?"

"Back into the dark. I expect many horrors ahead of us, so keep your big-boy pants on."

The Gilas and their brother-in-arms left unmoving behind them, Ferro and Drake set out anew. They didn't express any curiosity about where the "eggheads" had teleported to. That was Hudson's concern—but they didn't know where *he* was, either.

The dark engulfed them, and they pulled down the infrared goggles they had stored on their foreheads during the melee. Now they could see everything they wished they didn't have to see.

The same was true for me, put into this strange, ghostlike state where I could see everything, where my view was from all places at once. Maybe the aliens were used to this, but I felt like I needed to shut my eyes before I threw up from the horrifying complexity in front of me.

Goddamnit. The 4-space was apparently created inside my visual cortex, not my eyes, and so closing them did nothing to take away the magic vision bestowed on me by the alien pilots. Why did they do this? This would be of great help to us in our mission, and I had assumed anything that was good for us would automatically be bad for the aliens. But I didn't know that; I had only assumed it.

It then occurred to me that I had no idea what the full mission actually *was*. Ash had kept that information to himself and the Navy commandos, it seemed. But why? I couldn't *really* have refused to budge from Criminy Station—Ash would have hauled me out of there and shoved me down the tunnel anyway.

I wondered why the academics were being left out of this discussion. If you kidnap scientists, you'd better be able to—

I cast my 4-space gaze and saw *Colonel Ash* floating on his own disk down a far-off corridor. He hadn't remained outside in the bubble as he said he would. Why was he aboard? And where the hell was he going? And also, what the hell, he knew about the disks, too?

I headed toward the colonel on my magic platform, but something caught my eye immediately to my left (maybe not "immediately," but with my supernatural-like ability to see everything and drift through walls while in 4-space, one mile was covered almost instantaneously because I could move as the space-crow flies).

It was Stanton, and he floated in the air above some moving shadows, ovals of blackness that I had no idea how to identify. But I zipped over to my colleague in seconds flat, making him jump a little when I popped into 3-space right next to him.

"You about gave me a heart attack, man! That's the least-interesting way to die here."

"Sorry about that. Still figuring out these things we're standing on."

He laughed a little and said, "These things aren't so hard to drive once you figure out how to keep from jumping to new locations randomly. I don't like that—it's too much like when your ship goes into 'hyperspace' in the *Asteroids*, and you end up fatally teleporting into the middle of a giant space rock."

We both smiled, but then my gaze joined his in looking down at the migration of the tar-black things—which reminded me of the "portable holes" in that movie *Who Framed Roger Rabbit?* Then it hit me that these were the things Stanton had encountered on Venus. "Are those, um, *Venus Blobs?*"

"Look at the big brain on the exobiologist," he said with a smirk. "Yeah, these are the Blobs, and they will mess you up *bad*. Not a fan of dying by alien acid creatures."

"They're all migrating somewhere."

"I checked it out—there's a passage where the bulkhead leaves a one-inch opening at the bottom. I think this was by design."

"To allow these things to move freely? Why would anyone design such a thing?"

"Alien God works in mysterious ways."

A gave him a look and he had to grin. I did, too. "Should we follow and see where they're going?"

"Unless we can slip through that crack or travel through the walls after them, I don't think we're going to be able to track them."

"Um, Stanton, this is going to seem strange—"

"Oh, boy, haven't seen anything strange today."

"Yes, well, I don't know how this is happening, but … watch."

I approached the wall in 3-space so Stanton could see me, and then I slipped into 4-space and could see exactly where the Venus Blobs were going: out of the spaceship and up through the porous ice toward the surface. (Ice is very densely packed, but apparently any empty square micrometer would allow the blobs passage, since they acted as a superfluid that could squeeze into and work through anything even slightly porous.

I returned through the wall and dropped back into 3-space. "I know where they're headed."

"Whoa! How did you do that? Do the disks make us transparent to solid objects, or vice versa, or whatever?"

"No, it's—" That's as far as I got before I was out of Stanton's earshot. On his disk, he moved quickly toward the bulkhead I had just passed and then ran right into the wall. He bounced back, nose probably broken and a hell of a headache most likely brought on, but even as his body ricocheted, the disk remained firmly under his feet. (In truth, we had no idea how to get them free from the electromagnetic bonding holding us to our disks. We couldn't fall off them if we tried.) He floated back to me, his hand covering his smashed nose.

"What the—*why didn't you tell me mine can't do that?*"

"I tried, but …" I trailed off, nothing further to say about that. But I looked out with the strange perceptual power the pilots had given me (which apparently has a range exactly matching that of the volume of the ship) and seeing them slither and squeeze, as vertical as a plumb line, up the massive bulkhead and sizzling through the metal of the overhead of that section and up into the ice, which melted instantly at their tough.

I wondered why the acid blobs decided that right now would be the time for them to breach the hull of a *ship* meant to fly in *space*.

Then I actually said out loud, "They're *predators*. So there has to be prey." Somehow, the blobs could sense there was prey above them. Then the obvious slammed into my brain.

They're going to attack Criminy Station. Ten delicious sacks of meat awaited them … if they even ate anything they killed. The alien hunters wanted insanely aggressive predators to wreak havoc, chaos, melee—the beasts weren't necessarily motivated by hunger. I was beginning to realize that these things had been bred over the eons to hit their pleasure centers with the rush of causing fear, panic, and pain unto death.

I was absolutely certain the acid blobs were about to dissolve Criminy Station and everyone inside. And there was exactly nothing I could do about it—I tried to pierce the miles-high overhead with my four-dimensional hyperdisk, but my head banged painfully against the metal and told me that my superpowers, as I had already learned about with the 4-space vision, were limited to the inside of the alien ship. Stanton floated up next to me, stopping smoothly before he reached the top, looking where I was but unable to see the whole of the interior, not having been touched by one of the pilots.

I tried my radio, but the half-mile of ice above us would never allow my signal though. I thought maybe the magical alien disk would allow me to project my thoughts—after the consciousness-grabbing alien tablet, it seemed a not-unreasonable surmise—to the ten unsuspecting people inside the hard plastic cabin. Finally, I prayed for something, *anything*, maybe to God, the gods, the Fates, or to some all-powerful

mugwump

creature to intercede and give the poor bastards a warning, at least.

But no.

Prayer worked as well as it ever does, and I could picture the Venusian blobs bubbling up from the ice and spreading out. Two-foot pylons lifted Criminy Station to keep the blowing ice and snow from piling up against our surface base of operations. Everything I had, everything any of us had, was inside that reinforced plastic shell—every bit of our food as well as every bit of navigational, communications, and survival equipment we didn't bring down with us. Which was most of it.

If we lost Criminy Station, we would—every one of us and without question—die here.

Stanton made the situation very clear during his extemporaneous "briefing" of his fellow scientists in the living quarters when he returned from the Venus other-mind. The "living acid blobs" obviously survived, even thrived, in the most extreme environments. You just can't get more extreme and deadly than the surface of Venus. This frozen continent in the winter wasn't even in the running; the worst-case scenario here would be death in hours. Floating naked in outer space would boil your eyes while you froze to death, which would take about twenty seconds.

But on the surface of Venus, as Doctor Stanton saw for himself, you would die *instantly*. All of the gasses in your body would be tortuously—and fatally—compacted, if your rib cage wasn't crushed and your heart stopped in less than a second first. *That's* the place these acid blobs thrived. Ice and cold wouldn't faze them a bit. The things were *made* to travel through tiny fissures if they existed and just melt through anything else.

It was going to be an ambush and a massacre. Stanton and I were the only two people on the continent who knew what was coming for our compatriots upstairs. No one would be able to hear us shouting for help; the ship was too vast. I could use the 4-vision to find the others inside the ship, and then Stanton and I could zoom over to them on our disks … but to what purpose? They couldn't do anything, either. And even if Colonel Ash knew how to manipulate the energy beam to push us all the way through the tunnel to the surface—I was sure he had some kind of exit strategy so we could actually get to the surface again—there would be no way to get Ash to the tunnel in time to offer help before everyone was killed.

The goddamned things were on their way up.

And spread out as we were in the ship down here, we wouldn't know whether our compatriots at Criminy Station were alive or dead until— and unless—we were able to return to the surface.

18:45: AMBUSH

Now that the explorers were out exploring, Criminy Station was pretty comfortable, all things considered. Doctor Vasquez drank tea with the Air Force crew that stayed behind: Major Elden, Airman Bishop, and Airman Frost, all of whom preferred coffee.

The icenecks were arranged on the couch-like furniture that bolted and unbolted from the wall for easy setup and storage. Stripe drank a near-beer; Suntan was sipping at a mineral water; Ski Mask wished he had violated the rules and brought vodka; Michelle Rodriguez was gnawing at a plug of bubble gum stowed in her cheek like it was chewing tobacco; Pinkie was asleep, his head back and mouth open; and Big John was reading what had to be the most boring trade magazine in the universe, *National Driller*.

Doctor Vasquez and the icenecks, the Air Force's Major Elden and Airmen Bishop and Frost, could do nothing now except wait for the team to return.

Or never to return, Vasquez thought. They wouldn't know whether their compatriots were alive or dead until—and *unless*—the reconnaissance party returned to the surface.

"Bishop, your patrol," Major Elden said. At the top of each hour, he sent Bishop out to check on the alien laser whatever-the-hell-it-was, make sure the tunnel was still open. At the bottom, it was Frost's turn to live up to his name.

He knew it didn't really mean a whole hell of a lot to check on the tunnel, since the expedition had no alien-magic way to make a new one or any way to extract them from the anomaly even if they *could* make a new tunnel with the force-field thing. Which they couldn't. But it did keep the energy in the room less stagnant and gave *somebody* something to do, even if it was incredibly dangerous.

A hard wind gust rocked the building. The occupants were almost used to it after several hours … almost, but not quite. There was still that instant of complete terror before one felt silly, the way that turbulence terrifies airline passengers for half a second before they exchange sheepish smiles. Or they remain terrified as the plane crashes and they die, much like the crew at Criminy Station would if the wind knocked it over.

"Jesus," Frost yelped, then added with that same kind of smile, "Excuse me, everyone."

Spike laughed with the others and said, "Glad we got the barriers up around the force-field thing. This is *weather*, man."

Antarctica was the one place where mentioning the weather wasn't just small talk. Even so, there wasn't a whole lot of conversation to be had about it when conditions were highly unlikely to change for the next four months.

But there was small talk, and Big John would make the other icenecks laugh at something he read in his squeaky voice out of *National Driller*. Of course, it was all lost on Vasquez and the Air Force guys, but they laughed along with the others because laughter begets laughter, and laughter begets escape from worry, if only for a moment. It was the only respite in the whole mission thus far, and the occupants of Criminy Station kept the joking going for as long as possible.

When Elden's wristwatch beeped to notify him that it was now the bottom of the hour, he said, "All right, Frost, your turn."

Frost acknowledged the order and stood to get his outside gear. A look crossed his face and he scanned the room. "Sir," he said with growing dread, "didn't Bishop come back?"

Immediately alarmed, Elden counted off every person in the room. So did everyone else. Michelle Rodriguez and Ski Mask took on the search inside the building, which took less than thirty seconds to execute and come up empty.

It was this movement that finally awakened Pinkie, who immediately was told that a desperate search for Airman Bishop was underway. Other than that, Pinkie didn't need anyone to tell him the night soil had hit the fan—he was maybe a foot away from the mumbling, writhing Major Elden, whose legs were up on pillows. Those weren't the sort of things that "just happened" at once. No, the situation had gone FUBAR, and he didn't know what was going on enough to know if it was a fixable kind of FUBAR or the kind of FUBAR that spiraled into total chaos and everyone died.

He shook his head to clear hit and thought: *"Where everyone died." Lovely! Quite the Debbie Downer right now, aren't ya?*

Michelle Rodriguez and Ski Mask returned.

Bishop was not with them.

They all came together in the common room again, just as the wind rocked the structure again, harder this time.

"Did you try his radio?" Stripe asked Frost.

"Of cour—sorry—yes, I did. He didn't copy back. Major, sir, should I ... "

Elden's skin had turned pale green. He was slumped in his chair, his eyes open so wide they showed no lids at all, muttering, "I shouldn't have sent him out in weather like this. But the *mission*, the mission is bigger than any of us ... God, I never should've sent him out in weather like this ..."

"Sir? Are you all right? Should I—"

"It all seemed so cool, y'know, so secret? Like in the movies. I'd be one of the first humans to encounter extraterrestrials *and* we'd make the world safer. Yes, safer. The ultimate weapon ..." Elden looked up at them all standing in the room and deep concern on each face.

Doctor Vasquez stepped forward as he continued to mutter, looking like he was going into shock. But *why?* Another man had died already, the SEAL, but Elden hadn't taken it like this. Was it because Bishop was under his command? It didn't matter, but the poor man looked utterly *stricken.* "Major, I need you to lie down on the couch, okay? Airman Frost is getting pillows to elevate your legs and I'll keep close watch on you, okay?"

Elden kept going, his voice strengthening and weakening as he pleaded with them. For what, Vasquez wasn't sure. Forgiveness? Sympathy? Anger at Colonel Ash? "They'll kill me for even saying this, but this mission was supposed to change the world ... creatures bred for pure aggression ... slash and burn through any population ... we could study them ... breed supersoldiers ... *Jesus! We have to get to the ship before the Russians!*" The icenecks stood him up and were leading him to the couch while he muttered and raved.

Bishop placed the two pillows as Vasquez instructed, and together they made it so Elden's legs were raised and his head kept low to counter the shock, if possible.

Stripe stood next to Doctor Vasquez and said very quietly, "What the hell was *that*?"

"I believe *that* is the fact that our Major Elden has always been on the intelligence side of things in his Air Force career. I'd bet you that this is the first time he's directly ordered a person under his command to his death."

"He didn't mean to—Bishop and Frost, they did it ten times already, zipping out to check the status of the tunnel and zipping back in."

"I was a doctor in the Army after they gave me a free ride all the way through medical school," Vasquez said. "When I was Afghanistan, I saw the sanity of some lieutenants—these were field commanders—fall to pieces when a soldier he ordered to do something was killed as a direct result." She shook her head almost imperceptibly at the memory.

"Like PTSD?"

"No, Scott. PTSD can be treated with specific techniques to ground the sufferer in reality and show him or her that there is no danger." She smirked a little. "At least, no danger as imagined during their PTSD episodes. But insanity is different; we don't call it that anymore in medicine, of course. 'Severe mental illness' or 'acute mental disorder,' even 'mental derangement.' But these field officers I'm talking about … they lost their minds. It's not like with PTSD; it was nonspecific—they just went *insane*."

"Jesus Christ," Stripe said, and their conversation was ended by Airman Frost's cry: "I have to go get him! He could still be alive! And the thing may have toppled over in the wind, so there's an operational reason to go. I'm going out there!"

Big John had slowly and silently made his way along the bulkhead behind Frost to the first hatch that led to the outside hatch Colonel Ash had used to toss out Captain Davidson. For such a tall and large man, it was quite the feat that he was able to inch his way without anyone taking notice of him doing anything other stand than standing on the outside of the common room.

When Frost rushed to get his outer gear stowed in the space between hatches, he ran right into—and bounced right off of—Big John, whose huge frame of cold-weather fat and a lot of muscle now blocked every square inch of the hatchway.

"All due respect, airman, but us on the drill crew are the ones in charge inside Criminy Station, and *we* say you are *not* going outside," he said. "We're not losing another redshirt."

"Funny," Frost said. "I think I'll hit the head while I'm laughing about my friend dying out there."

"Aw, hey—I wasn't thinking when I—"

Frost pushed past the other icenecks without a word and walked with tight steps toward the bathroom.

Big John looked ill as he shut the hatch—and locked it, showing all the key going into a pocket a layer or two under his parka.

"We're all stressed and upset," Doctor Vasquez said. "We need to put all that aside and focus on what we're doing here."

The icenecks looked a little confused. "We should focus on sitting on our asses?" Suntan said.

"I meant making history. This expedition will be ..." She kept speaking as if there were nothing wrong.

But something was wrong, *very* wrong.

She just didn't know it yet.

***

If Airman Frost had been permitted to go outside to search for Airman Bishop, he would have found him exactly where he thought Bishop would be and doing exactly what he thought his fellow airman would do. Between the shielding of the force field device and the device itself, hunkering down for protection against the wind. *It's the wind that kills you, not just the cold*, Colonel Ash had told him before they set out for Antarctica. *If you get knocked down and can't get up, make some kind of shelter against that wind first thing you do.*

That's what had happened to Frost: a 100-knot gust practically picked him up and dropped him to the ground. It didn't matter how diligently he tried to right himself, the wind would not let him get to his feet. He had landed on his radio and broken it. He was alone, even though he wasn't 100 feet from Criminy Station. There was no way they could see him or hear him; he'd have to stay protected until the Condition One storm let up a little bit.

Remembering the colonel's advice, as soon as he realized his predicament, got him crawling to the shielding, the specific purpose of which was to block the weather from interfering with the alien device. That was ideal, and once he got ensconced, he gratefully soaked up the warmth coming from the force field generator. He even fell asleep for a while.

He was awakened by a tickle on his face, the only exposed part of his body. He rubbed where the sensation was—

—and his fingers were burned off to the knuckles.

"*Jesus fucking Christ FUCK!*" was all he could say as he screamed, as he saw the oil-slick creature wind its way around his triple-layered forearm and—*GOD AIEEEEEEEEEEEEEEE*—melt clothing and flesh away like a candle in a flamethrower.

Bishop puked in agony, most of it ending up down the inside of his parka. He didn't know if he was hallucinating because of the cold, thinking frostbite was a black blob melting his flesh—but it didn't matter. He was going to get up and run like a bat out of hell back to the station, wind be damned.

But now one *oozed out of the ground* and sizzled through Bishop's boot at the ankle, his foot and the boot it was inside dropping off as if they had been chopped off with an axe.

His screams were losing force as he struggled to stay conscious in spite of the fierce bolts of pain wherever the acid blogs touched him. And they were touching him all over now, burning through every layer of clothing, then every layer of skin to the bone. And then the bone, too.

They slithered over him, under him, suddenly dozens of black holes consuming every bit of matter wherever they touched him. He was conscious when they finally reached his heart, his stomach, his spine, his skull; and it was horrible, *horrible*, until the Venusian predators finally dissolved his brain.

Now came the flood of acid blobs, oozing up from the ice everywhere but very shortly afterward undulating as one toward the prey within the shell of Criminy Station.

***

A blood-curdling shriek of pain and terror came from the direction of the bathroom.

"Oh, for Chrissake," Stripe said with a sigh, speaking louder as he went to take a look, "there must be a goddamn crack in the shell blasting Frost's pants-down ass like an ice gun. I'd scream, too."

"Wait!" Major Elden's voice sounded from the couch. "I thought you guys said this thing couldn't break."

"No, no," Ski Mask said in his thick accent, "we said that nothing could penetrate the shell. That's different."

"Ah," Elden said. He was breathing easier and feeling much better now. He sat up on the couch. "The—the, um, *news* about Bishop threw me for a loop. I mean, I knew this assignment was extraordinarily dangerous, but I didn't think anyone would actually *die*."

Vasqucz said, "No, of course not. None of us think that." She was very deliberately trying to keep everyone's attention on Elden and not on Frost's shrieks of terror and agony. The shrieking stopped all of a sudden. She assumed it was Stripe saving Frost from the bitter cold whistling through the crack in the shell.

It was not.

***

The main body of Criminy Station, like all modern outposts in Antarctica, sat upon high-grade reinforced plastic pylons, which kept it high enough to avoid snow accumulation and limit the force with which the station would be hit by high winds. It also would make it much easier to disassemble—if they were to be disassembled. But Colonel Ash had made it clear to the icenecks that they would be abandoning the structure at the end of this expedition. Researchers could take over Criminy Station and do what they pleased with it. *Consider it a gift to the scientific community*, Ash had said.

The acid blobs oozed onto the surface just underneath the raised research station, having melted through the half-mile of solid, nonporous, two-hundred-year-old permafrost. It looked a bit like oil bubbling up from the ground, only oil didn't immediate snow and ice immediately begin to melt; also, oil didn't slither in undulating black ovals across the ground.

But the acid blobs of Venus did.

In the darkness and the wind and snow, the acid blobs surfaced until the entire ground underneath the station was flooded with black waves of them. Several blobs could stretch to stick onto the underside of the structure and burrow right through it.

A few seconds later, Airman Frost started to scream.

The rest of them were able to focus on bringing the prey to them, spot the two-foot pylons, and break into four equal masses—each headed for a different corner, where the steel supports held up Criminy Station.

It took seconds for the steel to sizzle away in each location, not exactly synchronized but close enough that the whole structure fell to the ground like it was dropped.

***

Everyone inside the station let out a cry of shock, including Big John, even as he tried to comprehend what had happened to Frost. Big John had no trouble forcing the door open with one shove from his shoulder.

He was looking at an abattoir.

Frost—or what were the airman's viscera, skull still able to shriek until the black globs melted his brain. It smelled like a cookout. It looked like … hell, Big John didn't *know* what he was looking at, but the deck was like Swiss cheese and unholy cold rushed in through the charred and melted foot-size holes—the globs did erased anything it touched like carbolic acid. These must have been the spaceship's *aliens*.

"Sweet Admiral Goddamn Ackbar, it's a trap," Big John said out loud. These hellspawn black globs had tricked them into coming here, and now … everyone in Criminy Station was utterly defenseless. They would be slaughtered, just like the oth—

BAM! BAM! BAM! BAM!

Criminy Station first shook, and then each corner of the building fell hard onto the permafrost. Every occupant's stomach lurched and, an instant later, ankles and knees and backs took the impact hard. There were sprained ankles and an ACL tear in Major Elden's right knee, but no one noticed their own pain.

What they *did* notice was Big John screaming and fleeing into the common area, wisps of smoke rising from his body … the back of which was covered with something *horrible*. In the few seconds it took for Big John to reach the far bulkhead of the room, he was dissolved before the eyes of everyone there.

They were all too stunned to scream—it happened so quickly that no one could had yet registered what they saw. Once they did, once they saw the acid-oozing creatures where Big John was supposed to be, they *screamed*.

The things spread up the far bulkhead and the smell of burning plastic had Doctor Vasquez and the icenecks retching. Major Elden passed out again.

"What the hell are they doing?" Pinkie managed to say before it became obvious exactly what they were doing.

They were melting away the far bulkhead. On the other side of that wall was Antarctica.

The acid blobs fell in clumps once they ate through the shell—and hell came with them. The full force of Condition One—frostbite in seconds and death in minutes, all in darkness—slammed into the crew, knocking every one of them off their feet. No one was wearing a parka or jacket. No one had goggles on.

At least this isn't the WORST worse-case scenario, Scott (the head iceneck Weaver called Stripe) said to himself, trying desperately to distract himself from the brutal and burning sensation your body gave you when its flesh was going to be gone in less than a minute. *This way the wind bounces off the air inside, since there's no opening on the other side to let it flow through.*

The acidic slime creatures had slithered around the station and gotten to work on the bulkhead opposite the one it had already consumed. It soon fell away, and now everyone inside lurched to grab something bolted down to keep from being swept into the night.

All right, Stripe said to himself again, *THIS is the worst case scenario.*

Criminy Station went dark.

Stripe could see nothing as the wind ripped away his body heat, as his face starting stinging with incipient frostbite. It was like being blind, and he would be if he kept his eyes open a few seconds longer.

But before he shut his eyes, he thought he saw a glimmer, a weak and variable point of light—two points—and it came to him that The Vehicle was always kept running so it could be moved if ice tried to seize its huge tires.

The Vehicle's lights had been kept pointed right at Criminy Station for this very reason. Not specifically for acid blobs from Venus, but if the power went out, the heat, the lights, the communication system. The Vehicle was a hundred feet or so away, close enough that the crew could walk against the wind to the behemoth, where it was warm and dry and they could radio for help.

Of course, that plan assumed that the people scurrying from station to Vehicle would be wearing their full gear. Stripe was in long johns and sweat pants. He knew he might not make it—but he had to try; all of them would die if he didn't at least try. He didn't know if anyone else was still alive, or even conscious. He wouldn't have been able to hear their shouts or screams anyway.

He had to *move* now. He stood against the wind and, literally, a red parka hit him square in the face. He practically leapt into it and pulled the hood tight over his head. Then he saw some night goggles reflect the headlights enough to make one blink, but that was enough for him—they would keep him oriented towards the heat signature of The Vehicle. He stepped forward against the unreal wind, then took another lurching step, slowly, making his way in the direction of their salvation.

Doctor Vasquez had shielded herself, Michelle Rodriguez, and Ski Mask (who was, unfortunately for him, not wearing it at the time of the ambush) behind a long table meant to be used for common meals. The three of them were able to lever it back and forth, and finally, they could bend it so they could huddle on its lee side while it remained bolted to the wall. Now they had a shelter in which they could just freeze to death instead of—

Michelle Rodriguez kept her infrared goggles clipped to her belt, and so she had them and could pop up every ten seconds or so to see if anyone in front of them was alive in the weakening structure. There was no one behind them at all, Major Elden having been swept out with the first open blast. "Hey. *Hey!* Somebody's standing up!"

"What's that?"

Michelle Rodriguez had to lean over to Vasquez and force her mouth against the doctor's ear in order to be heard at all. The loud and unrelenting wind made hearing impossible unless the words were shouted directly into the listener's ear.

Vasquez took the goggles and shot her head up, then back down. She told Michelle Rodriguez, and then told Ski Mask, "It's Scott! It's got to be! He's the biggest and strongest of us now!"

Vasquez handed the goggles to Ski Mask; he looked and told them directly in their ears, "That's him, all right!"

Michelle Rodriguez took another look, and then the goggles went to Doctor Vasquez. She didn't pass them back. "He's moving forward, really slowly!" she yelled into the icenecks' ears, her voice straining against the intense pain of her unprotected forehead freezing and dying. She would need skin grafts if they ever got back to civilization.

When, she scolded herself. *WHEN we get back.*

What was Scott trying to do, anyway? He knew there was no point in walking away, into the storm. Maybe he had gone nuts and felt hot, how one feels right before dying of hypothermia. Where could he go?

He's going for The Goddamned Vehicle! Vasquez thought with joy. *He's going to get in it and drive it over and save us all!*

She came back down again and shouted her realization in an ear of each of her shelter mates. Infrared goggles don't resolve faces well, but she hoped they were hanging in there. Flesh be damned, she rose again to watch their savior—

He was still there, but his forward progress had stopped. Then he fell forward, the wind seeming to slow his fall as Stripe sunk slowly out of sight.

He did not rise again. The snow and ice covered him so quickly, his heat signature faded away. Doctor Vasquez could feel a tear form in the corner of her eye and instantly freeze; the pain was horrific and she turned and slumped down with her back to the table. She had thrown the goggles off, and they were instantly whisked away and lost.

***

Stripe didn't fall down against the wind, as it looked to Doctor Vasquez that he had.

He was determined to get to The Vehicle and save the day, rescue his friends, and not die of exposure. It was about one hundred feet to the thing, not far, but looking a million miles away to a man with just long johns and jeans on.

But that didn't matter—even if he was able only to save himself, he could bring The Vehicle to the mouth of the force-field tunnel and load them all right in as they came up from the Anomaly. He steeled himself and took the first step out of what remained of Criminy Station—

—and every nerve in his right foot exploded.

He couldn't see a damned thing, but he knew instantly that he had stepped right onto a carpet of acid blobs. His ability to think was then scrubbed away by the monstrous pain as his foot, then his ankle, then up his shin. It was like every bone in his legs was being broken, producing that moment of sparkling agony when a bone first cracks—but that tortuous level increased exponentially with each new bit of his leg dissolving. He couldn't pull himself back, since he had nothing to push on, and he screamed and screamed as he fell onto his hands, his arms sizzling down to his shoulders. Then his torso, then this other leg, and then his face, which for one more instant bore a rictus of agony it could no longer shout.

***

Vasquez couldn't see anything, but her hand touch brushed against Michelle Rodriguez's shoulder, so Vasquez sat up to tell her that it was all over, they were going to die; advise her to make peace with whomever or whatever she believed in; tell her that it was an honor to serve with her, and that she … should …

But no. The girl was sitting on the deck the same as a moment before, but when Vasquez leaned into her ear, she was already frozen to death.

Vasquez thought she could hear something not above the wind but weaving through it. A man's scream—Ski Mask's!—reached her but was abruptly cut off. Maybe it was just the deathly storm knocking something against something else, not Ski Mask at all. But it was, she knew this; his shriek sounded just like those of Airman Frost.

She leaned against the table blocking the wind. It was so cold her skin adhered instantly, through her lightweight shirt, to the metal. It didn't matter now, nothing did. The wind continued to knock her about, but she very mindfully made peace with herself and with those she loved. Ready for her passage in mind and body, she now would just close her eyes and drift away. Slipping away into hypothermia was quiet, peaceful, dignified.

"HOLY SHITE! AAAAIEEEEE!" Vasquez screamed as an unprecedented agony ripped across her chest, the burning erasing every thought, and it burned right down to the bones of the arms she had crossed for warmth.

The acid blobs had come. She couldn't see in the blackness but she— *"STOP! GOD, STOP! GRRMFUUUUUAIIIEEEEE! STOP! STOP!"*—knew what they were, what was happening, even as they ate down to her organs, melted away her uterus and digestive tract, and spilled the contents of her intestines onto the ice and snow around her.

The last thought of Doctor Julieta Vasquez was *They taunted us, tormented us, not like animals but ... sadistic, like humans ...*

And the last moment ever experienced by Doctor Julieta Vasquez was one of unbearable pain, her final intake of breath fouled by the stench of her own burning flesh.

***

If they could have seen into the winter darkness and through the roaring storm, noticed anything at all beyond their own agony at the victory of the Acid Blobs, they might have caught a glimpse of Colonel Ash. His disk floated high enough in the force-field tunnel to poke his head out of it, allowing him full sight of the massacre at Criminy Station via powerful infrared goggles. He watched every second of it, taking in the entire scene of fear, then panic, then screaming while consumed by the blobs from Venus.

Then he sank back down into the tunnel, the last part of him visible being the very top of his head, where the aliens' telepathy skullcap blinked in the ultraviolet as it collected Ash's most recent memories for transfer and reward.

19.00: MUGWUMP

I could see through the bulkheads and overheads and decks of this enormous vessel. I saw my SEAL cohorts moving out of the vast space where they had forced the Titan Gilas into suicide by deceleration trauma. Many were still alive, but they couldn't follow Drake and Ferro as they climbed the mass of dead or dying creatures. With so much of the herd dead in front of them, the remaining Gilas milled around their fellows, unable to move ahead but not going back into the recesses from which they had come.

After they crossed Mount Death, they reached the passage Stanton and I had taken. They were at the disks set into the floor, and god, I hoped they would accidentally activate them by stepping—*yes!* They both lifted off the deck; and they both started their search for hostiles once again. Radios didn't work within the ship, so they would have no idea where the others were. They must have been given a rendezvous time to meet Ash at the hatch we had entered through.

No one had given *us* any rendezvous time … or any other information. Was Ash planning to leave his scientists behind? I smirked at the noir-movie sound of this, but *did we know too much?*

Probably not. But that didn't mean he'd care much about finding us within the ship if it struck him as inconvenient. I was intensely glad that the pilots, whatever their reason, had touched the disk and made me a human x-ray machine. I would be able to lead Stanton and myself out, but if Ash planned to leave the SEALs behind as well, I could …

I had been watching the colonel float down this corridor or that, but now he moved in a different manner.

He was moving *through* the bulkheads. He could do what I could do, and probably from the same cause.

It appeared to me that he was headed for the exact center of the leviathan. Not zooming, but moving with intent now, not meandering from that straight line. Then he turned his head and looked at me. Not in my general direction—he was looking directly at me.

So, he had the 4-space vision, too. I didn't know what to do under his eagle-eyed glare, so I waved. I made one wave of my hand, like I was his secret pal in elementary school.

He didn't wave back. Instead, he put out his arm and pointed his hand at me, then made a sweeping upward arc towards himself. He was saying *come with me*. He was inviting me to something in the center of the ship. I didn't know how to accept this invitation, but I wanted to be near the one person who would *definitely* be getting out of here alive.

I waved again, feeling like a moron at the beach trying to get Mom's attention, and I started my own path to the center—

Stanton stopped me with "Whoa, Weaver, where are you going? I can't follow you through the wall!"

I had been so absorbed with what Ash was doing that I totally forgot about the geologist. "Sorry, it's just that I saw Ash floating on his own disk towards—"

"Wait. Colonel Ash is *aboard?* Why did he come inside? Does he even have a SEAL with him? This is risky beyond any expected value of return."

"You sound like an insurance adjuster," I said. "He's going straight at something in the center of the ship. He can do what I do, 4-vision and pass through solid metal."

"Must be nice." Envy is automatic in academia.

"He wants me to come with him."

"What? Why?" Stanton said, then his eyes widened. "He's going to use you as a meat shield! Or something else dastardly—you *cannot* trust him."

"I don't. But I need you to stay right here and wait for me. I'll collect the, um, surviving commandos and get us all together."

"If Ash doesn't kill you or feed you to something, or both."

"I can go through bulkheads—walls—at will and see everywhere inside the ship, just like he can, so I'm not worried."

"But who knows what else he can do? Maybe it's something you can't."

I could do nothing but shrug. "Our survival depends on Ash. Regardless why, he has summoned me. That's it." I pointed to the deck and said, "Stay here."

Before he could raise any further objections, I passed through into the next cabin headed towards what, I could not tell. The center seemed shrouded from my 4-space sight, and that scared me more than if I could see it filled with a thousand invincible space monsters.

But what I saw behind the shroud almost vaporized what was left of my sanity.

***

As I raced on my levitation disk to intercept Ash on *his* speeding track towards our mysteriously cloaked target, I noticed that the shroud's opacity lifted in inverse proportion to my distance from it, but so did my über-vision. By the time I reached the rapidly lightening cloud of distortion at the very center of the ship, I could see only what was already within the cabin—the shroud now between myself and the rest of the ship—which included a just-arrived Colonel Ash, who twitched with anxious anticipation that I had never seen in him before. I don't think anyone had. In fact, it was the look of a man possessed by deep need and on the cusp of having it fulfilled.

The expression he wore, the need in his eyes, was directed at what was in the center of this opaque sphere of murky smoke. I followed his eyes to the thing I had spied only darkly as the shroud slowly abated at my approach. At first, my mind couldn't comprehend the information my eyes were sensing; after a horrible moment, I wished that visual perception was refused and I was struck blind, like those who could not tear their eyes away from the awe-ful true face of God.

In the center of the cloaking maelstrom, sitting directly on the deck, was a bulk of dun-colored, living biomass. It slowly pulsed in size, larger and smaller, like it was breathing. I thought "like it was breathing" because it had no mouth I could see, no symmetry from which I could divine eyes, or a mouth, or anything. I thought perhaps it was sucking what was needed from the atmosphere in the ship in the way that insects "breathe." But this nauseatingly pulsing pile was several orders of magnitude too big for any spiracular system. The organic-ochre heap of

191

fat, patches of hair, and fecal texture formed a lumpy mountain at least one hundred feet high and five hundred wide, looking and stinking like a landfill left to rot in the sun.

I knew what this thing was. I had seen it inside my alien hunter's other-mind and drew away, back into my own consciousness, to avoid seeing that which made the alien heave in anticipatory pleasure.

Before me was the *mugwump*.

Ash looked like a heroin addict ten days after rehab, handing himself over to the desires that, he knows full well, own him now and will own him until it kills him. The sight of the once-intimidating and formerly dignified Air Force Colonel was gone, replaced now by this quivering junky about to be given his fix.

But first, payment. I didn't know just what narcotic this ghost-Ash was buying; I didn't know what he planned to pay with; and definitely had no idea why in God's black universe Air Force officer and Above Top Secret–cleared son of a bitch Colonel Jonathan Ash was pulling something from inside his jacket while approaching the

mugwump

in reverence, sublime terror, and unmistakable hunger.

I'm a ghost to them, I thought. *They haven't noticed I'm here—or just don't care.*

I realized that I wasn't invisible; just completely irrelevant and ignored. There was nothing and no one that could pull them away from each other now

Colonel Ash and the Mugwump had begun *communion*.

***

Ash stepped very close to the eyeless, mouthless, heaving mass, still wearing his alien hunter skullcap. The mugwump seemed to quiver as Ash pulled one of the luminescent metal tablets from a large pocket somewhere in his layers of cold-weather gear.

The colonel, the telepathy headgear, the alien slate—Ash already knew the secret of the tablets, somehow he *knew* not just what they did, but how they worked. Now he would use the artifact to … what *was* he using it for? How did he know about the idiot god residing within the very heart of the hundred-mile-long spaceship?

It occurred to me that his secrecy wasn't just for "national security concerns." How the original alien artifacts he referred to were found in the first place; how he knew there was an eons-old alien spacecraft under the ice here; how he discovered the purpose behind the metal tablets and the force-field technology and everything else—the secrecy was kept as a bulwark against anyone knowing his real purpose in coming here.

Ash inched forward, still on the disk that kept him a foot off the deck of the shrouded area. He had 4-vision and he could travel through the vessel's walls—in other words, he could do everything I could do. He had been given these gifts by the alien pilots, no doubt, just as I had. I could understand why it was given to him, but why to me? Would I end up in thrall to the mugwump? What the hell would that even mean?

After carefully positioning himself against the pestilent, puffy thing, Ash pressed his tablet firmly against the mugwump—and the whole garbage pile of a creature shuddered, goose pimples rippling from the spot and covering every square inch of its flesh.

Jesus Christ! I retched, paused for an awful moment, and then projectile-vomited the contents of my stomach onto the cold surface beneath me. I would have fallen off my disk if it hadn't automatically corrected for my near-faint and kept me upright.

I wished I had been allowed to pass out. I would have preferred darkness, *blindness*, instead of watching the enormous mugwump quivering in ecstasy.

But at *what?* What did the tablet contain? Chaos, panic, pain, as the alien hunters would share with the thing after a melee or massacre?

I didn't get a chance to wonder long, because my floating disk rushed me forward—it had to be commanded by the pilots—against the side of the revolting being, forcing me into contact with it, with Ash, and with the tablet all at the same time.

And I *saw*.

It was as if I were watching from a safe distance as the Venusian acid blobs dissolved Criminy Station, eating everyone alive. I could see that I was floating half-in and half-out of the force-field tunnel. In front of me, Airman Bishop was consumed, flesh bubbling and sizzling away, the most horrible death one I could never have imagined.

They all screamed, panicked, huddled together against the tortuously frigid wind that swept through the channel the acid blobs had made of our home base. Within minutes, everyone had died in bewildered, bottomless agony.

I wanted to tear my eyes from my head, but that wouldn't have stopped my witnessing of the horror and chaos and unspeakable pain—it was in *my* mind now, as if I were inside Ash's own "other-mind" because of contact with the tablet.

A heaving wave traveled through the mugwump and broke my connection with it and Ash and the metal slate. I wondered if, had I remained connected to them, if I would be clutching at this monster to do what I could see Ash about to do.

Ash was waiting for his reward. As the mugwump ate up the misery and pain and fear contained in Ash's telepathic tablet, anthill-like pores puckered up out of the thing's sparsely haired skin. The tip of one risen and rugose nipple squeezed out a drop of something viscous, glistening, and black.

Then another drop squeezed out of another tip, and another, and another, until the entire mass of the mugwump was shimmering with oozing black ichor. The stench was like someone had emptied their infectious bowels onto a burning tire.

Colonel Ash dropped the metal artifact and placed his open mouth against the closest risen pore, lapping up the foul excretion like it was mother's milk. I could see the black pus rise again to fill the small cavity in the mugwump's distended nipple, at which Ash again lapped up like it was syrup being tapped out of maple trees.

My body convulsed into dry heaves, nothing left inside me to expel but saliva mixed with bile. I lost Ash as my vision blurred—the stench was too much; the sight of him suckling tar lactated by the acephalic, limbless abomination was too much; the cold and the fear and the images of my cohorts burning to death while Criminy Station fell all around them—it was all too goddamn much. I fell from the levitation disk …

… but it remained fastened to me. I had merely fallen into the six-thirty position, hanging upside-down now. I wanted to faint, prayed for unconsciousness, but no such gift was bestowed upon me. I could still see Colonel Ash, his parka and jacket and face and hair were drenched in black goo, even as he continued to suck up as much as he could from the million nipples of the panic-sated being.

However, I could see that there were more figures in the room now, a dozen shapes rushing by my upside-down magic disk. They *flew* on disks, these bipeds, to press their gleaming tablets against the rind of the mugwump, pulling forth further ecstatic secretions that they then consumed with a junkie's desperation. Represented was almost every kind of hunter I and others had seen in the other-minds—scaly, bushy, insectoid, reptilian, everything but the gecko pilot creatures—and they partook with raw hunger that had nothing to do with food.

Maybe it was because I was seeing the whole horrible scene from a weird vantage point, but all at once, I understood. Everything from the other-mind I inhabited and the stories from my fellow scientists—everything from what I had seen on the ship and through Ash's tablet, all of the monsters and terror and pain—everything I knew about how Colonel Ash got to this point, starting when those alien artifacts were first found and reported to him as the head of the government's black ops on steroids XSC program—everything made sense now, as I saw Ash fall under his levitation disk like I had. His eyes were open but unfocused, his mouth dripped with drool, and his arms hung down like sleeping bats. He was insensate with pleasure, filled with a diseased kind of bliss. He was *high*.

Every alien hunter soon slid into motionless after sucking up its fill of mugwump opium. Some of them gently landed their disks onto the deck and rolled onto the floor. Others hung like Ash and me. Still others collapsed against the side of the malformed alien biomass.

I certainly wasn't high, although the blood pooling in my head was making me feel like I would finally pass out, right when I didn't want to. I worked the disk so I stood upon it once again. The area defined by the smoky obscurance with the mugwump at its center was now populated with a dozen homogenous, semi-conscious aliens, some floating aimlessly on disks, others completely motionless on the deck.

I got it now. I couldn't think of anything more horrifying, but I finally had put it all together:

This pirate ship of literally astronomical proportions traveled the cosmos—maybe just in our local collection of solar systems, maybe coming from other arms of the Milky Way, but always traveling, never repeating its path. It was hundreds of millions, probably billions, of years old. It was so ancient that its voyage may have been aided by the expansion of the universe itself.

The gecko-like pilots were the ones who built this colossal ship and began this endless trek. One of them gave me the 4-vision and the other impossible aspects of my disk; at least one of them was in every other-mind experience of my colleagues; and they were the only ones in this gallery of hunters not here lapping up the inky seed of the mugwump.

I didn't know why the geckos bestowed upon me these magical-type powers, but I had a suspicion, and it shook me to the bone. They were not partaking of the organic drug, and I was not partaking, even though I could see on every different species' faces that it was the greatest bliss they had ever known, that any sentient being could *ever* know.

These aliens weren't hunters.

They were *slaves*.

The geckos had recruited these disparate species over the ages—shanghaied them from their home worlds, maybe, or offered adventure, or simply allowed the more curious among them to board the leviathan's daughter vessels on the surface, sweeping them to the stars once they were trapped. However they did it, the geckos created a hunting party that would last for untold epochs. I imagined that they replenished the crew as old slaves died, enlisting new ones from species from newer worlds.

The various aliens weren't slaves just because they had been pressed into hunting service aboard the massive ship. No, I could see now, they were slaves because they were rewarded with the mugwump's secreted pleasure-tar, its pan-galactic opium paid out at the end of every hunting mission.

This payout was the reason for the translucent metal tablets—it was within these, God knew how, that the hunters stored their experiences of violence … extinction … chaos … panic … horror … *suffering*. The "other-mind" we scientists had temporarily occupied wasn't a side effect of the weird slates—it was what they were for in the first place.

The hunters came to the mugwump on the levitating disks, traversing the miles between themselves and their desire in minutes. They flew right through bulkheads, decks, overheads, every surface a ship possesses, to deliver the wretched tablets and collect their reward. Whatever they could bear witness to that was terrible, agonizing, paralyzing with fear—this they brought to the mugwump, and were sent to heaven for a time.

A *long* time.

The ship had captured a fearsome dinosaur and rested on the soil of Antarctica before the first permafrost formed. Before that, the hunters spent hundreds of years, perhaps much longer, collecting various horrible predators from Earth's solar system. Saturn, Jupiter, Mars, Venus, then doubling back to Earth for a long slumber.

But *why?* Doctor Yutani was witness to the capture of the Rhiasaurus on Earth, so there was obviously a fierce predator here that they wanted, and they took it.

But they never left. They parked the ship back when Pangaea was the only landmass in existence, 200 hundred million years ago. This was also the time of the End-Triassic mass extinction, when half of all life on Earth was obliterated due to a singularly massive release of deadly methane from the vast ocean.

I would have bet my life that this was not a coincidence. Slow asphyxiation, starvation, and agonizing death was exactly what the mugwump fed on, and any race with the means to build that ship and stay alive virtually forever could have the means to cause half a planet to die for its own ecstatic entertainment.

That wasn't the aliens' only goal, however. I now saw in front of me a plan executed over deep time, long enough for continents to split off and drifted on their tectonic plates; long enough for dinosaurs to rule and then vanish in their own extinction event; long enough for animals of a higher cognitive order to develop emotions and, much later, thought.

Long enough for Earth's creatures to feel the most acute *suffering*.

The bastards collected every horrible monster they could round up in our solar system, set the wheels into motion to allow new species to flourish in empty niches, ultimately resulting in creatures that could feel pain much more acutely than a trilobite or a primitive marine animal.

But, again, *why* would they do this? Would the world's sentient beasts living so many eons in the future provide enough sadistic thrills for the mugwump? And if so, how in the hell could the geckos *know?*

Seeing the degenerate condition of our mission's leader in that moment, lost in narcotic dreams as he hung from his magic disk told me everything I needed to know.

They *didn't* know what exactly would evolve on this planet, no matter what extinctions they arranged or seeds they planted. But they knew complexity would grow, possibly enough to find the engraved tablets bearing the experience of a dozen extraterrestrial races. Once the tablets had imparted their information to the discoverer—or to the XSC chief who was the first to handle them—that being, whatever it was, would not stop until it reached the buried ship and fed at the mugwump's vile teat.

Colonel John Ash was that being. This immersion into decadence was the climax of not only this entire present expedition, but also of his entire career climbing the ranks of the darkest black ops to command the modern versions of Project Blue Book, MK-ULTRA, Project Stargate, PK and ESP development, and whatever the hell it was XSC stood for. Once hooked by a taste of the bliss awaiting him in Antarctica, Ash looked upon his life in Above Top Secret intelligence service as inexorably leading to the moment when the metal artifacts were presented to him.

I didn't know how the aliens lived so long, or how old the mugwump was. If there were universes beyond our visible one, maybe the mugwump drifted from there. Maybe the geckos were only the builders of *this* vessel; maybe the mugwump had been housed in an older ship that came to the gecko planet, and they built the present one.

Could the mugwump be eternal, or as eternal as any collection of subatomic particles could be? It had no intelligence I could detect, but it radiated its addictive promises across the universe, or universes, nevertheless. Waiting 200 million years for discovery, with the geckos, alien hunters, and myriad predators all possibly in cryogenic animation until the hull was breached by us humans, would seem like a short nap for this blind idiot god of the wretched and the damned.

And whenever the mugwump was awakened, the ship's contingent of hunters and predators would awaken as well. This expedition had awakened the mugwump, just as Ash had conceived it, planned it, and executed it.

That was all I could work out. It was a *lot*—a great synthesis in the way that only scientists and dime-novel detectives could create—but something vital was missing: It told me nothing about what to *do*. No matter why or how all of this plan had come to fruition, Criminy Station had been destroyed and most of our best-of-the-best crew was dead. That had to mean the rest of us, wherever Stanton and Ferro and OTHER SEAL, were as good as dead, too, no alien monsters needed.

None of us could make it to The Vehicle before freezing to death, even if it weren't pitch black out there. My brain instantly responded: *if there's even one-hundredth of one percent chance of reaching the vehicle and getting to the plane and flying out of this frozen hellhole, that's 100 percent better (technically infinitely bitter, since one is multiplying zero) than our chances of surviving otherwise, which is nil. In fact—*

An ear-shredding animal roar-shriek exploded in my ears, and I was snapped into the present moment along with Colonel Ash. He jerked and came to, seemed to recognize the ice-shaking sound, retook his position on top of his disk, and immediately flew through the 4-vision obscuration. Or, rather, not *immediately*—he took a moment to gaze back at the mugwump, who was covered in the thing's tarry expectorations. It was the look of a junky imploring his pusher to be remain there until he returned, his current high still at full force.

None of the hunters seemed to notice the sound, which repeated to the same effect: I slapped my hands to my ears, but the drugged extraterrestrials remained in their blessed stupor.

The roar, call, shriek, whatever it was, made me think of Goldsmith's description of *Cryolophosaurus* on ancient Earth, the mega-carnivorous dinosaur renamed *Rhiasaurus* for the continent's then-warmer climate. I admit, what I knew of dinosaur roars was pretty much limited to the *Jurassic Park* movies, but this sounded like Spielberg knew what he was talking about.

I could see no reason to remain in the den of the mugwump, as no one seemed like they were going to be moving for quite a while, and I still needed to locate my colleagues and the remaining SEALs if they were to make the dash with me to The Vehicle. That is, if we could get back to the tunnel to the surface.

And if there still *was* a tunnel.

But the plan, the geckos' and other hunters' plan and no doubt now Ash's as well, the plan required a tunnel, some way for beings on the ship to reach the surface of the planet. The Venus blobs just ate their way to the top, but the Titan Gilas and the Ginsu Balls and the Rhiasaurus and all the rest of the killer things would need a tunnel—and a wide one at that. Once on the surface, I was sure, the monsters would find their way to the other continents, reproduce, and never stop their attack on every living being they could reach. They needed a way to the top so they could sow chaos, panic, fear, murder, pain, horror; that was the point of this whole venture, from 200 million years ago to now. They would feed the mugwump through their experience-laden tablets, feed on honeydew, and go back to collect more terror and agony until they all were sated. I didn't know what the plan was from there—would they fly off after squeezing every drop of pain, headed to new hunting grounds? Could this ship break out of the ice in the first place?

I didn't know, of course, and I didn't care. It wouldn't matter to every sanity-drained being left alive on the planet whether the aliens moved on or not. They—*we*—would already be as good as dead.

Stop wasting time, I scolded myself, and levitated on my disk through the top of the 4-vision–opaque bubble. I could see everything. Ferro's and OTHER SEAL's weapons the bottom of the vast sea within the ship, and I knew one of the dozens of Europan Ice Serpents I could see curling and wriggling in the frigid water had just enjoyed a meal.

I could see Goldsmith, sliced into ribbons; Yutani, his outline almost unrecognizable as human after he was trampled into paste; Hurt was pierced so thoroughly I could see *through* her; and Hudson, his body intact but as dead as the others.

Startled at another roar, I took my attention from locating all humans on the ship and focused on the source of the sound—or, rather, *sources*: two Rhiasauruses being herded to the side of the ship opposite the tunnel we had come down. I couldn't tell if Ash had some kind of ray gun or sonic "whip" to force the giant dinosaurs forward, but it was definitely he who was flying behind them on his disk and goading them on.

There was a figure in front of the Rhiasauruses, a human hovering on his own flying disk: *Stanton!* And he was shouldering a hunters' railgun, the weapon they had used on Titan—he was going to shred those goddamn things, and maybe Ash just for good measure.

I almost shouted his name out loud, but I remembered that he was at least thirty miles away. I wasn't sure how fast I could make the flying disk go, but I could get there in time to help Stanton. I tipped forward on the disk, and a gecko pilot was suddenly in front of me. He used his bare ear-foot to tap my levitation disk—

I was no longer thirty miles from Stanton and Ash and the dinosaurs. I was now more than a hundred miles away, back in the cockpit command center where I had stumbled upon the pilots earlier. Where one of them, fresh from cryo-sleep, touched my disk and gave me superhero powers.

I was back there now; the pilot had taken the 4-vision away. I was sure I couldn't float through the bulkhead, either. I was trapped in the cockpit with the three gecko-aliens.

The disk descended and turned my back toward the pilot, something I certainly was *not* making happen. It put his hand through my parka and lower layers—but didn't tear a stitch of my gear. There were more abilities here than I knew about, obviously. Using an appendage "coated" with some kind of force-field glove, the alien reached and pulled something off the bare skin of my upper back and pulled it through the jackets equally without damage to the clothing.

Except there hadn't been anything on my back or anywhere else on my person, as far as I knew. *I'm not injured*, I marveled, *so what did it take from me?* The disk turned to face me at the pilots. The one closest to me held a translucent metal slate in its covered hands.

That was *my* tablet. It just recorded my witness to horror.

The pilots had put it on me right through my gear, gave me the power to see everything horrible happening to my friends, and let the tablet absorb the horror and shock and even the disgust I felt at the mugwump itself. The pilots would press it to their god-thing, creating a loop of my disgust and the mugwump's absorption of it and the aliens' tripping balls on the resulting secretions of dank space-opium.

That's why the superpowers. They wanted me to see everyone dying, dead, or about to be dead. Those sons of … wait …

Stanton wasn't dead, at least not yet! I had to see if his railgun ended the Rhiasauruses and maybe Ash as well. Maybe I could help! I tipped the magic disk forward to race around the corridors if I couldn't pass through solid metal anymore. But before I could get the disk to move, the pilot holding my tablet reached forward with an unshielded hand and touched it again—

23.20: DARKNESS

—and I found myself hurtling through the blasting storm, shot up and out through a tunnel on my mutinous disk. It stopped on a dime at the top of the tunnel, and my momentum did the rest. I rolled as I hit the concrete-hard surface of permafrost and got to my feet, but I was shoved backward by a monstrous burst of wind and fell hard onto my back.

Even out in the elements, disoriented as hell from my sudden ejection from the ship, I could tell I wasn't expelled from the small tunnel Ash opened for all of us to get to the anomaly. No, this one was a much wider tunnel. Wide enough for a dinosaur or two to be levitated through, in fact. And mating pairs of predators from Titan, Mars, Venus, and God knew where else, come to be unleashed on Earth and destroy everything and anyone they could reach.

I could also swear I had gotten a glimpse of The Vehicles, one tethered behind the other, very near the wide mouth of this second, secret tunnel. The only reason I could see even this was that the force-field envelopes around the massive dinosaurs—protecting them from the conditions, I would guess—gave off a blue glow. For an instant, I saw a human inside his own glowing protection. It had to be Colonel Ash.

I couldn't see any sign of a second human. Stanton was either dead inside the ship or inside the stomach of one (or both) of the Rhiasauruses.

Trying to stand up once I hit the ground, I was knocked over immediately by the incessant storm, which had to be severe even for Category One. Luckily, by falling flat, I had less surface area exposed to the frigid nightmare world. Standing, I would be like an open sail against the wind, but rolling over onto my stomach on the ground, I would be more like a furled sail, offering much less resistance.

I turned painfully onto my stomach and pointed like a puffy red torpedo in the direction that I thought the Vehicles were. I knew in an instant that Ash was stuffing them full of extraterrestrial monsters to take to the plane, himself encased in a protective force field, and unleash them on the world.

The predators must have been temporarily stunned inside their force fields as they were lifted by glowing levitation disks into the rear Vehicle. Even the Venus blobs were within a force field—acid can't eat through a charged-particle barrier—and, although it couldn't be all of them that I saw burning up to the surface, it was certainly enough to multiply and lay waste to anything and everything alive near it.

Once I hit the ground and rolled over, I had to keep my eyes squeezed shut so they didn't immediately get evaporated by the direct wind. Then I remembered—I had night-vision goggles stowed in my layers of clothing! I managed to pull them out and strap them onto my head.

There was no green-phosphor glow. Everything was black, even blacker than seen by the naked eye, since the force-field envelopes gave off light but not heat. No infrared.

That could have meant any number of things, none of them good. The sensitive infrared device had succumbed to the minus-85°F conditions. Or the fact that visibility, already less than 100 feet when I was standing, was much less at ground level, so any heat coming from the Vehicle would no longer be detectable by the goggles. Or it could be that the Vehicles, the only place in thousands of miles where I wouldn't be dead in an hour, had already begun its 25-mile creep towards Wilson Airstrip, where the computer-piloted C17 cargo planes awaited. The planes would be "idling" as well, burning fuel as they inched along the makeshift landing strip. They had to do this, I remember Spike telling me, to prevent their wheel-replacing sledges from freezing against the ice. There would be no way to thaw them for months once that happened.

God, how I hoped they had frozen. No flying, thus no mugwump-feeding apocalypse.

Even if the tank-tread behemoth couldn't move any faster than 10 mph through the sadistic weather, I would never be able to catch up once it moves. Right then, I didn't know if I can "catch up" as it sat there, idling. But not to keep on was to accept death, to *inflict* death on the world. So much death.

I desperately wanted to quit, just stop trying to move, trying to save the world from the very beings I had devoted my career to. Take off the parka and its hood and lie on my back, hoping Antarctica would put me out of my misery. Struggle or don't struggle—either way, I would be dead in minutes.

But goddamnit, I moved on my elbows towards where I thought the big tunnel mouth was, where the Vehicles were. Damn it all to hell—I *crawled*.

I kept struggling, trying to reach the Vehicle if it was still there, dying horribly and alone—to be quickly followed by the rest of humanity—if it wasn't. I didn't even know what I would do if I got to the thing, like a dog who catches up with a car it's chasing. If Ash and the creatures were protected from the cold and I wasn't, I might as well quit now and enjoy the coming permanent darkness.

At this point, I didn't really need to make a decision between quitting and dying versus struggling on: the muscles in my arms were already awash in lactic acid as I pulled myself forward. My ability to breathe in the unholy cold, already slight, was being affected by the whitening death of my nose and lips—I'm already feeling the unbearable pain of frostbite radiating from my tongue as I breathed through my mouth. The goggles were working, I found. They showed clouds of my relatively warm breath, which were then whisked away by the wind. My breath I could see, but there was no sign of Ash and his monstrous menagerie.

My brain announced: *Give up.* My body couldn't have agreed more.

I flopped over onto my back to stare straight up to spend my last minutes gazing upon the Large and Small Magellanic Clouds, wondering if there were any friendly civilizations out there, any exobiological specimens that weren't bred for violence, any peaceful aliens who didn't fill a mile-long space transport with horrors.

There probably weren't. But it's not like humans are a particularly friendly lot, either: our evolutionary opportunities were fueled by violence. We are horrors in a universe of horrors, but mere neophytes to pain and suffering compared to the race that built the spacecraft below me.

There was no point seeking solace in the sky, anyway; I couldn't see any stars, let alone Magellan's wispy galaxies. I don't know why I was expecting anything different—I'm fully sealed within a whirling hell of cold and ice and wind.

The icy winds were ripping away any warmth I might have been building up. I wanted to take the infrared goggles off, but that would leave my eyes unprotected against the wind. I'd be permanently blinded in seconds, even though my "permanently" could now be measured by stopwatch. The useless goggles may have been frozen to my face, but were protecting my eyes for the last few minutes of my misspent life.

The uncovered skin on my face alternates between wholly numb and fresh explosions of agony, like someone's pressing my forehead, my nose, my entire face against a glowing-red stove burner. I tried to scream, but my cry was stuffed back down my throat by the force of the wind. But I knew I couldn't shift position to avert the damage from the wind—I'd lose any slim chance of orientation toward the Vehicle, and catching up with it was a hell of a lot more important than even the worst pain of torture. I scream against the most horrible agony I've ever experienced, but I move despite the pain.

I thought we gave up, my brain said.

"I'm a scientist," I groaned back at it. "Can't be too attached to outcomes."

Think about why *your face is screaming in pain.*

I understood—and let out my own scream. It didn't matter if I was going to live or die. By continuing to struggle, I must have held some hope of surviving somehow. So, no matter what the odds of actually making it, what was happening to my face sent me into panic.

It was frostbite.

My face was being destroyed by frostbite.

I pissed myself inside the layered gear, and as the clothing was overpowered by the cold, that urine was going to freeze right onto my genitals and kill them by insanely painful frostbite as well. Then this sanity-shattering pain would shoot knives into me down there as well. Then that area would die and go numb.

If I lived that long.

23.35: RHIASAURUS

Frostbite *will* kill you. Even worse, it does its job with enthusiastic cruelty, killing each exposed cell individually. You experience the agony of being burned alive, bit by bit, until you die.

This was happening to me as I faced the sustained assault of air so cold that it evaporates every atom of moisture from whatever it touches. One's flesh is freeze-dried, withering like a rose without water, whitening as it dies. That dead, frostbitten tissue will soon turn ice-white and fall off.

My face would soon be just the front of my skull. My nose, all the skin on my face, was turning snow-white as the wind took it 100 degrees below zero. Because it's wind-chill and not just air temperature, my feeble 98.6 degrees of skin heat can't warm up, each caloric unit leached away as soon as it was touched by the wind, which then gave way to new wind, over and over until the flesh temperature matches the wind chill. Human flesh can't live at that level of cold … and so it dies.

My unbelievable pain—now spreading to my ears, too—meant the skin, muscle, and fat weren't *quite* dead yet. They were turning frost-white and would die soon, meaning they'd have to be cut away before infection set in. It was too late, anyway—my face would soon be gone, my eyes eaten away from behind since their fronts were behind the goggles, and a human cannot live without a face.

The skin and fat and muscle were afire, but the pain was decreasing now, a horrible mercy because of what it meant. It was going numb, and it would stay numb.

Crawling like a salamander, torso against the ice, I was sandwiched between that heat-stripping wind and a "ground" consisting of permanently frozen, millions of years of accumulated ice that stole my remaining body heat like a thermal vampire.

Then came a new sonic blast: *HWONNNK!* That was the roar-shriek of the Rhiasaurus, loud enough for me to hear it with my frostbite-ruined ears. That meant—

The Vehicle! It hasn't driven off yet! I couldn't do anything about my face, and the condition of my face wouldn't matter anyway if I died out here. So, I ignored the dead flesh of my face flapping in the brutal wind like a Tibetan prayer flag and scramble, slipping and sliding against the ice as best I can—*for God's sake, give up!*—definitely moving. I kept dragging myself toward the source of the sound, which came from directly in front of me—or at least I believed it did, the storm acting like a silencer to keep a sniper from having his location determined. I think—

HWONNNNNNNNNNNNNNNNNNNNNNNK!

Closer. I knew I was closer now. My goggles were frozen and broken, so I was as blind as I would have been if I hadn't had them in the first place. But I could just about pinpoint the source and now scuttle in that direction, the pain fading away as I died in pieces.

HWONNNNNNNNNNNNNNNNNNNNNNNK!

I was so close now that I could *feel* the roar through the ice. I was so damned *close* … but to what purpose, I still didn't know. The infrared goggles, like my dumb ass still struggling to function, buzzed and showed me the green-phosphor heat signature of the Vehicles, bundled predators in the one *not* containing Colonel Ash, and two towers of prehistoric malevolence ready to stomp and bite and chew and swallow anything in their path.

Of every impossible thing I'd seen in the past twenty-three hours—blind computers flying airplanes, the torment of Antarctica, alien hunters, flying with superpowers on an alien frisbee, the hazy skies of Titan—the *most* impossible (if I may modify an absolute in my death throes) was two thirty-foot-tall prehistoric monsters tethered now to the Vehicles fifteen feet away from me. If either of them noticed me, I would surely die about ninety seconds before my time.

At least it would be warm inside its stomach.

The green of the front Vehicle's heat signal flared in my barely functioning goggles, but it was enough to know that Ash was pulling up stakes with a world-ending collection of outer-space predators behind him.

There wasn't a goddamned thing I could do about it, either. All I could do was lie there and die.

That's when I remembered the words of my high school basketball coach: *If you're too far behind for a win, make the other bastards pay for theirs.* It was a scorched-earth policy, but satisfying as hell.

I turned my numbed and shredded face toward the wide mouth of the second tunnel, its slightly less frigid signature visible only for an instant before my infrared goggles died for the last time.

But I saw it, just ten feet or so away.. And goddamn if I wasn't going find a way to make the bastards pay for their imminent apocalyptic triumph.

I survived long enough to at least get to the opening, then slipped head-first down the tunnel to the hunters' ship.

23.45: PILOTS

The tunnel was wide enough that I could right myself with my feet on the bottom in time to avoid breaking my neck upon landing. The rush of air made me scream with pain as it struck the remaining nerve endings of my peeling flesh, and the night-vision goggles fell off because the skin around my eyes was dead. Where the skin split, though—I learned right away that my eyes could still form tears.

Seconds after I finished turning right-side up, I was almost split in half by a fork in the tunnel; but, fortunately, I was on just enough on the right to slide into that branch without horrible injury to my almost-frozen testicles.

Once again fortuitously, the branch of the tunnel I happened to go through opened, after at least half an hour of sliding full-speed down at least a 50 percent grade, near an open hatch on the ship Ash had never mentioned—that made at least two he kept secret, and on a 100-mile long spacecraft, there were probably many more.

The fortuitous part was that through the open hatch, I could see the three gecko pilots inside the cockpit, which was *right there*. I assumed it would have been at the fore end of the giant ship, but then realized spacecraft don't have or need a "fore end" as such. The Space Shuttle notwithstanding, spaceships weren't flown like airplanes, with pilots needing to look out a window. This force-field tunnel branch had to have been created specifically to take the pilots to the surface and back.

In fact, the cockpit was empty. They could have been at the surface that very moment.

But why would the pilots go to the surface? I tried to puzzle it out. *What would they possibly want—*

My gaze fell upon what were plainly stands for the experience-transfer tablets. One was next to each of the three pilots' seats, or what I could only guess were seats.

They were missing from their stands. I supposed they could be doing something somewhere within the ship. But I didn't think that's where the geckos were. They went to the surface, and for some reason, the pilots must have taken their tablets along with them, needed them for something up there. But what? Were they wishing Colonel Ash a final farewell? They wouldn't have needed their mugwump tablets for that; it was terrible for Earth but surely not at all unpleasant to the aliens. They needed to feed their hungry god scenes of terror, of pain ... of death.

They had been watching *me*.

The one pilot had shot me like a cannonball through the tunnel I had just slid down, throwing me to the elements. There was nothing but my panic and despair and excruciating pain from the most sensitive nerve endings in the human body.

The mugwump would—literally *and* figuratively—eat it up.

When I slipped down the wide tunnel, then, the show was over. If they had followed me back down the tunnel, they would have reached the cockpit, and me, already.

No, I knew where they were. They had gone to feed the mugwump and, slack and blissful, would soon float to the floor and stay there until Colonel Ash had collected every experience he could in person and on every bit of media he could find. He would witness until his slate had absorbed the entire planet's worth of fear and sorrow.

That could be a year later, or ten, or a thousand, or a million. Ash had partaken of the narcotic immortality juice, too, and so he would live awake just as long as the others would live in their heavenly hallucinatory world. But he would return one day, and on that day he would awaken the pilots, the hunters, and the mugwump would awaken so they all could once again drink the eldritch milk of paradise.

As this all flashed through my mind, my pain was driving me toward unconsciousness, a state from which I would never return. I had to hurry if I were going to do something.

What is it you think you can do here, cowboy?

"Shut up," I said, but my brain was right: I didn't know how to stop Ash and his caravan of carnivores, even if I understood every bit of alien technology in the cockpit in front of me. I moved as quickly as I could (which was slow as hell, but at least I was moving) to find something, *anything* that I—an exobiologist, the greatest expert on hypothetical alien life in the scientific community—could use to ... I had no idea. But I kept searching the weird alcoves set into the bulkheads and equipment, checking and rechecking, looking at everything twice. The computer display–like panels, four chairs for the pilots, what appeared to be star charts ...

Wait—weren't there three chairs before? I remembered taking note that the three tablet-stands, one next to each pilot's weird seat, were empty, meaning they must have taken the tablets with them, and so on. But, in a part of the cockpit area that was shrouded in darkness, I saw a fourth seat for a fourth pilot.

As carefully as before, I made my way to that fourth seat and turned it around.

There was a silvery uniform "sitting" on the chair. The suit bore some penetrative-looking holes, and a kind of mashed powder distributed in the seat's nooks and crannies. The equipment here was shattered and dented.

The geckos must have had a fourth co-pilot when they came to Earth, but it looked to me like that being was killed during landing—a planned landing that ended up in a crash, maybe. With the ship being so epically gargantuan, even if the ship *did* crash, the most damage sustained by its predator and hunter passengers would be getting thrown forward. With the size of many areas of the spacecraft, no walls or other obstacles would necessarily be present for them to be thrown into. There also could have been some kind of lockdown with everyone and everything tightly belted, since they knew they were going to land either way, but this was based on airplane travel. In all my writing and studying, I never once considered what the cockpit of an alien spacecraft would be like.

This fourth pilot, though—it wasn't belted in. The restraints were *under* the ancient uniform he must have been wearing when he was killed. The others just left him there, I supposed, but whatever happened, he was dead and gone to dust hundreds of millions of years before Amundsen showed up at the South Pole.

I also believed he had been dead a long, long time because a still-gleaming, iridescent metal tablet was in its stand next to the dead alien's seat.

I did a cartoonish double-take at the tablet, and tried to think as quickly as I could: Colonel Ash was headed for the C-17s, taking with him both Vehicles to ferry his world-ending horde of interplanetary horrors; Criminy Station was destroyed; no commandos or scientists or icenecks were alive except me; I had no idea how to go *up* through the tunnels; even if I did get to the surface, my excruciating frostbite would finish its job in minutes, maybe seconds; and I would die of infection within a week, even if there was obvious food and water on the ship—which there wasn't.

There was no way out, no escape. Everyone else had died, the *world* was going to die, and I was definitely going to die down here in this immense spaceship.

A *spaceship*.

I looked again at the dead pilot's slate, an undoubtedly idiotic idea forming in my mind from sheer desperation and disorientation. *If they set this thing down deliberately, maybe it can be forced back up.*

Through half a mile of Antarctic ice shelf? my brain mocked. *Maybe with a giant force-field generator, but it would have to be as big as this ship. Give up and die with dignity, for Christ's sake.*

I told my brain to blow it out its ... brain-ass, whatever, just shut the hell up. I had an idea, something formed from the first time I had ever heard of the Wilkes Land gravitational anomaly. Since then, "gravitational anomaly" had just been a part of my vocabulary; there was something under the ice with much greater mass than anywhere in the rest of the continent. Sure, crackpot "alien experts" said it was a giant spacecraft and crackpot conspiracy theorists said it was a secret World War II Nazi base—but both of those ideas implied that there would be *less* gravity in that area, *lower* in mass.

This spaceship should have been like that. It was almost unfathomably enormous, but most of that volume was empty. How could there be *more intense* gravity here?

Something rustled in my memory, something I saw while in the gecko hunter's other-mind that made me think of gravity … and then I had it: the smaller daughter ships that came down to herd the Titan Gilas crushed everything they flew closely over.

There can't be anything *resisting* gravity that doesn't push against the attracting mass. Regular things sit on the planet, their weight being how they push back and don't fall into the Earth. Landing airplanes flatten anything under them because of the compressed atmosphere holding it up. Their lift was their anti-gravity.

The daughter ships had some kind of actual antigravity technology, but the rule remained the same: the only way not to be pulled down by gravity is to push back. This mothership would have to have had an enormous force to counteract gravity while skimming over the surface of a planet or moon.

If that technology remained in operation—it would have to be powered by something unimaginable in order to keep working for 200 million years, but as I had considered, that length of time could be seen as short for these inter-universe travelers and their magical mugwump— then it would still be maintaining a constant and greater force than the Earth's gravity. Hence, the anomaly.

In other words, the geckos kept the anti-gravity mechanism idling. They had to have had a plan to leave Earth one day, after all our planet's living things had been tortured to death for the mugwump's pleasure. From what I could figure out, that plan including letting the engine run. If the ship was primed and pumped and ready to go at all times, that would mean the geckos could raise the ship through the ice of untold epochs.

That meant *I* could raise the ship, if I knew how to do it.

My gaze remained on the dead pilot's tablet. It would most likely contain some experiences translatable through the other-mind; that was what the things were *for*. Maybe one could select an area of experience instead of just seeing the pain and horror the mugwump got off on. Maybe I could access the pilot's knowledge, its memory, as some of us had done within each of our other-minds.

Maybe I could learn how to fly the ship. Maybe enough to get somewhere that I could warn the world, stop Ash and the predators before they even started on the first inhabited continent.

I could touch the tablet and know what the dead alien knew. I literally had no other option that wasn't, essentially, lying down and dying, doing nothing to even try to stop the ruination of life on Earth.

There would be time to absorb all I could, then return in time to stop Ash, because time didn't pass in the outside world while one's consciousness was inside the tablet owner's other-mind. I could also enter and never leave—the fact that none of us had been trapped forever didn't mean that we *could* have been sealed into a never-ending existential nightmare.

But to hell with worrying about that. I had been a smooth-skinned academic all my career, thinking and speculating about extraterrestrials in a glass-bead game that helped nothing and no one. However, I knew about extraterrestrials now, not in theory but in reality, and it was time to get my hands dirty if there was even a scintilla of possibility that I could save the world.

I reached out and touched the tablet.

23.57 GRAVITY

I don't know how long my consciousness resided within the other-mind of the dead pilot; it might have been a year, it might have been a hundred years. I was taught as the alien had been taught. I gained experience as it did. I understood how to fly the immortal spaceship at the moment my alien had understood.

I didn't know how long it was, but it was a long, *long* time.

When I was released from the other-mind, I had no idea where I was or even *whom* I was. My mind had been inside the other-mind for longer than I had lived before touching the pilot's slate; I felt that I *was* the alien pilot.

But only an instant had passed in the real world, as I knew would be the case. It didn't take me long to snap back to whom and where I actually was, but it was weird as hell being *me* again.

I knew how to fly the ship. I had learned the secret of how to lift through the ice shelf and anything else I needed to pass through.

I didn't have an inkling of what I would do once I broke through the ice, but now all I had to do to get the ship shooting up was push the dead pilot's uniform and remains off the seat, sit there myself, slide three levers, and tap one single button.

The first lever sealed every hatch and filled every hole created by any creature that had lived on the ship.

The second lever engaged the antigrav engines, making every surface hum with vibration. It also brought up a display that showed a 4-vision representation of the exterior of the ship. I could see the Vehicles and the Rhiasauruses trudging behind them.

And the third lever—the ace in the hole to escape the ice—wrapped the entire ship in the blue glow of a force field. The tunnel-making device *did* have to be as large as the ship; forming the field around the leviathan made it exactly as large.

All that was left was to press the blinking button, and, heart in my throat, I did.

Immediately, the giant spacecraft roared to life and pushed upward against the ceiling of the ice cave, melting through it like a bubble rising from a scuba tank. There was some shaking and the whining of engines not revved up for millions of years, but the ship made it through the half-mile of us in less time than it had taken us to slide down the tunnel in the first place.

We were free, and the 4-vision cameras (if they were cameras) illuminated the eerie landscape, the wall of blowing snow and ice, and the creature convoy led by Colonel Ash.

The ship was at least twelve miles high, and I set it to hover once the hull bottom was five hundred feet or so above the surface. The immensity of the thing had left me thunderstruck at first sight, but it was only while trying to pilot it that I understood how gargantuan it really was.

I couldn't tell if Ash could see the ship through the storm, but the dinosaurs knew something huge and dangerous had risen from the ice— they started freaking out, scrambling to run in ten directions at once, not only stopping the Vehicles but dragging them first in one direction and then another, and then yet another.

I eased the craft toward them. Even inside the massive ship, I could hear Antarctica's permafrost shell groaning and cracking and buckling under the force of the antigrav drive.

I wished I could see Ash's face via the ship's 4-vision as I approached, creating a trench one hundred miles long and fifty miles wide, the shiny hull reaching as far as the eye could see even if it were in daylight. I wished I could know the pain and anger every alien hunter, would feel when they awoke and learned that their evil dream of 200 million years had been, quite literally, crushed. I wished I could know the untranslatable agony of the mugwump when it was not fed for another epochal stretch of time.

But I could live without it. I drove the ship slowly forward and compressed Ash, the alien melee predators, the Vehicles, and the dinosaurs into a reddish-gray smear. The paste-like remains of the machines and creatures would soon be swallowed up as the winter's tectonic pressure sealed the tunnels and ground up the trench like soil being tilled. No one would ever know what had been here, not until global warming returned Antarctica to a green place once again.

I rumbled on the twenty-five miles or so to the XSC-built cargo planes, grinding them into particles as well.

As academics do, I prematurely congratulated myself on a job well done, saving the world and all. But I hadn't saved it yet. There was one more thing to do.

24.00: ESCAPE

I had to get this ark of despair and cruelty far away from Earth. One day, the mugwump and the geckos and the other hunters and the many predators still on board would wake up from their nap, and they would start anew on my planet for their supper of insanity and pain.

I moved more sliding levers and the ship, bigger than some moons in our solar system, rose through the atmosphere of Earth in less time than it would take the inside of an egg to fall from its shell onto a frying pan. I felt the G-forces, but it wasn't any worse than a fighter pilot at an air show enduring a sharp change in direction.

Once I was in space, I set the drive to accelerate at eight Gs, eight times the gravity of Earth, which would knock me unconscious in a few seconds. In science fiction, spacecraft are often crashing into moons or flying into stars, but that shows a real lack of comprehension regarding the emptiness of the universe. A ship could travel forever and never even be captured by a body's gravitational field, let alone run smack-dab into it. It would require great planning and perfect execution to deliberately hit some bit of space flotsam like a planet or a moon. Even with the dead pilot's training downloaded into my brain, I would have no idea how to pull off something like that. But I could keep the ship slowly accelerating to eventually come a few percentage points of the speed of light. It would take centuries, even millennia, for the ship to reach that speed at Earth acceleration, but the mugwump's opium made its addicts sleep in never-aging stasis for much, much longer than that.

I had learned from the alien pilot's training that the ship would never run out of fuel as long as protons could still be scooped into its massive ramjet maw. Protons wouldn't begin their decay for at least 100 billion years, so it would have fuel for at least that long.

It would just keep speeding up and speeding up, and, when the things finally awakened from hunger and need, time dilation would have taken them so far into the future of the universe that there wouldn't be another living thing anywhere for them to feed from.

Science fiction tells us that all spaceships, from the *Enterprise* to the *Nostromo*, have self-destruct systems ready to go. I didn't learn of any such thing from the dead pilot, but all I needed to do now was let the eight Gs take me into unconsciousness, then death, and the alien craft would be as good as destroyed.

So, after my lifetime of devotion to everything extraterrestrial, I ended up saving the mundane old Earth.

Typical, my brain said.

"You go to hell," I wheezed with a smile before passing, as the ship would fly, into eternity.

CHECK OUT OTHER GREAT
SCIENCE FICTION BOOKS

IN PERPETUITY
by Jake Bible

For two thousand years, Earth and her many colonies across the galaxy have fought against the Estelian menace. Having faced overwhelming losses, the CSC has instituted the largest military draft ever, conscripting millions into the battle against the aliens. Major Bartram North has been tasked with the unenviable task of coordinating the military education of hundreds of thousands of recruits and turning them into troops ready to fight and die for the cause.

As Major North struggles to maintain a training pace that the CSC insists upon, he realizes something isn't right on the Perpetuity. But before he can investigate, the station dissolves into madness brought on by the physical booster known as pharma. Unfortunately for Major North, that is not the only nightmare he faces- an armada of Estelian warships is on the edge of the solar system and headed right for Earth!

BATTLEFIELD MARS
by David Robbins

Several centuries into the future, Earth has established three colonies on Mars. No indigenous life has been discovered, and humankind looks forward to making the Red Planet their own.

Then 'something' emerges out of a long-extinct volcano and doesn't like what the humans are doing.

Captain Archard Rahn, United Nations Interplanetary Corps, tries to stem the rising tide of slaughter. But the Martians are more than they seem, and it isn't long before Mars erupts in all-out war.

CHECK OUT OTHER GREAT SCIENCE FICTION BOOKS

FURNACE
by Joseph Williams

On a routine escort mission to a human colony, Lieutenant Michael Chalmers is pulled out of hyper-sleep a month early. The RSA Rockne Hummel is well off course and—as the ship's navigator—it's up to him to figure out why. It's supposed to be a simple fix, but when he attempts to identify their position in the known universe, nothing registers on his scans. The vessel has catapulted beyond the reach of starlight by at least a hundred trillion light-years. Then a planetary-mass object materializes behind them. It's burning brightly even without a star to heat it. Hundreds of damaged ships are locked in its orbit. The crew discovers there are no life-signs aboard any of them. As system failures sweep through the Hummel, neither Chalmers nor the pilot can prevent the vessel from crashing into the surface near a mysterious ancient city. And that's where the real nightmare begins.

LUNA
by Rick Chesler

On the threshold of opening the moon to tourist excursions, a private space firm owned by a visionary billionaire takes a team of non-astronauts to the lunar surface. To address concerns that the moon's barren rock may not hold long-term allure for an uber-wealthy clientele, the company's charismatic owner reveals to the group the ultimate discovery: life on the moon.

But what is initially a triumphant and world-changing moment soon gives way to unrelenting terror as the team experiences firsthand that despite their technological prowess, the moon still holds many secrets.

CHECK OUT OTHER GREAT SCIENCE FICTION BOOKS

SALVAGE MERC ONE
by Jake Bible

Joseph Laribeau was born to be a Marine in the Galactic Fleet. He was born to fight the alien enemies known as the Skrang Alliance and travel the galaxy doing his duty as a Marine Sergeant. But when the War ended and Joe found himself medically discharged, the best job ever was over and he never thought he'd find his way again.

Then a beautiful alien walked into his life and offered him a chance at something even greater than the Fleet, a chance to serve with the Salvage Merc Corp.

Now known as Salvage Merc One Eighty-Four, Joe Laribeau is given the ultimate assignment by the SMC bosses. To his surprise it is neither a military nor a corporate salvage. Rather, Joe has to risk his life for one of his own. He has to find and bring back the legend that started the Corp.

SERENGETI
by J.B. Rockwell

It was supposed to be an easy job: find the Dark Star Revolution Starships, destroy them, and go home. But a booby-trapped vessel decimates the Meridian Alliance fleet, leaving Serengeti—a Valkyrie class warship with a sentient AI brain—on her own; wrecked and abandoned in an empty expanse of space. On the edge of total failure, Serengeti thinks only of her crew. She herds the survivors into a lifeboat, intending to sling them into space. But the escape pod sticks in her belly, locking the cryogenically frozen crew inside.

Then a scavenger ship arrives to pick Serengeti's bones clean. Her engines dead, her guns long silenced, Serengeti and her last two robots must find a way to fight the scavengers off and save the crew trapped inside her.

www.ingramcontent.com/pod-product-compliance
Lightning Source LLC
Chambersburg PA
CBHW051435170626
46809CB00006B/2469